Coming
Home
to the
Cottage
by the
Sea

May 2014 -

March 1942

BOOKS BY REBECCA ALEXANDER

Rebecca Alexander

Coming Home
to the
Cottage
by the
Sea

bookouture

Published by Bookouture in 2023

An imprint of Storyfire Ltd.
Carmelite House
50 Victoria Embankment
London EC4Y 0DZ

www.bookouture.com

ISBN: 978-1-83790-654-3
eBook ISBN: 978-1-83790-653-6

To my father, John Alexander, who has filled me with a love of learning and history, from which these books flow. My childhood walks were always full of stories.

PROLOGUE

MAY 2014

Libby took his hand, the burnt skin papery and silver now with age. 'Grandad?' she whispered.

'I'm still here,' he breathed, then turned to look at her. His snowy hair spread out over the pillow; he hadn't got it cut for months as he let go of living. The tiny window was rattling in the wind, and when Libby moved to close it, he held fast to her hand. 'Leave it,' he said. 'I reckon it's your grandma coming to get me. She must be impatient by now.'

Libby could feel tears creeping over her eyelashes, dripping down her face.

'I don't want you to die.' Her voice broke.

'I'll die when I die, maid. How's university life, then? Your ma says you have a new boyfriend.'

She sniffed back more tears, dried her face with the back of her sleeve like a child, not a twenty-year-old costume designer. 'I have. But...' She couldn't finish the sentence. She had never been able to lie to him.

'Still Jory Trethewey, then, is it?'

'No!' she said, her face hot. She pulled her hand free to

stand at the low window. The sea rolled on, exactly the same as it had every day of her childhood, yet always new.

'Not exactly.' She perched on the window seat her grand-mother had covered with cushions.

'When I saw your grandma the first time, back in 1942, I knew,' he said, his voice small and raspy. 'I just knew. Only I wasn't sure *what* I knew, just that it was something very important.'

'Did you fall in love, just like that?'

'I didn't know what it was. But the world was different because she was in it. The sky was clearer somehow, the winds sharper. I knew, whoever I married, wherever I lived, she had changed me.'

'I've never felt like that,' she said, returning to the chair.

'Haven't you?' His thin voice sounded just like her grand-mother's, who had died ten years ago. 'Do you remember Grandma sliding down the dunes outside, right down to the beach?'

'I do,' she said, smiling at the memory. Her grandmother, over eighty years old, landing at the bottom in a heap of sand almost too hot to touch, struggling to her feet to walk barefoot into the sea up to her waist, clothes and all. Sometimes up to her neck.

'For me, falling in love was like that. Sliding down to land in a heap at the bottom. I might have been buried, I might have got a face full of sand, I might even have been swept away by the sea. But I'd never feel so alive. When someone makes you feel like that, don't hold back, maid.'

He dropped back into sleep. A robin buzzed up to the windowsill, cocked his head on one side. Her grandmother had always fed them, right from her fingers. Libby took a few crumbs from his discarded plate – he was hardly eating now – and held out her hand. Tiny claws clung to her fingertips, the sharp beak pecked for the biggest crumb and he hopped back onto the windowsill to eat it.

She sat in the armchair beside the bed and covered herself with the blanket she had once crocheted with her grandmother. The squares Libby had made looked more like spiderwebs, but they had been included. The cottage smelled like laundry soap and baking; her mother's response to her father's illness was to cook. The more she baked, the less he ate. The cottage pressed in on Libby, like a hug. The cracked ceilings, the deep windowsills, the masses of flowers nodding outside between the wall and the beach beyond enfolded her. The floorboards were patchworked with rugs and scraps of carpet, light curtains billowing into the room in the wind.

She curled up in the chair, listening to the roar of the waves at high tide, reaching almost to the dunes surrounding the cottage. For a moment, she thought she heard a voice, calling, whispering. Something compelled her to look at her grandfather. He looked smaller than before, as if he had shrunk away. There was a smile on his face; he looked peaceful, his eyes just open a little. His gaze was distant.

Libby slid off the chair and walked back gently. As she reached the window, the robin came back, sitting on the windowsill, his head on one side as if to ask the question. She took a deep breath and spoke to the bird.

'He died,' Libby whispered to him, before she turned to call to her mother downstairs.

PRESENT DAY, 19 APRIL

The helicopter took off very gently, hardly a ripple on Libby Elliott's coffee, but the sound was horrendous.

In all her years growing up on the islands, Libby had never arrived by air before. She looked down at the islands she called home, sitting in the silvery-blue water, just poking their green heads above the mist. Libby had always loved their iconic shapes: the fat crab of her destination, St Brannock's; St Petroc's, with its internal lake and tropical gardens; and the hook-shaped Morwen Island sticking up, rocky and rugged.

Her trip back to the islands was being paid for by the production company, along with an allowance for accommodation, which was enough to rent her parents' holiday let, which had once been her grandad's cottage. He had died eight years ago, and although her parents had stripped it out and used it as a holiday rental, it was more shabby than chic.

The cottage needed a lot of work to bring it up to the standards that holidaymakers expected. The ceilings and windows were low and irregular, the stairs and floors creaked and sand drifted in the door, but every window had a stunning view of the dunes or the rolling sea. She would have to manage with the old plumbing and kitchen while the rewiring work was being done, but the back bedroom would make a great studio for her work. She had adored her grandad, and she longed to be in his home once more, to feel close to him again. It would be like stepping back in time to her childhood, when her beloved grandparents had lived there.

Libby looked back at herself in the salt-crusted window of the helicopter. She looked into her own pale blue eyes, wide under dark hair. She had treated herself to dyeing it on her twenty-ninth birthday, and her mother hated her new colour; she was always arguing that she should go back to her natural shade. But whatever she called it – strawberry blonde, auburn – nothing could get around the fact that Libby was ginger. And anyway, Libby thought brunettes looked more serious, more professional, which felt more important to her now she had her new job. But her mum had one thing right, Libby thought as she gazed at her reflection: dark hair made her look pale.

She looked beyond her reflection and out of the window, hugging the idea of her new job – costumer on the new show, *Polzeath Manor*, a Victorian tale of Cornish folk cruising in the slipstream of *Poldark*. She'd been working with the BBC for several years, mostly doing repairs and adapting costumes for minor characters. But now they had a new male character coming in – played by the engaging Callum Michaels – and *she* would be meeting him in Penzance in a few days, to take his measurements and explain the designer's plan for his character.

The helicopter had reached a height that offered a view over the distant islands. No matter how long she was away, she always yearned for just a day or two back home. A voice next to her cut through the engine and rotor noise and she jumped.

'Almost there, maid. Are you ready?' called Ben Maitland, who had been in the year above her in school. He had welcomed her at the heliport earlier that morning with a rough hug that lifted her off her feet. 'Skinny little thing!' he had scoffed. 'Don't you eat in London?'

'Don't have time,' she had replied. 'Anyway, I'm not skinny,' she had added, 'I'm *tall*.'

'I'm ready!' she called back now, her own words lost in the sudden increase in engine noise.

She involuntarily grabbed the arms of her seat as the helicopter leaned into the turn, the sea filling up half the window. The low hills behind the airport pointed along the coast to the furthest point, where her grandparents' cottage sat just off the beach. Only a grey square of roof showed above the low ridge overlooking a strip of sand, before the aircraft turned into the green of the old aerodrome. A few sheep grazed by the runway, and the helicopter flew past the control tower and swung around over a large disc of tarmac.

I'm home.

Libby looked out over the grass to the reception building, just a cabin on the edge of the landing area. Her mother Joanna was in the doorway, along with Beth, her younger sister. Her nephew, Stevie, was held between them, desperate to get to the barrier and the aircraft beyond. It made her feel like a child again, when she was actually poised on the edge of the most adult thing she had ever done.

The pilot and Ben, who was wearing a badge that said co-pilot, handed her bags out of the hold.

'I thought you'd have loads of stuff,' Ben said, hefting a case of clothes. 'You know, sewing machines, or a movie star or two in your bags...'

She smiled back at him as they walked across the tarmac. 'My equipment comes on the ferry tomorrow,' she explained, her voice coming out a bit prim. 'And the movie stars probably rent a private plane.'

'Well, a load of us from school are meeting up on Friday

night, if you fancy a proper catch-up. Unless you're too *Hollywood* for us now?'

She managed a crooked smile. 'Oh, shut up, Ben! Bargeman's Rest, about eight is it? You haven't changed, you know. You still look ten years old.'

He grinned back. 'Oh, and Jory's going to be there.' There was a pause. 'He's moved back to the islands, you know.'

Libby swallowed. 'Oh.'

Memories flooded into her mind: Jory's grin, his broad shoulders, his eyes... *There lies madness*, she thought.

'I haven't seen him for years. Not since his sister's wedding.'

'He's set up a boat building business on West Island, in the old harbour, with his brother. Designing racing boats or something, proper engineering.' He pushed open the gate.

'That's good,' she said quickly, wanting to change the subject. Picking up her pace, she reached her mother. 'Mum!'

Caught in her mother's hug – a mist of laundry detergent and the indefinable smell of the sea – Libby's eyes filled with tears.

'Oh Beth, Stevie!' Libby said.

More hugs, and the tears crept over the edge of her eyelids, although she sniffed them back. She never really cried; it was an odd thing, but coming home was the closest she got to it.

Pulling away, she smiled at her family. Beth and her mum looked more alike than ever, with long faces and auburn hair, like her, although both of them were curly. Just a few silver strands at the temples made her mother look older now. 'Where's Dad?'

'He's keeping an eye on lunch and playing with the puppy.'

'*Puppy?*' She looked at her dark-haired nephew, reached out for his warm, wriggly body, and picked him up. 'What puppy, Stevie?'

'He's a fat face!' two-year-old Stevie shouted joyously, if not very distinctly. 'He's a fuzzy felt!'

Her mother rolled her eyes. 'Your dad can't decide on a name so he gets called all sorts of nicknames. I wanted to call him Bingo but Paul says it doesn't suit.' She sighed with a smile. 'He's a cross between a poodle and a cocker spaniel. I won't tell you the nicknames he gets called in the middle of the night, when your dad has to take him out to pee...'

She curved her arm around Libby's waist as they walked towards the terminal and Stevie wriggled to be put down. He happily took Libby's hand with slightly sticky fingers while Beth followed with Libby's bag.

'How are you, Mum?'

Her mother looked trim in simple jeans and jumper. There were a few more lines on her forehead, but other than that she looked the same as always.

'I'm fine,' Joanna replied. 'Doing more at the shop, now the season has started. The holiday flat's fully booked for the summer. You should see it, it looks lovely.'

'Thank you for letting me have Grandad's cottage. I know you'd get a lot more money with visitors—'

'Oh, shush,' her mother said. 'It needs too much work to let it out as it is. And as long as you let the workmen in, we're happy with the rent. Let me know if it's too much. And if the work is too horrible, you know the summer house in the garden is habitable too.'

Libby took a deep breath of the fresh, salty sea air before turning into her parents' front gate, set between stone walls. It smelled like home, the warm air feeling different against her skin from anywhere else she had ever lived.

I'm home.

For the first time in her life, Libby wasn't staying in her childhood home, and it was a strange feeling. She was torn, impatient to get to her grandfather's cottage – her new home for the next seven months – but she also wanted to spend time with her family. Her dad had made a Korean soup served with rice, which was fiery hot and made her gasp, but as they all tucked in she looked across to see Stevie sipping his from a cup without discomfort.

'It's the gochujang paste,' Paul said with a smirk as he noticed her glance. 'I add it at the end, except for Stevie's of course. I love it.'

Her father looked great, Libby thought. He'd slimmed down a bit and his dark hair was longer than usual. Everyone in the family had thick, curly hair, except for Libby.

'Where do you get the ingredients?' Libby choked.

'Online,' said her mum, laughing. 'You should see his spice rack.'

Beth laughed, but even she was sniffing from the heat. 'It's making me hiccough, Dad – that's the sign that you put too much in.'

'Water it down with some more soup,' her mum advised. Over the sound of conversation, she added softly to Libby, 'Your dad had a health scare, love. He's decided to eat more healthily and, for some reason, he fell in love with this cookbook.'

'What scare?' Libby whispered back.

'I'll tell you in a minute. You don't have to eat the soup if it's too much.'

'I'm not complaining, it's delicious. It's just really... *hot.*'

Her mother got up and returned with a few small glasses and two cartons of milk, one plant-based. 'This will help.'

'That defeats the object!' her father objected, but the rest of them drank some milk anyway. Stevie, sporting a milk moustache, happily continued eating rice with his fingers.

As they sat around the table, Libby decided she couldn't wait any longer.

'Mum tells me you had a health scare, Dad?'

'It turns out to be nothing much, but I realised it was time to cut down my dependence on pizza and beer. I am fifty-five, after all.' Giving in to the heat at last, he poured himself a little glass of oat milk and raised it in a toast. 'To our Libby. And to a summer of the family being back together again.'

At that moment, the puppy jumped up at him, yapping.

'Paul, you've been feeding the dog at the table again!' her mother said, rolling her eyes.

The puppy, a bundle of black curls, started bouncing up and down, appearing above the table each time as if he were on a trampoline. 'I'll take him out in the garden,' Paul said, grabbing a couple of dog biscuits out of a jar on the sideboard. 'I'll have a scoop of that coconut ice cream when you get round to it,' he called over his shoulder.

Libby turned to her mother. 'Mum, what happened?'

'I don't want you to read too much into it,' Joanna said. 'Beth, can you get the peaches out of the oven?' she added, as if playing for time

'*Mum?*' Libby pressed.

'He was having problems getting up at night, just getting older, we thought. Only when he went over to the mainland for tests they found it was very early prostate changes.'

Libby's heart sped up. '*Cancer?*'

Beth put the tray of caramelised fruit on the table. 'It's not as bad as it sounds, Libs,' she said. 'It's not going to kill him.'

'Why not?' Libby stammered. 'I mean, if it's cancer, does he have to have an operation to take it out?'

'We hope not,' her mother said, taking her hand. 'The doctors are watching it and he might have some radiotherapy.'

'Why didn't anyone tell me?' Libby's eyes filled with hot tears, and she started to shake. 'Beth? Mum?'

'Because there wasn't anything you could do. And to start with, Dad was a bit shy about talking about it.' Her mother smiled. 'He'll talk to anyone who'll listen about *you*. You'd just got the new job, he was so excited. We wanted to tell you about the cancer face to face, when we knew it wasn't serious.'

Libby couldn't conceal her hurt. 'Would you have told me if it was bad news?'

Joanna stood, gestured to Libby to do the same and enfolded her in a hug. 'I love you, darling, but this was our problem. You don't tell us everything you do. Thank goodness!' She laughed. 'And of course we'd have told you if it was bad news.'

'I *do* tell you all the important stuff,' Libby said, settling her chin on Joanna's shoulder for a moment.

'If you did, then we'd all know about you and Jory,' Beth added with a grin, coming back in with the ice cream.

Libby made a face. 'There's nothing to know,' she said crossly.

But her cheeks were burning.

2

MARCH 1942

Nancy Baldwin hefted her single suitcase along the walkway on *Islander II*, the Atlantic Island ferry.

The entire crossing to St Brannock's Island had been spent clinging on as the ship lurched from side to side as well as up and down. She had been too scared and cold to be sick, but she felt wrung out as she dragged the heavy bag towards the gangway. She had travelled as far as the ferry by train from an agricultural college near Winchester, armed with six weeks of training in farming, milking and tractor maintenance. One of the other land army girls who was travelling with her, Henrietta, paused long enough to spit over the railing into the sea.

'At least they know we won't run away,' she said, her face white as paper. 'I couldn't face the voyage again.'

Nancy reached her free hand for the handle on Henrietta's huge kit bag. 'Let me help you with that. What have you got in there?'

'Extra jumpers. My mother's convinced I'll freeze to death,' she answered. 'And she tucked a few treats in afterwards, off-ration confectionery mostly. If we get searched, I'll end up in prison for dealing boiled sweets on the black market.'

Nancy laughed as two of the other girls walked up behind them. 'Let's hope there's transport to our billets,' she said as they reached the gangway.

Fortunately, a tall woman in smart uniform awaited them, crisp breeches, shirt and tie under a mackintosh, her dark hair confined to a bun. As the six bedraggled female travellers arrived, the woman pulled herself up smartly.

'Audrey Westacott, senior land army supervisor and voluntary representative,' the woman said with a crisp, sharp voice. 'Welcome. You'll all make a splendid contribution to the war effort.' She looked over the group. 'Didn't anyone tell you to come in uniform?'

Only Nancy was dressed in her proper outfit, and she had a non-regulation coat over it. 'Most of us haven't received our full uniform yet,' she explained. 'We've come from three different training courses.'

'I'll make sure we get sent the appropriate supplies,' Miss Westacott said, looking each woman up and down. 'Line up, girls, and give me your names.' She pronounced *girls* as *gels* and sounded like she was from a good, county family. Nancy was getting used to the fact that the Women's Land Army came from all parts of society, but she'd noticed that the better-educated ones tended to rise to the top.

Miss Westacott ticked names off a list and then stepped back to reveal a battered old lorry with an open top. 'Up you go. We have temporary accommodation for you for training, then some of you will join the girls already on the farms. The rest will turn half of the aerodrome into good, growing land.'

Nancy, as the tallest and strongest, found herself helping people up and handing their bags up after them. Finally, she climbed in to the lorry and sat down on a hay bale. 'How far is this place?' she asked, pushing her thick, dark curls back from her face with one hand.

'You'll need to tie that hair back, too,' Miss Westacott said, sitting perfectly straight with her heels together, tucked neatly to one side. She wasn't snippy, just factual, and Nancy quite liked the twinkle in her eye.

Henrietta shrank against Nancy a little. 'I hope it's not far,' she murmured.

'You seem very young, Penhale,' Miss Westacott said.

'I'm almost eighteen,' Henrietta said. Nancy had only known her for three hours, but she already felt protective towards her.

'They don't pay the full allowance until eighteen, if I'm not mistaken,' Nancy said. 'But we will be able to celebrate your birthday,' she added, with a smile. 'How many land army women are there on the island?'

'Twenty-three across all six islands,' Miss Westacott said. 'You could be sent to any one of them, provided they are exclusively growing food. Not just daffodils.' She rolled her eyes. 'It's very behind here, hardly any mechanisation, a lot of hand-digging and horses. But the farmers are very grateful for the help and we're starting to make a difference.' She looked around the small circle of women. 'Food on the islands is in short supply.'

The truck pulled up a hill out of the narrow street and along the edge of what she assumed was the airport. A newish-looking hangar sat beside a two-storey building with a tower and a runway. All around was grass, some of it confined in temporary fences and grazed by sheep with lambs beside them.

'Will we do any lambing?' Nancy asked, with trepidation. 'We didn't cover that.'

'I know lambing,' one of the girls piped up. 'My dad keeps sheep.'

'That's good to know,' Miss Westacott said. 'We'll need to find out what you have all learned from your various training schools and experience.'

It turned out that only Nancy had trained with tractors or

car maintenance, and her grandfather had run a garage. Another of the girls was experienced with rearing poultry, but Henrietta shook her head at each question.

'I did kill a chicken, once,' she said, finally. 'But it made me feel faint.'

'You'll get better at it,' Nancy said, smiling at her encouragingly. 'Oh, is this it?'

The truck turned into a small access road, with tall gates and a manned guard post. The young men who stopped the truck cast their eyes over the girls but didn't say anything after Miss Westacott stared them down.

'You'll need to sign in and out when you leave the base,' she said, as they rolled further into the aerodrome. 'Curfew is ten on weekdays and eleven at weekends. Coming in late will incur a penalty of ten shillings. No exception.'

Out of twenty-eight shillings a week? Nancy looked at the other women, but they all looked so tired and dispirited that she didn't complain.

'Most of the beaches are going to be mined,' Miss Westacott said, 'but the main beach along this side of the island will not be. It's well served by gun emplacements and the fishing fleet – no one will sneak in here under cover of darkness. But the other side of the island is heavily protected. Stay on the paths as directed. Ah, here we are. Your temporary home.'

The truck rolled up to a cleared area of grass on which was pitched a mildewed and patched tent.

'Is this where we're staying?' another of the girls said. 'In a *tent*?'

'It's temporary,' Miss Westacott said briskly. 'New billets are being constructed as a priority, and a small washhouse and kitchen will be adjoining. Remember, some of you will lodge at the farms you work for, and there is a small hostel on St Piran's for land army girls there.'

Nancy jumped down and reached up to help Henrietta off

the truck. 'But these are acres of productive land,' she said. 'We'll be fine here. And the weather's already warming up.'

'That's the spirit, Baldwin,' the supervisor said approvingly. 'Now, I've organised some food this evening. I'm certain you will all be hungry after your long journey.'

Looking around, Nancy couldn't agree. Three hours of seasickness had done nothing for anyone's appetite. 'Maybe we'll all feel better after supper and sleep?' she suggested to Henrietta hopefully.

The tent itself smelled stale but was large and had several small lanterns and a primus for tea. Metal buckets filled with clean water were already installed in a sort of kitchen corner, and two canvas 'tent toilets' adjoined the sleeping quarters.

Even Miss Westacott looked a bit defensive. 'It will be like the Girl Guides,' she declared. 'And the bunkhouse will be a luxury afterwards.'

No one spoke until Nancy broke the silence. 'We're all here to do our bit,' she said. 'I've seen enough food shortages in London – we all have.' She looked around the bleak tent. 'We'll make it homely in no time.'

3

PRESENT DAY, 19 APRIL

'I think your grandfather would have loved you to have the cottage this year,' Libby's dad said. 'He was so proud of you two getting your degrees and all your jobs.'

Paul and Beth were helping carry Libby's bags along the road towards the old cottage. They dropped Joanna and Stevie back at their house, and collected the puppy. The island had a long, curved coast, with an attached islet that created a perfect harbour. The cottage was a full mile away, out of the town along the edge of the old aerodrome. It had acres of grazing, going all the way to the furthest corner of the island.

'Nursing isn't quite as glamorous as making TV costumes, though,' Beth chimed in, making a face.

'But essential,' Libby said. 'No one dies because I sew a sleeve in back to front.'

'Can you do that?' Beth said, looking over her shoulder at the back of her fleece. 'Oh, I suppose you can.'

'So, sweetheart, tell me about your latest client,' her father said as they continued their walk, the puppy prancing about on his lead.

'His name is Callum Michaels, and he's going to play the younger half-brother of the lead, played by Sam Worthing.'

'Oh, that Sam was brilliant last year. Especially when he waded out to rescue Kerensa from the shipwreck.' Beth changed the bag over to her other hand. 'Do you want to carry this bag with me, Libs?'

The sisters took a handle each, her flight bag over Libby's other shoulder. 'I've got the more valuable fabrics in there,' she explained. 'All the authentic linens for the shirts – I didn't trust them on the cargo boat.'

As they reached the end of the road, the footpath stretched through the grass, nibbled by rabbits and trodden by dog walkers. A single gatepost marked the way to the cottage.

'Oh,' Libby breathed, stopping abruptly as she saw the cottage.

With the sunset behind it, white-capped rollers just brushing the sand, the house looked snuggled into the dunes like a toy. Above it, among stiff dune grasses and wild flowers, was a blue outbuilding blasted grey in places with sun and sand. It was hard to believe her grandma wasn't cooking in the kitchen, and her grandad wasn't tending his raised beds, moaning about the sand that drifted in over the vegetables. The house had once been washed pink, but had now faded almost to white again in the salt-laden sea air. Small windows sat either side of the silvery door, almost devoid of paint.

'It's still lovely, isn't it?' Paul said. 'Your mum prefers it to our house. I think she would retire here if she could. We tidied up the summer house because you'll need to move out of the cottage when the worst of the rewiring is going on. I moved Grandad's old table upstairs for a studio while you can work indoors. And we can always carry it up to the summer house when you need to move out completely.'

Libby looked at the small windows nestled under the blue slates. 'I'll work in the cottage during the day as long as I can –

the light will be brilliant for sewing.' She smiled at her father. 'Why don't you and Mum move in here one day?'

'She's torn. She wants to be near Beth and Stevie, and she would miss her friends in town. And it was a pain looking after Grandad when he got old. We were walking up every day at the end. That would fall on you two eventually.'

'We wouldn't mind,' said Beth. 'We'd do it for you old fogies, if you needed it.'

Paul pulled a key out of his pocket. 'Look at this sand, right up to the door again. We had a windy winter and the beach is starting to get blown into the garden again.'

The winter winds moved the dunes around, and sometimes sand blew up over the low wall. It filled the space between the wall and the house, like drifted snow. It was piled up a few inches high against the door.

'It's still lovely,' Libby murmured, humbled that she would be able to enjoy the cottage while working on the project.

'Don't get too excited,' Beth said with a grin. 'Mum and Dad robbed all the good furniture and put some touristy stuff in. And the plumbing is *dire*.'

'I can swim in the sea if I need a shower,' Libby replied, still breathless from the climb, as she looked out to sea.

'I love the romantic idea,' Beth said, laughing, 'but the water is still *freezing*. And the salt will make your hair like straw.'

Libby turned the key in the old lock and stepped over the sand on the threshold. Her grandparents had put oddments of carpet down to soften the flagstone floors, but they had gone. In the main living room, painted red by the sunset, the settle was covered with cushions she remembered from her grandma's time, twenty years before. A small dining table and two chairs were modern, the kitchen was dark pine from the eighties, and the cooker looked older than she remembered. The fireplace had been boarded up years ago when it became too much for her grandparents to look after.

'Thank you so much for helping me. You can put the bags down here,' Libby said. 'I kind of want to explore.'

'The bed is new and all made up,' her dad said. 'There's a few basics in the fridge, although your mum thinks it should be condemned. And you can come to ours any time you want.' He moved closer. 'Seriously, we would love to have you stay.'

'I bet she'll be back soon enough to wash her new dyed hair, if nothing else,' Beth joked, stroking the puppy who had sat down on her foot. 'We're going to have to carry Bingo home, Dad; you've finally worn him out.'

'I've told you, he hasn't found his name yet.' Paul reached out to Libby with bear-like arms. 'Come here, maid. You'll be fine here, but you come over any time you like. And you get an OK signal outside, and you've got internet laid on.'

Libby hugged him back, feeling like a child in his arms. 'Thanks, Dad, and thanks Beth. I'll be fine and I'll see you really soon. But I'm looking forward to some solitude, to be honest. There's not a lot of that in a shared house.'

'You'll see us soon,' Paul said. 'Because we're getting the gang together. Your Auntie Jane and Uncle Nick have invited us to get together for Sunday lunch next week, with all the kids.'

Beth rolled her eyes. 'All the *kids* being in their twenties and thirties,' she joked. 'And *getting together* meaning going next door.'

Jory's parents and their kids.

Jory.

4

For the first week in the land army, Nancy dug up old roots from hedges that had once bordered the aerodrome. The grass beyond the airport ran gently down towards the long sandy bay, where dozens of boats – from pleasure yachts and dinghies to trawlers and open boats – bobbed at red and blue buoys. There weren't many trees on the islands, and those that grew were pushed over and stunted by the prevailing winds. It wasn't surprising the roots had grown deep, and were twisted under the soil. But they needed to plant some crops – some areas of the country were chronically short of food in this hunger gap of March, the last shrivelled vegetables already sold from storage.

She hacked an exposed root with a saw. Getting the land alongside the runway of the airbase ready for growing food was a challenge in conditions where the wind almost blew her over, even though she was five feet eight, and well-built.

Miss Westacott, leader of the land girls, was walking up and down advising and helping the others. Nancy dug deep over what she hoped would be the last big root. The farmer was expecting to be able to plough the whole area and wouldn't thank them if his equipment got damaged on debris. Her new friend Henrietta was moving rocks the size of her head, leaving them in piles to be picked up.

'How you doing, Hen?' Nancy hissed over.

'Not bad,' Henrietta replied breathlessly. 'Just two broken nails. We'll just have to go to the pub in gloves and pearls, like society ladies.'

Nancy laughed. Hen had come from a well-to-do family in Truro; at least being in the land army gave her a uniform and a purpose. Several of the girls were working on the new barracks, putting tin roofs on. One came from service, another had grown up in an orphanage. Nancy's upbringing had been poor, but at least she had grown up with her widowed mother. The thought stung, like salt in a cut, at the memory of her mother's death during the Blitz.

The pub was something to look forward to. They could have a half pint of shandy and ogle the new American trainee pilots and crew on the bombers. They all seemed to look like film stars, and sounded like them too, with their accents. They were absolutely forbidden to fraternise, but Nancy reasoned the Women's Land Army only owned her for the fifty hours they were paying her wages. Not much more than a pound a week, taking the rest off for her present canvas accommodation. Maybe the barracks would be better. She had seen a couple of stoves arrive, although what they would be able to burn in them was a mystery. There was no wood available, and all the coal had to be delivered by boat. At least it looked like they would be here several months; she didn't want to be moved off the islands. It had taken a lot of manoeuvring to get here.

She hit another root with her spade, managed to hack through it and pulled it clear. Perhaps she should dry them out to burn them. Just as she was thinking this, the whistle blew. Audrey Westacott must have finally called a tea break, as someone was boiling up a kettle on a portable stove.

'Tea, Baldwin?' No amount of effort had persuaded Miss Westacott to call anyone by their first names.

'Thanks.' It was strong, with very little milk and no sugar but at least it was proper tea. She cupped her hands around the tin mug, huddling with the other girls.

'There's that bloke again,' Henrietta said, as a slim figure approached from the distance. 'Burned to bits, poor thing. Maybe he's up at the garrison.'

Several hundred soldiers were stationed to defend the islands. No one had forgotten the German invasion of the Channel Islands, nor the rumours of their miserable lives under occupation.

Nancy watched. Under a uniform cap his hair was a dull red, his scars covering half his face. She shuddered to think how he got those burns, maybe trapped in a burning plane. He had a limp, too, favouring his right leg. 'No, he's RAF, I think.'

She lifted her cup in salute as he passed, just glancing over at them. He nodded, and carried on, head down.

'Shy, isn't he?' Hen said. 'Where is he even going?'

'There must be some houses beyond the aerodrome,' Nancy said, standing on tiptoes. 'Mary, what's back that way, away from the town?'

Mary, their only local girl, looked up. 'There's an old cottage. My mum used to clean for the old couple who owned it. It's been sold recently.'

'To that man?' Nancy said, watching him turn the last corner.

'No. A woman, from Morwen, she's a bit odd. That's Oliver Pederick. I knew him from school. He's working with the RAF, looking after the planes.'

Nancy finished her drink already cooling in the strong wind, and turned back to the girls. They had all been changed by the war, but while her grief ran deep inside, his was showing on the outside.

.   .   .

At the end of their first week, getting ready to go to the pub was hard work. Hot water had to be brought up in buckets from the airbase kitchen, lukewarm by the time it arrived. The enamel basin was filled and refilled as two girls at a time had a strip wash, and dampened and styled their hair, while a couple of others stood guard over the tent flap. There were only two lanterns for the whole tent, and everything from spiders to mice ran across the mildewed groundsheet. Nancy washed with one of her last bars of soft soap, dried herself on a rough towel that was becoming damp, then moved along to allow Henrietta her turn.

Putting on fresh clothes, the old ones sweaty and earthy, she did what she could with her hair. Away from London, it had reverted to its mousy frizz, only the ends attractively sun-bleached. She stared, in the last of the light, at her round face in her compact mirror.

'I look old,' she said with a sigh.

'You look rosy-cheeked and healthy,' Henrietta said, 'whereas my face is chapped and dry.'

'Go on with you,' Nancy said, patting a little powder over the Pond's Vanishing Cream she had just applied. 'You still have baby skin.'

'I have *spots*,' Hen said, peering at herself over Nancy's shoulder. 'And windburn.'

By the time the girls were ready, and had put their first week's wages in their purses, it was already dusk. Fortunately, the single road into town alongside the airbase was fairly level. When they reached the outskirts of the town they could see a small group of young men in American uniforms huddled by the war memorial to the first war, smoking like there wasn't rationing.

'Excellent, girls. One of those is mine,' Nancy threw over

her shoulder to laughs and replies.

It was as if the five young men had been waiting for them. They all headed into the pub, and within minutes had formed a noisy, jokey group in the corner. Nancy sipped her drink, a port and lemon paid for by an attentive officer who almost certainly expected some reward for his generosity.

In the bay window of the pub, four young people huddled around a table meant for two. One was a short young man, his arm around a giggly girl who didn't seem to mind. The other two looked like friends who had been asked to form a foursome. One was the young man who had walked past the aerodrome earlier, Oliver Pederick. His burn scars were more flushed, perhaps with the warmth of the alcohol, although he didn't seem to have touched his drink.

The girl beside him was pretty, in a fragile, fairylike way. She was talking non-stop to him, just allowing him the odd smile or word. She seemed fascinated by him, and was wedged against the window, their chairs touching.

Henrietta squeezed in beside Nancy. 'Oh, I so much prefer using the bathroom here. Roll on proper bunkhouses.' She leaned over to see what Nancy was looking at. 'It's hard to look away sometimes, isn't it? I mean, does it still hurt? It must have been agony when he was getting burned. Maybe he was unconscious.'

'He wasn't,' Mary cut in, waving an American cigarette over them. 'My mum told me. He was rescued by the secret service, brought back from France last year.'

'You really know him?'

'He went to school with my sister. He was quiet even back then. He joined up at the beginning of the war, went away to train. I think he was a rear gunner. His aunt Bernie couldn't have been prouder, she told everyone about her hero nephew. Until he was shot down and washed up in France, and she thought he was dead. Poor thing.'

'He doesn't look like he's enjoying himself.'

'I don't think he's been in here since it happened,' Mary said. She turned to the landlord, who she seemed to know a little more. 'Is this Ollie Pederick's first night out?'

'It is. That's his first pint, I sent it over. Maybe he and his girl will come in regular.'

Nancy studied the couple, and was startled when Oliver looked right at her, before his gaze fell back to his drink. 'God, what am I doing? Staring at him.'

Henrietta nudged her. 'Drink up. Then you'll get another one from that gorgeous airman over there.'

'Yes, but what for?' she asked.

'He's good-looking,' Hen said, lifting her glass in salute.

'You have him then. I know where that ends.'

Hen laughed at her. 'He's just out for a bit of a flirt.'

Maybe men did want just that from youthful Henrietta, with her boyish figure and her pretty face, although she had resisted the temptation so far. But men seemed to want more from Nancy, with her hourglass figure and wild curls. She'd been there before.

'I'll be going home after this drink,' she said. 'I'll take Sue, Joan and Kathleen with me.'

The other girls were already getting silly, having had several drinks and no food since tea. She could see Oliver leaning away from the pretty girl as she moved in to speak to him.

'That's sweet,' Henrietta said. 'Maybe she really likes him...'

'Why shouldn't she?' Nancy could see the flush on his face. Maybe embarrassment. She decided in a flash to rescue him.

She finished her drink and approached their table.

'I'm sorry, it's Mr Pederick, isn't it?'

'Pilot Officer Pederick,' the girl said, tucking her hand into his arm.

'I am so sorry to ask this, but I have responsibility for those young land army recruits. Just girls, really; their first drinks have gone straight to their heads. I know you walk along the aero-drome road – I wonder if you would mind escorting us? I would hate them to get any unwelcome attention.'

Since one of them was being fed chocolate by an American and the other was squealing with laughter, holding two drinks, she was confident she had made her point.

Oliver climbed to his feet, straightening his arm. 'Actually, I can't stay late, I should be going. I'd be happy to help.'

His friends pleaded with him, but she could see the relief on his face. He pulled his coat on, his scarf half around his face and pulled his cap down over his eyes.

'Thanks, Johnny, Frieda, Joy.'

The girl jumped to her feet. 'I had a lovely time. Maybe we can do this again? My mother makes a lovely picnic.'

Under pressure, Oliver mumbled something like 'maybe' which was jumped on as a definite.

He turned to Nancy, who had linked arms with one of the girls and Henrietta, who had taken two more in tow.

'I didn't want to spoil your evening, Henrietta,' Nancy said.

'It won't be as much fun without you. And I don't quite trust those boys to walk us home.'

Oliver held the door open for them, and they stepped out. The cold air off the sea hit one of the girls and she reeled, Oliver helping to catch her other arm.

'She might...' Nancy warned as she steered the girl towards the gutter. Oliver stepped back to avoid his shoes getting spattered. 'Sorry,' she said.

'No worse than air force recruits.' His voice was warm and low, and full of humour she hadn't expected. 'And these ones look young.'

'Pretty well just eighteen,' Nancy said. 'There you go, love. No harm done. Stay with Hen.' She watched the group ahead, arms linked for support, as they started chatting.

He had fallen silent again. She liked the silence with him; it wasn't awkward. 'So,' he finally said. 'Where are you from?'

'London, originally. But I've moved around.'

'So you're a long way from home?'

'I'm never at home.' The words sneaked out before she could censor them. 'I'm sorry, I don't know where that came from. I mean, I'm not attached to any one place. How about you?'

'I'm an islander, born and bred. So what would make you feel at home?'

She took a long time to answer. 'Being with my people, I suppose. Family, friends.' Her throat closed up and roughened her voice. 'I just lost my mother. Bomb, direct hit.'

'I'm sorry.'

Another hundred, quiet steps. Another of the girls stopped to throw up, and Nancy stopped as well. 'We weren't that close at the time,' she explained. 'And at least it was just her, no one else was hurt. She went back to get her dog.' She managed a sad laugh. 'Ironically, he made it, although he lost a leg. The neighbours took him in.'

'Another lame duck. The war seems to have made a lot of those.' He carried on walking, and this time she felt awkward.

'Are you talking about yourself?'

He managed a laugh. She stumbled on the edge of the path, unable to see where the grass started in the darkness. 'Here.' He switched on the red glow of a blackout lantern, illuminating a few feet in front of them. 'It's been hard getting back to normal life,' he said. 'Of course, I'm lucky, it's the poor souls who didn't make it back that deserve our pity.'

She thought over his words. 'Was that the first evening out since your injury?'

'It's been very quiet. Since you and the Americans turned up, it's got a lot more lively.'

'Not in a good way?' she guessed from his tone.

'The landlord is *thrilled*,' he said, with that low laugh again.

'I just went to keep my friend happy. He asked a girl out, but she wasn't allowed to go unless there was another couple there. Hence me and Joy.'

'She's pretty.'

'She is.' He didn't sound interested. After a long pause he added: 'She likes the idea of walking out with a *hero*.'

'Well, who wouldn't?'

'I would rather someone walked out with *me*, Oliver Pederick, local boy, who loves planes and gardening.'

'Oh. I see that. I mean, people see a land girl and they think haystacks.'

He laughed out loud. 'They do?'

'They think we're all a bit loose in our morals,' she said, making a little laugh out of it. 'Girls in trousers, *shocking*, isn't it? This is our entrance. And, I'm sorry if I stared at you.'

'It's OK. I stare at the burns sometimes in the mirror. They look hardly human, like they're painted on. But at least I don't have to shave the burnt bits.'

'It wasn't even the scars I was looking at,' she said, thinking about it. 'You just looked so uncomfortable. Lots of people were looking at you, I could see you didn't like it.'

'So you stared as well?' But there was still laughter in his voice.

'I thought I would rescue you. And me, frankly. One of those Americans was very interested. They pick the older girls, they think we're more likely to...' She couldn't find a polite way to explain it to this young man.

'Find a haystack?' he asked, raising an eyebrow.

She laughed. 'Thank you for walking us home, I appreciate it. I'd better go, Henrietta's struggling with them now.'

'Thank you for rescuing me.' His words floated back to her as she hurried to where one of the girls had fallen over and was now giggling, struggling to stand up.

'Any time,' she called back.

5

PRESENT DAY, 21 APRIL

Libby spent a disturbed night in her grandfather's cottage, listening to the old house creak and move as it settled, and the different sounds from the sea. High tide sent the waves whooshing onto the sand dunes, hissing as they pulled back, just to return again. Far off, seabirds called, sounding like a child weeping. As the tide dropped, the sound became more continuous, a whispering that eventually lulled her to sleep.

After a breakfast of toast with some of her favourite peanut butter, roasted on the island and supplied by her mother, Libby explored her new studio. Her family had already set her up with the original dining table from the cottage, which had been carried into the largest bedroom. It couldn't have been easy, up the narrow stairs, but under the window she could work looking out to sea. Her dad had slipped an old office chair under it, while her grandad's old wing chair was sat in the corner. He had also included a couple of decent work lights and an extension lead with four outlets, the room just having one wall socket. She'd have to be careful not to overload it.

She checked her phone for the cargo boat's arrival time and found she still had an hour before she had to go and pick up her boxes. She walked down the stairs, scratchy with sand, and headed out to the beach. She pushed open the gate to stumble and slide down the gully that led to the sea. It was cool, the early chill not yet burned off, and the tide was out. Wisps of dry sand were lifted up by the breeze and twisted and danced along the beach.

The scent of the air tickled the back of her throat. She could pretend her grandparents were still sitting up at the cottage, talking, always talking. They liked so many things. Her grandmother sewed and knitted, read history and listened to the most eclectic range of music. Her grandfather loved the cricket but only on the radio; TV coverage was boring, he said. He would listen to it while working on his woodcarvings, making walking sticks for all his friends. For the children, he told stories around the fire. He was an armchair traveller, reading or listening to adventures and then magically retelling them as if he'd been there personally, standing by the subject's side.

She walked along the beach, the hard-packed wet sand contrasting with the powdery dry at the top. Her grandad had always rated the sand by sugars. The white sand of St Piran's was caster sugar; the grainy amber sand of St Brannock's was mostly demerara. But on this corner of the island, the sand was fine, and pale gold like soft brown sugar. Half a dozen birds landed further down the beach. Oystercatchers, they set up their call to each other from red beaks, prancing on scarlet legs. On the remains of an ancient stone pier, a cormorant popped up and spread its wings. 'Drying his laundry,' her grandma always used to say. Libby found she was missing her grandparents more now she was back in their world.

Her phone beeped and she was slow to look at it, reluctant to start her day.

'Schedule for week starting...' read the email, with a long list of times and dates. She would have to be in Penzance early in the week, and one of the other costumers could put her up in the tiny studio she had rented close to the main filming location. The email had included the detailed measurement forms that Callum had provided, and looking at the production schedule it looked like he would be in Cornwall next week, too. She could do dynamic measurements, too, seeing what extended movements he would need to make in his performance. He could be riding a horse or fighting with swords – it wouldn't do to have his shirt pulling out of his breeches all the time.

She consulted the ferry timetable and decided she'd catch the mid-afternoon ferry on Monday. By then she would have put away the contents of all the boxes arriving on the boat, met old friends in the pub this evening, and done the big family Sunday lunch. It would be a relief to get all the family stuff out the way so she could start work, the biggest job of her career to date.

I'll be better when I've spoken to Jory. When we've put all that teenage stuff behind us.

She took a deep breath to settle the nerves that jangled when she thought about seeing Jory. She could recall every plane on his face, the way his eyes narrowed when he was amused, the curve of his mouth before he said something funny. The darkness of his eyes was like plain chocolate, lit by grains of gold. She shook off the poetic sighs of her youth. He couldn't match up to the mythical creature of her dreams.

She was nervous about walking into her past, where she was the skinny ugly duckling to his popular, charming group of kids. She turned her back to the wind, walking towards the cottage. The window frames had been completely bleached on the sea side, from the salt and afternoon sun, and were flaking down to the old wood. Her studio was dark, and appeared to be looking up, over the sea to the islands beyond.

.   .   .

Libby set out along the aerodrome road to meet the cargo ship. She could see it approaching the islands, a dark blotch out to sea. Wrapped in one of her hand-printed overshirts, made as a student piece, she walked down to the port, the breeze warming up already on her face, whipping her hair around. Her father was standing on the quay, sipping a drink from a takeaway cup.

'Hi, Dad!'

Paul squinted into the sun as he turned. He held up a spare cup for her. 'I hope you still drink caramel lattes,' he said, smiling at her. 'And I brought the van.' He waved back at the vehicle behind him. 'How much stuff have you got coming?'

'It will all easily go in there.' She took the cup and hugged him, feeling his bulky shoulders, his solidness. He was the same height as her – she had picked up her height from her mother – but she noticed his beer belly had diminished. 'Have you been working out?'

'At my age, you have to,' he said. His smile was almost a wince. 'You get to fifty and start falling to bits. Everything that's wrong with you turns out to be a disease. You get pills for everything.'

'Well, cancer *is* a disease. What aren't you telling me?'

'No, you've got all the news. It's just sitting there, not doing anything. That might be all I need, they call it active surveillance.' They sat on the wall.

'What's that?' She tucked a hand into his arm, his plaid shirt soft against her skin.

He shrugged. 'They have to monitor it, that's all. I get blood tests every now and then, and I'll have a scan next year. Most people don't need anything else, but the oncologist suggested I lose a bit of weight and maybe give up dairy.'

She started laughing. 'Give up *cheese*? Dad. You love...' Her voice trailed away as she saw his expression. 'Dad?'

'You've got to do what you can, don't you? It came as a shock, I can tell you.' He sat on the wall overlooking the quay, where the boat was inching its stern in. The tide lapped the wall, climbing higher as the water was pushed ahead of the cargo ship. 'Giving up cheese might be giving up cancer. It was an easy decision.'

'Why didn't you tell me?'

He looked at her, his eyes the same light blue as hers, round and wide. 'I couldn't talk about it for ages. We didn't tell anyone, just headed for the mainland and told people we were going on holiday. Friends thought we were having marriage problems, you know, being all quiet and disappearing on and off.'

'Oh, Dad.' She sheltered against his side. 'You could have told *me*, you know that.' The ship crept forward, against the quay, and a man jumped off to tie it up, the engine whining in reverse to pull it in tight. A crowd of gulls screeched and dived into water churned up by the propellers.

'But you weren't here, chick. And you were just getting your dream job, if you remember.'

'I was mending clothes for extras mostly, but yes, it is the dream job.'

'And you would have wanted to do something to help, that's who you are. And you *couldn't* do anything, that was up to me and the hospital.' Finally, the gangway was rolled from its position on deck and onto the quay. The crane started lifting a case from the bows. Paul jumped off the wall and held out a hand for Libby that she didn't need. 'So, what have you brought?'

'Just plastic boxes and a couple of machine cases.' They walked over to where the crew were moving crates. 'For Elliott?' she said.

He called the name over his shoulder, waved to her dad and lifted the first of her industrial sewing machines. He helped her father carry it to the back of the van and heaved it in. The overlocker was next, equally heavy, while she lugged the boxes of fabric and pattern paper. Last, and most creepy, was her tailor's dummy, swathed in black plastic.

'It looks like a torso,' one of the crew joked.

'It's for a film star,' she said on impulse, then felt like she was boasting. 'One I haven't met yet.'

'You working on that TV thing on the mainland?'

'Sort of... I'm one of the people sewing costumes.'

'Will you do any of that Kerensa's sewing? She's a looker, she is...'

Libby squeezed the last of her boxes in, with shears, rotary cutters and boards. 'No. I'm working for a new male character.'

'Well, you should bring some of them back to St Brannock's. We'd show them a good island time.'

Local beer and every flavour of crisp under the sun? Maybe not.

She said her goodbyes, and her dad beckoned to her to join him in the van. 'We're picking up some muscle along the way,' he said, starting the engine. Her heart lurched. 'I don't think we can carry those machines upstairs very easily on our own.'

'Who?' Her heart fluttered at the thought of it being Jory.

What's wrong with you? she asked herself sternly. *You're not fifteen any more.*

'Kris. He said he'd help me out. We'll stop at his house.'

Jory's younger brother Kris was standing outside his parents' house. It was one door down from her mum and dad's place, who were their best friends; they had brought their kids up together. They had even put a gate through the garden fence. She squeezed over to let Kris in. Five years younger and slighter than his brother Jory, he was still easy on the eye. The brothers were both dark-haired and dark-eyed, but Kris was taller and leaner. He gave her a quick hug in a cloud of some woody aftershave.

'Hi, Libs. You look great. How's it going?'

'Good.' She waited until her dad headed up the airport

road, past lambs wagging their tails, feeding from their mothers. 'It must be snack time,' she said, laughing at them. It was lovely to be surrounded by green fields, the huge sky overhead and the sea lining the beach.

'Not a care in the world.' Kris glanced out, smiled at them. 'So, I hear you're going to be making clothes for a film star?'

'A rising *TV* star, anyway. He's been in a lot of series and done small parts in films.' She grinned over at him. 'I'm pretty excited to meet all the cast. I'll be working on his main wardrobe, but it's sixteen pieces, so will keep me busy.' She lifted her paper cup. 'Better than a few years ago when I mostly picked up dry cleaning, sewed on buttons and did coffee runs.'

'Did you hear about me and Jory?'

Just hearing his name made her jump; she turned her hot face into the cool air from the open window. 'Something about a boatyard?' His shoulder was warm against hers.

'Boat design, building and modification. We took over one of the units in West Island's old harbour. Colley's yard, by the old dock.'

'I know where that is, we used to sail around there, me and Beth and Dorrie. Building yachts, though? A bit of a step up from repainting the old ferries.'

'At the moment we're repairing them with some design modifications. I'm loving it, but Jory's the one with all the big ideas.'

'How did he even get into it?'

At that moment, her dad pulled over at the end of the road, half on the sandy verge, as close as they could get to the cottage. She got out with Kris and went to the back of the van.

'He did a boat design course at college. Well, university, I suppose.'

'Jory? He used to be dead set against education at all.'

Kris lifted the first of the machines. 'Oof. I think we'll do these one at a time. Grab that big plastic box, Libs, it's not that heavy.'

'Always the gentleman,' she joked and got a smiling glance back.

'Amber talked him into it. Do you know Amber? He met her while he was crewing at Dartmouth four years ago.'

'No, I don't know her. And I didn't know he'd done that either.' She'd had her head in her job so long... She put the box down and pushed the unlocked door open for them. 'Racing?'

'He was quite good at it,' Kris said, looking up at the stairs. 'But it doesn't pay. It was good for networking, though.'

'You'll have to lock the cottage from now on, maid,' her dad called over his shoulder. 'Lots of strangers on the islands now.'

'I suppose. And I don't want to lose any of the expensive equipment.'

Paul grabbed the other machine. 'Upstairs, then, love?'

'Yes please, and thank you for the amazing workroom. The table will be a great surface for cutting and construction.'

'Grandad's table wouldn't have looked right at our house,' he puffed as he put the machine down. 'Over there, Kris. Just three more trips, then, Libby?'

'Just bales and boxes.' They did it in two, Kris piling boxes in pairs and racing backwards and forwards, possibly showing off his lean shoulders and brown arms. She put the kettle on. Her mother had put her father's new favourite green tea in the cupboard. 'Very healthy,' she said, scanning the box. 'Green tea with cranberry.'

'Thanks love,' he said, smelling the steam. 'Disgusting, but good for me. If I drink this, I get a decaffeinated coffee as a reward back home.'

Kris accepted his builder's tea with thanks and stood looking over the beach. 'This is a gorgeous view. You doing it up to rent out for holiday lets again, Paul?'

'You know what it's like, we don't have enough money to

make it posh enough for the visitors. Last time someone complained we didn't have a steamer oven, whatever that is. But we're doing the plumbing and wiring. Then we'll try and get someone to replaster all the bits that we've cleared off. Tart it up on the cheap.'

'It would probably be better to take it all off, plaster again,' Kris said, looking around. 'I can give you a hand. Jory's at the design stage with the clients at the moment. I don't mind labouring for cash.'

Her dad looked over at her for a moment, then smiled at Kris. 'I might take you up on that. I hear you're going down to the pub tonight with Libby?'

'The usual crowd from school,' he said, and finished his tea. 'We're all looking forward to seeing our seamstress to the stars.'

All of who? Libby wondered, as she finished her tea.

'Well, I definitely owe you a drink for moving all the boxes.'

She smiled brightly, trying to not look like she was thinking about Jory.

6

MARCH 1942

Nancy didn't see Oliver for over a week, as they were all needed to construct their barracks, do basic training in horticulture and wait for two elderly horses to drag a plough up and down the field. The girls enjoyed petting them on their occasional breaks and chatting to the even more ancient farmer. He was short and slight, but he seemed strong. He was full of the tales of the first war, when his daughter had been a land girl in Cornwall. He brought them all a basket of slightly wrinkled store apples which were sweet, and his wife had furnished him with some pastry twists for the girls to share. It was almost like having apple pie, even if the pastry was made with lard.

'What will we be planting?'

He cackled at their ignorance. 'We'll need to plough first, then break up the sod with a harrow – grass roots are tough. Then we'll sow turnips, roots, potatoes. Anything that will store through the winter and help feed the islanders. We'll plant mangel-wurzels for the cattle, too.'

Nancy hadn't heard the word before, it seemed hilarious. 'I'd love to learn to plough,' she admitted, putting her fingers on the handle. 'I have used a tractor for harrowing.'

He looked her over. 'You look sturdy enough to plough. Mind you, a pair of horses can pull you right over; you need to keep it moving. Like a bicycle.'

'Do you mind if I try?' She looked over at her superior. 'If you don't mind, Miss Westacott.'

'Certainly, Baldwin. But don't get in Mr Allison's way. We need this field done as soon as possible.'

Nancy gave it a go. It was ridiculously hard. The plough was heavy, and if she didn't put a lot of her weight on it, it shot out of the ground. The horses wouldn't work for her, or one would but the other wouldn't, leaving Mr Allison almost helpless with laughter.

'No, maid, like *this*.' He put his bony hand beside hers and put all his weight behind it. It worked. The blade cut a wobbly furrow and turned it. 'I tell you what. You go to their heads and encourage them. Storm there, the bay, he's eighteen. He's already thinking of his stable. And young Star is a few stone lighter so they're an awkward pair. If you can keep them going, I'll be done in less time.'

'That would be lovely,' she said, and the afternoon began.

It was much more work than she had expected. Star was younger and flightier, would stumble to the side, pulling Storm with her. Storm would just stop unexpectedly, and Nancy would have to heave to get him moving again. The wind off the sea kept her hands and face cool, although the work made her hot. But the afternoon went by faster, and at the end of it she was filthy and stank of horses, but there was an area along the fence where brown earth was visible as the grass was turned deep under the soil.

For once, the supervisor was full of praise. 'You'll need a bath,' she said. 'In the absence of proper facilities, perhaps we should hose you down, clothes and all.'

She caught sight of a slim figure in the distance, walking head-down towards her. She squinted into the low sun, wondering if it was Oliver. 'I'd be grateful, Miss Westacott. Right now, even a horse trough would be heaven.'

'None of that, it's not fair for the horses,' the famer said, frowning. 'Go on with you. You did a good job, maid. We'll get it done by the end of the week, Missus.' He tipped his cap to the supervisor. 'Then we'll get harrowing. Your potatoes will be ready to go in.' The ministry was sending crates of seed potatoes and they had been told they were precious, none were to be wasted.

He walked off, Miss Westacott behind him, as Nancy leaned against the fence to knock the clods of earth from her boots. She hadn't been this tired since... well, for years, anyway.

A sound made her jump. 'They've got you ploughing now?' Oliver, smiling at her, was standing on the grass on the other side of the fence.

She turned to face him. 'I rather enjoyed it. The old horse was getting so tired I was a bit worried the farmer would yoke me up alongside the young one.'

He laughed, the tough skin holding down his smile on one side. 'You look tired.'

'And dirty. But I'm sure you're too much of gentleman to mention it.'

'No. I was about to say if you had potatoes in your pocket they would be sprouting already.'

'Nothing that being hosed down by freezing cold water won't fix,' she said. 'I have to go, we're not supposed to stand chatting to young men.'

'Of course.'

He stepped back, tipped his cap to her. She walked across to the larger group of girls, gathering up their tools around the new cabins. Being largely made of corrugated tin, they were going up fast.

'Any chance of a luxury bathroom, yet?' she asked, then yawned until her jaws ached.

'Actually – *ta da*!' Henrietta and a couple of the girls, laughing, stepped back outside the tent. A tin bath, presumably for the new barracks, had been given a few inches of water and – heavens be praised – a little steam came off the top. 'We've got a bit of canvas to give you some privacy as well.'

'Unless one of the fly boys circles the airfield,' she said, but her thick jumper was already off. One of the younger girls had two towels.

Hen handed her a bar of her own soap. 'For your hair. Don't go mad, I won't get any more for a month.'

Sitting in the water, shampooing and rinsing, scrubbing and then drying, she felt truly clean for the first time in weeks. She pulled a dressing gown over the top of the towels and headed into the tent to put clean clothes on. Her old ones went straight in the bath behind her for a rinse, and she heard the girls laughing about the mud.

Miss Westacott put her head around the tent flap. 'Ah, there you are, Baldwin. I've arranged boilersuits for any girls who wish to help with the more physical tasks. They are old ones the engineers aren't using. You can ask at the small door at the side of hangar B.'

'Thank you, Miss Westacott.'

'Next time, go through me before you decide to do something unexpected.' But her nod held approval.

While getting dressed, Nancy thought about Oliver again. She was curious about him, there was something so sad about him...

'So, Nancy, what are you doing on Sunday?' Henrietta nudged her arm. 'Some of us were thinking of going over to one of the other islands. St Piran's or West Island, or that little one, the one they call the rocky isle.'

'I could do with a quiet day. I might go to church.' She tried to smile. 'And I've got some letters to answer.'

Hen frowned. 'Who from?'

'Old friends. People I've neglected. It's too dark in the evenings to write.'

Her friend wound her arm around Nancy's waist. 'Oh, do come!'

Nancy stared out the tent flap, over at the sea in the west and south, islands in the distance. 'I'm not ready to be seasick again,' she joked. 'And I have to put up with you lot all day as it is. Like a flock of parakeets.'

'That Ollie might be at the pub, if you want to come down....' Hen watched as Nancy dressed, putting on the cardigan she had only just finished knitting.

'Ollie is just a boy I feel sorry for. He must be five, six years younger than me. I feel like an old lady going around with you lot as it is.'

'He's the same age as Mary's sister, who's about a year older than her, twenty-one. He's old enough to get shot down, brought back to England and be training for air crew again.'

'What?'

Hen handed her a hairbrush. 'That's what I heard. He was on desk duty, then he moved to ground crew to do some engineering stuff, now he wants to go back in the air.'

'I would have thought he'd had enough of danger and excitement.' She started tugging at the tangles in her mass of curls, now almost to her shoulders. 'I need a haircut. Perhaps I should get it shorn off, like the boys do.'

'It's your crowning glory,' Hen said, throwing back her artfully tonged brown hair, usually held in a ponytail. 'It's so dark and curly.'

'It looks like a swarm of bees have sat on my head,' Nancy said, without rancour. 'And it takes forever to get grass seeds and brambles out.'

'Please, Nancy. If you don't want to go to the pub, let's go out, just you and me.'

'And end up with everyone else at the only pub that will serve us?'

'We'll just go for a walk. We can sit and chat. You don't look happy, and I've got – well, I need to talk to someone, too.'

Nancy's attention was caught. She sighed, gave up on her hair and crammed it into her hat, and nodded.

'Just a short walk, Hen. I ache all over and it will be even worse tomorrow.'

They walked along the road away from the town, the road that Oliver had walked in on. It petered out to two wheel ruts, then ended at a low stone wall and a small gate. The sign said *Capstan Cottage*. Underneath was a scribbled instruction, painted on by hand. *Private*.

'That must be where Ollie lives,' Henrietta said. 'It's a bit creepy. He lives with this old woman, people say she's a bit odd. Maybe mad.'

A footpath went through the wall, a small gap leading to a route carved in the dunes towards the beach. 'I'm sure she's not mad,' Nancy said. 'She'd be locked up if she was.'

'She's probably kept in the attic,' Hen said, 'like poor Mr Rochester's wife.'

'Oh, don't be daft.'

She scrambled down the path to the sea, curving away from the cottage. The tide was out, and the sand was lit fiery red by the sunset. Stiff grasses held the soft soil underfoot, more sand than anything else. Mounds of sea pinks were just topped with buds, wrapped in silver hairs like spiderwebs. They were both out of breath when they reached the beach.

'The tide's going out,' Henrietta said, pointing at the lacy edge to the ripples. 'We can walk all the way back to the harbour.'

Nancy wrapped her coat tighter around her neck and

started walking. The wet sand was pristine, not a footprint, even from a gull or dog. 'So, what did you need to talk about?' She couldn't imagine Henrietta having any secrets, she was such a sunny person, so open.

'Do you know why I joined the land army?'

'To see the world, get rich?' Nancy joked. 'I just thought you needed to get away from being a child, living with your parents.'

'My mum and dad are the best, kindest people.' She walked on ahead, ramming her hands into her pockets.

'Well, that's good, isn't it?'

'They own a sweet shop.' Her voice was so sad she might have been telling Nancy they had died.

'Hen, what is it?'

When she turned back to Nancy her eyes were glistening. 'They have a plan. I will marry George Pinter, and we'll take over the sweet shop and raise our children there.'

'You've never mentioned him.' Nancy caught her arm. 'What's wrong?'

She moved closer. 'He says we have to get married, because of what... what we've *done*.'

'Oh.' Looking back at Henrietta, she could see the corner of Capstan Cottage, now blood red, the light fading, the clouds purpling. 'Well, that's all nonsense. You can just say you don't love him enough, and you want to meet someone else.'

'He says he'll tell them. He'll tell everyone in the town.' She sounded desperate. 'My dad's a churchwarden, my mother's chair of the townswomen's guild.'

'Hen, what exactly *have* you done?' Henrietta shook her head. She started walking along the beach, the whisper of the waves and the wind the only sound. Nancy followed, the wet sand eating up any noise. 'Hen, you can't have done anything illegal.'

'Just... immoral.' Her voice broke up, Nancy caught her elbow.

'Hen, stop. We've all done something immoral at some point in our lives.'

The girl looked down. Tears were tracking down her face. 'Not like this.'

Nancy could see from her expression that she was ashamed. 'Exactly like this. When did it happen?'

Henrietta tucked her hand in the crook of Nancy's elbow. 'It started out as kissing and cuddling. Then it was tickling...' She took out a handkerchief. 'I knew it was wrong, even though he said it was just playing. Then he said it was all right because we were going to get married.'

'Dear Hen. It's all right.'

She stumbled in the sand and Nancy caught her, hugged her. It was almost dark now, she could just see Henrietta's wet eyes. 'It was wrong.'

'No, sweetheart.' Nancy put an arm around her shoulders, guiding her on. 'And you don't have to marry him.'

'But I couldn't persuade him to stop! I managed to push him away for a few months, but then he started again.'

Nancy was enraged at this man, preying on a young girl. 'How old is he?'

Henrietta blew her nose again. 'Twenty-four. He's six years older than me. My parents think he's lovely.'

'Did you join the land army to get away from him?'

'As soon as I was old enough. But now, Mother is talking about a wedding before he gets called up.'

'Why hasn't he been already?'

The half-moon reflected off the blackness beyond the sand. 'He was a train driver, a reserved occupation. Now they are recruiting more older drivers and women, he's freed up to enlist. He says he doesn't want to until he must. His mother relies on him.'

Nancy had to lengthen her stride to keep up. 'Hen, wait for me.'

Henrietta whirled around. 'You won't tell anyone?'

'Of course not. But he can't hold this over you. You mustn't think of marrying him.'

They walked on for several minutes until they reached another path up to the aerodrome road.

'I thought, if I grew up and moved away I'd be able to see a solution. But my parents want me to go home when I get leave, and he'll be there. Stroking my knee under the table, kissing me in the garden. I can't do it, I just can't.' She sounded hysterical, so different from the usual calm Henrietta.

'Would you like me to come with you?'

'What? Would you? Oh, Nancy, that would be so kind.'

'I warn you now, though. If he puts his hand on my knee he'll get a shock,' Nancy said grimly.

7

PRESENT DAY, 21 APRIL

Libby dressed especially carefully for the evening out at the pub, trying to work out which of her crumpled outfits didn't need an iron, then pressing two of them. Boho chic or business classy? Then she remembered the sticky seats in the pub, the blaring music and spilled beer and went for old jeans and an embroidered top she'd bought off the rails at a festival, which she loved.

As she got ready, she thought of Amber, Jory's new partner. She didn't remember ever hearing the name. Her parents hadn't mentioned that Jory was seeing anyone new, but then, she'd never asked. She wondered if he was still with her. Not that it mattered, she told herself, trying to dry some bounce into her flat, glossy hair. He was a childhood crush, that was all. Who hadn't wanted to kiss the most popular boy in the school? Jory wouldn't come out, anyway. And he probably wouldn't come to Sunday lunch either.

She shrugged a velvet jacket over her outfit, an exhibition piece she had made for her final year at university, and headed out. It would get cold tonight and she'd be glad of the coat on the way home. The stars were starting to show; it was a clear night, just space above. That's what her grandad had always said, and she felt a little sad at the memory.

She walked through the town to the Bargeman's Rest, which from the outside looked exactly the same as it always had. Except the smokers were vaping fruity clouds rather than smoke. She was just ducking into the low door when she bumped into someone coming the other way.

'Whoa, princess!' he said, before she registered the very short hair, straight eyebrows and glittering eyes of Jory Trethewey. '*Libby?* Really? Kris said you were coming!' He gathered her up into a hug before she could move. He even kissed her cheek. 'It's great to see you. I'm just taking the dog home, I'll be back in a minute.' As he walked down the road he shouted back, 'Don't tell them all your news, I want to hear it!'

And that was that, after all the years she'd spent wondering whether he meant anything by the kiss he gave her before she went to university, all the further speculation after they engaged in a hot and heavy kiss at his sister Dorrie's wedding... Questioning. Speculating. Yearning. Apparently, all that time was wasted; it seemed he had forgotten all about it, and to him she was simply his sister's best friend.

She slipped inside. The pub had been improved considerably; it clearly wasn't the hangout for students any more. There were a few couples, some older people. A call came up from Kris and his sister Dorrie who stood up when they saw her.

'Over here, Libs!' The girls hugged, the years apart falling away.

Dorrie studied her. 'You look fantastic, I love your hair.'

Libby hugged her again. 'You look exactly the same!'

The others crowded around. There were a couple of girls she knew from school, one of them recently engaged and showing off her ring, and Ben, the helicopter co-pilot. By the time she'd sat down and someone had bought a round of drinks, her own sister had turned up with Jory.

'I found this vagrant outside,' Beth said. 'I haven't seen him for ages. Where's Amber?'

'In London, dealing with the bank,' Jory said, squeezing on the end of the bench next to Libby. 'So, Libby. Everyone's talking about your new job.'

'It's not exactly a new job,' she demurred, but someone was talking over her about the show's male lead.

'I hear you help all the stars get dressed,' Dorrie said.

'It's really not like that,' Libby started to say, but someone had said something crude and she finally banged her hand on the table. Dorrie shushed everyone, and even Jory turned to look at her. 'I am going to be making the costumes for a new character on the show so, no, not Sam Worthing. I will be here all summer, except when I get to go to the film locations in Cornwall. *Which*,' she added, with enthusiasm, 'I get to start on Tuesday!'

There was a general round of applause. 'Still, you will meet the cast,' Kris said. 'Maybe work with them?'

She shook her head. 'It's a lot less fun than it sounds. I'm just making his clothes; I won't have a reason to meet the whole cast. But I will get to meet him, and I'll definitely make all his clothes once he's ready to start filming. But I'll mostly be in a draughty warehouse, sewing like mad with a load of costumers, moaning about the catering.'

Her sister showed her phone around. 'This is him. I looked him up,' she said unnecessarily. 'He's twenty-four and a rising star, rumoured to be the *major* new heart-throb now the main characters are hitched.'

Jory looked over. 'Callum Michaels... Hope he's not too much of a diva for you, Libs.'

She shook her head. 'So, how about you? Yacht designer extraordinaire?'

He laughed, shook his head. 'Kris should stop telling people that. We're not there yet. We have two repairs to do, both racing yachts, both with dodgy hulls. One hit a whale in the Southern Ocean, can you imagine that?'

She was intrigued. 'Kris said you did some racing, too. I didn't know.'

'I crewed for two seasons, just to make the contacts. There are always running repairs in fast yachts. I went to Dartmouth and Cowes. I really wanted to try the oceanic races but didn't have the experience. Maybe next time.'

She leaned towards him. 'I was surprised to hear you went back to study. You always said school was for children.'

'I said – and *did* – lots of stupid things when I was young. I was wrong.' He sipped his beer, looked away. 'Getting away from the islands made me realise that there were so many opportunities out there, if I just went and looked for them. Like you did; you paved the way for me.'

'I did? I was just the geeky, quiet girl in the corner.'

He smiled, shook his head. 'You never were, though, were you? You had big opinions, as I recall. You were always looking stuff up, trying new things. You might be quiet in a crowd but you're confident enough one-to-one. And, remember, you were the one who came up with the idea to lubricate our slide with bubble mixture. I nearly ended up in next door's garden.'

She nearly snorted her white wine out of her nose. 'I did have a lot of good ideas.'

'But then you got really shy, around sixteen.'

She nodded. 'You didn't have time for Dorrie, Beth and me. You were one of the big boys.'

'I did let sport go to my head a bit. And girls, oh my. Didn't have time for you young 'uns.'

'Is that how you saw me?' The words burst out of her before she could stall them. She could tell Beth was listening. 'I mean, I suppose we were all just annoying little girls.'

He smiled, turned to Beth. 'I liked to think you were cheering for me in the gig racing and the football.'

Beth rolled her eyes. 'Best footballer, best rower, biggest ego. Of course we did. You would have deflated like a balloon if we hadn't.'

The conversation became more general, but Libby could feel her pulse bumping uncomfortably in her throat.

'Another drink?' Beth asked.

'Just sparkling water. I have to walk back and I haven't had anything to eat.'

'I'll get some fries for the table if you like,' Jory suggested. This was generally well received, and Libby receded into the corner, watching the conversation. He was right – she wasn't as outgoing in crowds, but it was lovely to see the people she had known all her life chatting and laughing.

Jory leaned forward unexpectedly. 'I'll walk you back if you like. It's very dark along the path.'

She was so tempted to say yes, as she always would have, then spent the night obsessing over every look and word. But this was a new Libby, who wasn't going to be tempted, even if her heart *had* sped up when he asked.

'I have good boots, a torch, a mobile phone, and it's not like I'll get lost,' she said. And she smiled with something like relief, at a ghost being laid to rest.

8

APRIL 1942

Nancy thought about what Henrietta had told her. It would just be her and five others in their makeshift barracks for St Brannock's. Two girls were bunking in at the dairy farm on the other end of the island, Tors Side Farm. Several farmers had applied for land army help, but as part of their crop was flowers, they were not allowed help. But the cheerful fields of daffodils uplifted Nancy enormously, and she could imagine them doing the same to families all over the country.

She headed into the town a little early on Friday, bought herself a small paper of fish and chips, and settled on the harbour wall to enjoy them in peace.

A familiar male voice interrupted her thoughts. 'Hello. You had the same idea as me.'

She jumped, but the shock was a pleasant one. 'Oliver. Or is it Ollie?'

'Out of uniform, Ollie is fine. May I join you?'

She smiled at him, watched him manoeuvre himself onto the stone wall. He had a bad leg, too. He saw her staring, she didn't seem able to stop.

'I broke it in the crash,' he said, opening the corner of his paper. 'Look at those beauties. I'm sure Mrs Hammond gives me extra. People either don't look at me at all, or overcompensate for my injuries.'

'You've got twice as much as me,' she said with a smile, unable to keep the envy out of her voice.

'I'll share.' The side of his face close to her was the unmarked one, smooth. She liked the sprinkling of freckles across his face, but it made him look even younger.

She concentrated on her food. He was right; she was burrowing down for the last bits of batter when he held out his paper to share.

'Thanks.' She sighed with pleasure. The water was just choppy, lifting and dropping the smaller fishing boats. The wind rattled the ropes on the masts. 'That's lovely. I feel hungry a lot of the time. It's just knowing we're being rationed makes me hungry, they feed us perfectly well.'

'Lots of porridge, and bread with dripping?'

She raised an eyebrow. 'Don't kid yourself I was eating any better before the war.'

He reached over to pick up another chip. 'What were you doing?'

She took a moment to censor most of what she wanted to say. 'I was in a cotton mill in Manchester. Before that I was making wireless sets back home, in Braintree. What about you?'

He looked out to sea. 'I suppose I expected to end up doing something on the boats, but my mother and aunt got me jobs in the hardware shop. I did a bit of painting and decorating, too, odd jobs.' He pointed out to sea, where dozens of small boats rocked in the harbour. 'I've painted lots of those.'

His voice was soft and deep, despite his youth, and she smiled at him. 'You were probably still at school,' she said.

'I was fourteen. I got into the technical school in Penzance, I wanted to go into engineering. I've always had a thing about planes.'

'Then the war came along.'

'Perfect timing.' His voice was strained. 'I really wanted to be a pilot but that wasn't possible for someone like me. But I was happy to be air crew, I trained as a bombardier and rear gunner.' He was still staring at the sea, his whole face sad.

'I heard you want to fly again,' she said, spearing another piece of batter.

'I've applied for air crew, but they don't think I'll get through the medical.' His hand shook as he held the paper, the fingers curved by the scars.

She took a last chip, but he seemed to have forgotten the food, staring off to the other island. 'I would have thought you'd be scared to go back,' she said softly.

He managed a short bark of laughter. 'Scared? I'd be terrified. That's why I want to go back.'

Nancy couldn't understand it. 'I think you've given enough.'

That's when he turned to look at her, the eye in the middle of the scar tissue weeping, as if half his face was crying. 'The others gave their lives. It's the least I can do. To honour their memory.'

She wiped the grease from her fingers on a corner of the paper. She put her hand under his, shook the packet of food for a second. 'Eat up. I reckon you're too *skinny* to get through the medical.' His skin was cold, and she felt self-conscious at the way her heart skipped at the brief contact.

He half smiled then, taking another chip. 'Sorry. I can't explain it, it's just a strong feeling I have.'

'I can't say I understand, but I haven't been in your shoes, so I can't say anything.'

'You are the only person who *doesn't* express an opinion. My mother, my aunt, Joy, her friends, my friends... they are all determined to keep me safely on the ground.'

'So, you're seeing Joy now?'

'She's OK. She's nice to me, which makes it easier to get out more, even with... this.' He waved a hand at his damaged face.

Nancy took the empty newspaper and twisted it up neatly. 'Don't sell yourself short.'

But there was something she hadn't liked about the way Joy spoke to Ollie. Hero worship, like she was infatuated with his story rather than the man inside. She walked over to the bin and got rid of the rubbish.

She was surprised to see he had followed her, was at her elbow. 'That's good advice, but it sounds like you know from experience.'

She wanted to tell him so much, to tell someone. 'I've made a few mistakes, that's all.'

'Look, I'm going to see my cousin on Sunday. It's a lovely ride out to Morwen Island on the boat. Would you like to come too? I hate the way they stare at me over there when I'm on my own.'

The word 'Morwen' was like an electric shock. 'Uh,' she stammered. 'I'm not sure, I might be needed on the farm...'

'Well, let me know. I walk past every day or you can drop a message at the house.'

That helped; she could change the subject. 'I saw the cottage, it must have a lovely view over sea.'

'Too good a view. The sand gets blown up in the storms, and spring tides sometimes throw spray right over the house.'

For a moment she imagined the power of the sea, shaking the windows, spray rolling down the glass like on a boat's porthole. 'That must be incredible.'

He smiled. 'Next time we expect a storm, you'll have to come over for high tide.' He walked along the quay wall, around the harbour. Someone had fixed seashells along a stretch of the wall, mussels, scallops and oysters set in mortar. She ran her hand over them, sniffing back the beginnings of tears.

'What is it? Did I say something wrong?'

She turned to him then, worried that she had upset him. 'No, I'm sorry. I've had a rough couple of years, that's all.'

'Your mother died.'

It wasn't the only reason tears crowded into her eyes. 'It's all tough now, with the war. But mostly, I get by. I'm a cheerful sort of girl.'

'No one's cheerful all the time,' he said.

'Never mind,' she said. 'I'd better get back, a couple of the girls and I plan to play cards for clothing coupons.'

He laughed. 'Good luck with that,' he said. 'There's no cloth on the islands, anywhere.'

'I'll get the rest of my uniform soon,' she answered. 'An extra jumper and a mackintosh. I can't say the land army uniform is all that flattering, but it's good for planting acres of potatoes.'

Ollie turned around at that. 'Emma, my cousin, has been digging the garden to plant a few vegetables. On the land side, obviously, not the sea side. We could do with a few seed potatoes if there are any spare.'

'I'll see if we have a few left over. I'll think about going to Morwen. Anyway, enjoy your evening.'

She had nothing to offer Ollie, but she had to admit she was always pleased to see him. And, as she walked away, her heart ached a little at the thought.

9

PRESENT DAY, 25 APRIL

By Tuesday, Libby was on the mainland, trying to look composed and part of the crew as she walked past the service truck blocking the tiny roads that led down to the sea. She recognised the wardrobe designer, Magda, who waved her over.

'Great timing, Olivia. Or do you prefer Liv?'

'I'm normally Libby, but Olivia's fine,' she said, scanning the line of sand where half a dozen people were walking.

'Well, welcome to the madness, Libby. Your client is down there, walking the ground for the scene. He'll be in some of Sam's old clothes, it's just a torn shirt and soaking wet breeches. He's supposed to have fallen out of a boat, so he's going to have to wade out of the sea shortly.' She grimaced. 'It's *freezing.*'

Libby could see a younger man walking backwards and forwards with someone with a clipboard.

'What do I need to do?'

'Look, he's busy filming until we lose the morning light. Then after lunch he's going to meet his horse. All actors say they can ride a horse, but most of them struggle with *acting* on horseback.' She grinned. 'You can get your hands on him then, ask whatever questions you need. He has a lot of action – his outdoor clothes need to allow him to ride, have a fist fight with another character. And he has to carry one of the girls.' She rolled her eyes. 'Guaranteed to split shoulder seams, so make sure you reinforce them.'

'I always do,' Libby said, nodding. 'So, what's the idea for the character?'

'Young, reckless, brought up rough so a bit uncomfortable in his glad rags. We think he would find the transition difficult, so possibly making the coats a little ill-fitting – like they've been altered to fit him – would look better than tailored like Sam's. Neckcloths more romantic than starched and formal. Breeches need a bit of room.'

'Of course, for the horse riding.'

'Our animal manager has picked a big one for him, a bit of a stretch but he's got long legs. He's six foot one.' She smiled. 'No guarantee he can stay on his back, of course. We have four generic shirts for you to fit to him. His boots will be coming next week, so he'll be acting in wellies until then. When the crew break, I'll introduce you.'

'Do you need me for anything until then?'

'You know what it's like, we always need help with costumes. One of the girls throws the outfits on like they are yoga clothes – she tears stitches just getting her shift on. And this afternoon I could do with help sewing our lead lady into a gown.' She waved to the men on the beach. 'Come on down, I'll introduce you to Callum. He seems like a nice kid.'

Libby could feel herself tense as she walked down the soft sand on the slipway onto the beach. Several men were walking around, some making notes. One man was wearing a headset, and he walked up to them with another man at his side.

'Hi, Magda. Another one of your elves? This is Callum Michaels.'

Callum was tall, and looked older than twenty-four. His brown hair was a little sun-bleached at the front, like he spent a lot of time outside. He was slim rather than broad-shouldered like the male lead, Sam, and he had a dazzling smile.

They shook hands.

'Libby,' she said. 'I'll be your costumer.'

'Be nice to her, Callum, or she'll leave pins in cruel places,' Magda said. 'It's only his second day here, Libby, so you can find your way around together.'

'Nice to meet you, Libby,' Callum said with a smile. 'Where do you want me?'

'Magda suggested we catch up over lunch and I can start asking questions.'

'I'll look for you when we break,' he said, speaking over his shoulder as he was beckoned away. 'I have to practise running in the sand and not falling over. Very skilled work,' he shouted as he started to run.

Magda led her around the location, showed her the village, and they got a coffee from a café on the beach.

'It's not very different from the urban shows you've worked on, but the locations are more spread out.' Magda sipped her coffee. 'Honestly, a lot of it is mending. The main workshop is back in Bristol, and we'll be there later in the shoot. Callum was only cast a month ago and we only had a few costumes in storage that fitted him. I've designed his look to be brooding, a bit of a loose cannon, but I'm not sure that's where the character will go.'

Libby nodded, looking at the roughs Magda had sketched out. 'Will I get a copy of the script?'

'You will, so you'll be able to get ahead of the next block of shooting. We did take basic measurements but he's been working out, so they'll need tweaking.'

Magda opened the door of what must have been a boat shed at one point, now converted into a temporary office with electric wires taped to the ground, the smell of salty damp everywhere.

She led Libby to the back of the space, to bare planks forming steep stairs.

'Upstairs?' Libby asked.

'Upstairs. Introduce yourself around, offer to do a beverage run, and you'll be part of the gang. I'll let Callum know where to find you.' Unexpectedly, she leaned forward for a hug. 'Welcome to the team. You'll fit right in.'

Libby was still wondering what she meant by that when she reached the top of the stairs. It looked like a former sail loft and was filled with natural light cascading down from large roof lights. Four tables formed a loose rectangle, a couple of garments spread over each. There were several commercial sewing machines, but everyone was sitting around the middle of the room, sewing by hand.

'Ah, another slave to our little workroom,' a man said cheerfully, waving at the rest of the team. She either smiled or greeted them as she went around, being introduced but immediately forgetting their names. The first man, Brandon, was easier to remember as his T-shirt was printed with many different versions of his own name.

'I'm sure you didn't catch everyone's names,' he said. 'I mostly sew Sam's clothes, and I've probably been here the longest.' Brandon handed Libby a petticoat with a ragged hem. 'Let's see how you manage that,' he said, handing her a threaded needle.

Libby sat down, amused at the test. 'Why don't we use fusible tape instead of all that stitching by hand?' she said, teasing him. 'I could iron this up in thirty seconds.'

Brandon's face was a picture of horror at the thought before the others cracked up, and he grinned at her. 'You got me.'

There was a peculiar peace that always came over Libby when she did plain sewing. It was uncomplicated, and the sounds of conversation started to fall away as she stitched, rethreaded her needle, stitched again. When she got all the way around, half an hour had passed. She unpicked the first few awkward stitches she had made and replaced them with matched, almost invisible hemming.

Brandon picked up the petticoat and held it to the light. 'OK, not bad. You've passed the first test to join the elves.'

'That's very high praise from Brandon,' Sinead said.

'What's the next test?'

'Remembering the tea and coffee order.' She handed Libby a folded piece of paper. 'If you don't mind? There's a catering truck just around the corner.'

'I don't mind.' She hadn't noticed how thirsty she was while she'd been working. 'I'm just a bit unsure what to do with Callum when he's free.'

'Bring him up here. We have a fitting area, you can take measurements and fill out the liabilities and allergies questionnaire, and I'll be near if you need anything. Our characters ride horses and get into fights – it requires a bit of know-how to accommodate them so they don't look like they're wearing jodhpurs when they get down. There will be a few clothes for dances, too, later in the series. We'll probably have some in stock, but they'll need refitting.'

'I've been warned.'

She walked downstairs to get the coffees and teas, too many to carry on one tray so she went back for the second round. The caterer kindly marked up all the cups, which would help get names into her head. Just as she was balancing the last four cups and a packet of biscuits on her way back to the boathouse, she was called from behind. She turned to see Callum jogging towards her.

'Let me help you! You look like—' He just caught the biscuits as they slipped from her hand. He was soaking wet, carrying a bag. His physical presence so close to her suddenly made her face feel warm, and she hoped she wasn't blushing. She tried to seem nonchalant as they fell into step.

COMING HOME TO THE COTTAGE BY THE SEA   63

'Only because you startled me. Are you free now?'

'Well, it's lunch soon, but I'm free for half an hour.' He followed her to the stairs. 'Is this where they've got you?'

'It's the nicest workroom I've been in, on location,' she said, leading the way. She introduced Callum, handed over the biscuits and showed him around.

'So that is the fitting room?'

He pointed to a curtained area with drapes that didn't quite meet, a folding chair and a full-length mirror.

'Glamorous, isn't it?' Libby said. 'This is pretty good, really. I've fitted people in corridors before.'

'Wow.' He tugged at the curtains, starting to shiver. 'Not exactly private.'

'They never are. But you'll only be down to your underwear.'

He leaned forward and spoke under his breath. 'They told me I won't be able to keep my normal pants on when I'm in costume.'

'No. Modern waistbands show up,' she said, as breezily as she could. 'You'll be given a nineteenth-century equivalent, but that will come from stock, you won't have to be measured for that.'

His skin reddened quickly. 'Right. OK. I'm new to this historical stuff.'

'Me too.' She smiled, hoping it looked reassuring. 'But everyone is on your side, everyone wants you to be brilliant. Get changed, if you like. No one's looking.'

He looked away as a couple of people put their work down, started talking about lunch. 'Is it wildly inappropriate if we go back to my hotel instead?' he said, sounding uncomfortable. 'Then you could do all my measurements and stuff. My room-mate could be there, if you like.'

Libby was a bit surprised and aware of Magda looking at

them over her glasses. 'Um, I'll just ask if there are any insurance implications. It looks like lunch now, though.'

'I'm just a bit... *shy*...'

'I hope you don't have any major sex scenes to do, then,' she joked.

'Not so far.' He followed her down the stairs. 'But they did ask my agent about how comfortable I was with nudity.'

'What did they say?'

He winced. He shrugged on a sweatshirt from his shoulder bag, and they joined the back of a long queue. 'She did what she always does. She lied. According to her I can climb mountains, hang-glide and make balloon animals.'

She smiled at that. 'And ride horses?'

He laughed as they shuffled one step closer to the smells of something delicious. 'No, I actually *can* ride. But not do all the tricks in a Victorian saddle that they want me to. I have to have extra lessons with Horatio the stunt horse.'

'I used to ride,' she reminisced, surprised at how easy it was to chat to Callum. 'There was a pony-trekking company on the island, it's probably still running, I might give it a go.'

He smiled at her. 'You say "the island" as if it's the only one in the world. Which island?'

'Sorry. We literally are a bit insular. *Insula* means island in Latin. The Atlantic Isles, I come from St Brannock's. The pony place was on St Petroc's.'

'That's off Cornwall, isn't it?'

'Hours away by ferry, actually, but yes.'

He laughed. They were close enough to the counter for him to lean against the side of the catering trailer. 'How on earth did you end up working in TV?'

'I always loved making things. I started sewing when my grandma taught me. When I was about six, I made clothes for all my toys.'

'Brilliant. And now you're making clothes for me.' He waved her ahead of him.

She asked for a chicken salad and was handed a plate of rainbow-coloured vegetables and sliced meat. He ordered a vegan plate, and they both perched at a table nearby.

She moved closer, away from people passing them. 'How about you? Did you always want to be an actor?' Close up, he was remarkably good-looking, with long eyelashes over hazel eyes that were almost amber in the light.

'I was always a show-off, but not in public. I mostly performed for my nan's friends.' He smiled at her, and she laughed as someone approached.

'Hey. You must be Callum Michaels.' A woman in an African-print dress and huge earrings sat next to him. 'I'm Kalinda, make-up supervisor. We've got an appointment tomorrow, I'm looking forward to making you look even better. Great tan, by the way – that makes my life easier.' She didn't speak to Libby, but Callum introduced her anyway.

'This is Libby, she's making my costumes.'

'Hi.' A smile didn't quite reach Kalinda's eyes as she looked over Libby and turned back to Callum. 'So, Callum, you've got your script memorised already?'

'Uh, not yet.' He looked at Libby. 'Most of my character's work in the first episode is action. Libby's going to make me look good getting on and off a horse.'

'Great,' Kalinda said, shifting her body so Libby was excluded a little. 'So, where are you staying?'

'The Pebble House Hotel,' he answered. He spoke to Libby before Kalinda could reply. 'I have to share with Leo Fallon, one of the other actors, but I'm sure it would be better than being measured basically in public.' He raised his eyebrows as if he was pleading with her to say something. Kalinda seemed a bit full on.

Libby decided to rescue him. 'OK, how about this evening?

I have to get back to the island tomorrow afternoon, I'm just bunking in with one of the set designers for the night.'

Kalinda hadn't quite given up. 'A group of us are going to the Blue Note pub tonight, do you want to come along? It's a bit of a shoot tradition. Sam will be there.' She looked over her shoulder without meeting Libby's eyes. 'You can come too, if you like.'

'Another time. We've got to work this evening,' Libby said, and as Kalinda swayed off, Callum mouthed, *Thank you*.

10

APRIL 1942

Nancy read through the letter she had been sent, rerouted through three previous addresses and the land army. It had arrived already opened, although after two weeks of travelling the glue might just have failed. She smoothed it flat, read the few hundred words again, folded it.

Nancy's chest ached. She had always dismissed the idea that someone's heart could break, but this must be what it felt like. It was agony. She tucked the letter into the inside pocket of her kit bag.

Your request has been denied...

She pulled on her hat, more to keep the sun off her nose than to wear the correct uniform. She looked at her watch. Seven thirty, just in time for breakfast in the aerodrome's canteen. Soon they would have their own kitchen – the last touches to their hut were being added today. A working WC, a kitchen sink, room for a primus stove.

'Ready, Nancy?' said Henrietta, yawning. She seemed relieved to have told someone about her predicament, although she hadn't mentioned it since.

'Ready,' she answered. They were a bit late, so she thought she would miss seeing Ollie walk past on his way to work.

But she didn't. She was halfway through a bowl of heavy porridge, without milk or sugar, when he popped his head around the canteen door.

'Just getting a cup of tea for the base commander,' he told the woman behind the counter. 'And I was wondering if you could advise me on growing potatoes,' he asked Nancy. The other women turned to stare at her and she felt a heat rise to her cheeks.

Trying to ignore the others watching them, she smiled at him. 'Yes, I probably could.'

He smiled at her. 'I'll wait at the fence, then. How about tomorrow?' He spoke to the room in general as eyebrows were raised. 'Growing anything helps, right?'

Their supervisor nodded. 'But in your own time, Baldwin,' she warned. 'We finish early tomorrow.'

Nancy turned back to her porridge, her face burning, as Ollie took the cup and saucer and carried it carefully out of the room.

Nancy had never imagined that planting potatoes would be such a demanding job. The wrinkled tubers had been left out to grow little shoots, which were fragile and had to be left pointing up. This meant bending low and placing them carefully while someone else covered with a hoe. Despite regularly rotating the jobs, all of them were holding their backs by the time they broke for sandwiches. Any potatoes that had lost their sprouts were discarded into a bucket, to be replanted later when they had put up a new shoot or two.

When they stopped for a lukewarm mouthful of tea from a thermos, Henrietta sighed and leaned against her friend.

'I meant to ask you about something you said the other

day... Did you get close to getting married at some point? I mean you're a few years older than me, you must have had a beau or two.'

'A few young men. But I didn't have time for them,' Nancy said, unable to stop herself thinking of a wedding day that was meant to be the start of a lifetime of happiness and children with the man she loved. 'I'm not that much older than you, anyway, and I'm not the kind of girl men run after.'

'Well, I think you have a pretty face,' Hen said, and took another bite of one of the store apples. 'My dad would call you bonny, rosy-cheeked.'

'I think men like delicate, slender little girls like you,' Nancy said. 'But nowadays, women don't have to get married before twenty or risk being left on the shelf. Look at us lot, not a proper boyfriend between us.'

'No time for men,' one of the other older women said. 'Thank goodness, because there aren't many good ones left in the country.'

'What about the Americans?' one of the younger girls chimed in, giggling. 'Lots of them are good-looking.'

'They all have sweethearts back home,' Hen said. 'And they're not all nice. Just like our boys, there are mean ones.'

'I heard from the Camborne group that one asked a land army girl to marry him and she nearly did, before she found out he was already married in America.'

Nancy turned away and shut her eyes in agony. 'It happens,' she said, a little choked. Her stomach lurched, and she suddenly felt cold inside.

'Could we talk about something else?' Henrietta asked. 'Like the Easter dance?'

The local hotel had a small ballroom, nothing like she was used to in London, but they had started doing afternoon tea dances and had planned an evening dance on the Saturday before Easter, in ten days' time.

Nancy shook her head, wrapping her uniform cardigan around her. 'I'm not sure if I'm going.' The tickets were two shillings.

'But I don't want to go if you don't go,' Hen pleaded. 'Please, Nancy. I know you love to dance.'

Nancy was torn. Underneath the glamour of dressing up, putting on make-up, risking her one pair of stockings, was a darker undertone to these dances. Nancy had seen it in London: young men off to be mutilated or killed in the service of their country; girls seeing their brothers and lovers in the eyes of each dancer, wanting to give them a good memory to take off to war.

'Well, maybe.' She shook herself as she stood, clods of earth and grass falling out of her trousers. 'I might feel different nearer the time.'

'But they'll be sold out by then!' Hen said. 'Look, how about if I buy you a ticket? Then if you want to go, you can. If not, you could give the ticket to someone else.'

'And there was me thinking you wouldn't go without me.' Nancy smiled.

'Well, I wouldn't enjoy it if you weren't there.' She jumped up. 'Come on, there are baby spuds to put into their cribs.'

Nancy sighed. 'And then bury them alive, with a great big mattock,' she said, rolling her eyes.

'And then that young man with all the burns will be along to say hello soon. Maybe he will come to the dance...' Hen looked at Nancy, eyebrows raised.

Nancy could feel her temper sting. 'Is that all he is to you? The boy with the *burns*?'

'No, of course not. Sorry.'

'Pilot Officer Oliver Pederick. Who has volunteered to return to air crew. Our own *hero*,' Nancy said, as she stomped back across the grass.

Hen had to jog to catch up with her friend. 'Maybe *he* will ask you to dance,' she said, puffing alongside her.

'He has someone to dance with already,' Nancy answered quickly.

Joy. She was beautiful and innocent and probably much sought-after, and it was clear she had already chosen Ollie. Surely he would choose her too?

11

PRESENT DAY, 25 APRIL

That evening, Libby changed before she grabbed dinner with the sewing team. After dinner she walked up to Callum's hotel. Her colleagues had ribbed her a little about it, but mostly understood.

'He'll be stripping off in the workroom in no time,' Magda had said. 'And we probably won't even notice. Unless he's put on a few pounds, then, oh my *goodness*. What a nightmare.'

'Not as bad as Maria what's-her-name getting pregnant three weeks into the first series,' another one had said, and they all laughed.

As she walked into the hotel lobby, she felt a twinge of nerves. Callum walked down the stairs and there was a moment when he reached for her, almost dropped a kiss on her cheek, then settled for an awkward hug. She was engulfed by his scent – a fresh, woody smell that was not unpleasant.

'Sorry. This is all new to me. Actors are a huggy, kissy lot,' he explained as he led the way up the narrow stairs. The hotel was quite old-fashioned, in a retro way.

'Are most of the cast here?'

'No, they spread us around and mix us in with principal

crew. That way we all get to know each other at breakfast,' he explained. 'You?'

'I'm only here some of the time,' she said. 'I can go home if I'm doing an extended period of work, back to my studio.' It sounded grand. 'My dad set up the spare bedroom as a studio in my grandparents' old cottage. It has a lot of natural light.'

'Sounds lovely.' He unlocked the door to a large sea-view room with two single beds. 'My roommate is just in the bar,' he added. 'If you want a chaperone?'

She laughed. 'No, it's all fine. These are the forms I just need to run through with you. Then we can look at measurements.'

'Do I have to undress?' He looked anxious.

She looked at the clothes he was wearing. 'Something more figure-hugging than slouchy jeans would be better,' she said reassuringly. 'But the top is fine.'

He went into the bathroom to change. 'What questionnaire is it?' he called through the door.

'Just a health and safety thing. Because I'm working very closely with you, and because we're working with different fabrics, I just need to know if you're allergic to anything.'

He returned in gym shorts and a light T-shirt. 'Better?'

Wow. She tried to look unbothered as she quickly looked down at the papers in front of her.

'Loads.' To distract herself, she ran through a list of allergens, but all were clear, including wig tape and plasters that might be used to secure clothing. 'And there's nothing here about infectious diseases and we've all been tested,' she finished, hoping to sound completely professional. But as she looked back up at him she couldn't help but notice he was *very* attractive.

'Why do *you* have to be tested?'

She made a face. 'Because we're using pins and scissors. Who knows when we might stick our clients with a pin?'

'OK. Is this the time to tell you I'm needle phobic?'

'I haven't put a pin in anyone since college,' she said. 'Now, here's the list of measurements. It has to be detailed because there are less stretchy fabrics in our battery.'

She very quickly found out he was ticklish. He laughed a lot, which seemed to relieve his embarrassment about being measured, and it made it easier for her to touch him without it seeming inappropriate. Under his shirt, she could feel that his muscles were toned and, as she leaned in to read the tape measurements, she had to stop herself from inhaling his intoxicating scent.

'I was the fat kid at school,' he confided as she worked her way around him. 'I was always being pushed around and bullied. They called me Chubby.'

'Your old school friends will be so surprised when they see you in magazines, talking about the show,' she mumbled, pen in her mouth, her measuring tape now around his bicep. 'Can you flex your arm for me?'

'I doubt they'll recognise me,' he said, looking at himself in the mirror, making a face. He flexed his arm, and Libby felt the muscles move under the tape. 'And I had to change my name from Ben, there was already a Benjamin Michaels.'

'That must be a nuisance,' she said, having taken the pen out to write the measurement down. 'If it helps, I didn't have to change my name but it's really Olivia,' she confided. 'At school, I was known entirely as Ginge or Red.'

He laughed at that and peered at her head. 'You're ginger? What happened?'

'Modern hairdressing,' she admitted. 'There. I'll get on with the first outfits that have to be altered, then start on the coat. It's the biggest pain, because you have to ride and fight in it. Magda suggested I make a spare if I have time.' But she couldn't imagine, on the tight schedule, that she would have a spare two days to build a second coat.

As she rolled up her tape measure, she realised she really

enjoyed his company, and his insecurities made him more than a little endearing. She also appreciated being treated as more senior, as a costumer to one of the main characters. She was anxious to start working on the outer clothes, the most intricate and challenging coats and breeches. He was going to look fantastic in them, from his action scenes to the candlelit interiors in a few weeks' time, in the sets being finished in Bristol. She couldn't wait to see her jackets and cravats on film, especially with his broad shoulders and long neck.

He sat in the bedroom chair and watched her input numbers into her pattern-making programme on her laptop. 'What are you doing?'

'I'm looking at how much fabric I'm going to need for your shirts.' It seemed like a huge amount compared to a modern shirt. Of course, it would stretch almost to his knees and be tucked in around him. 'I may have to order extra cloth along with the laces. And the silver buttons for the riding coat are coming here next week, too.'

'I've never had to do this before,' he said. 'I've always done contemporary projects. It's a bit daunting.'

Since Libby had looked up several of his previous acting credits, she was surprised. 'I thought you were brilliant in that police drama... you know, the one where you got run over and it was told in flashback.'

'That was basically a version of me. If I was born up north, was five years older and joined the police as a kid, anyway. I could imagine myself in the role. This is different.' He looked vulnerable as he sat there, a little how she herself had felt moving to such an important production. There was a crease between his eyebrows and he was staring out at the sea.

'People are exactly the same now, at their heart. The rest is just how they spoke and what they wore, and we're doing all that for you.'

'There's a couple of lines that seem strange to me,' he said, biting his lip for a moment. Libby overcame the urge to reassure him. 'Olde worlde speak.'

'Tell the director. He'll listen, and if he explains it, you might find it easier. Or it might not matter, and you can change it.' She closed her laptop, put it back in its case. 'You're one of the leads, now. You can stand up for yourself.'

'Sam did it so well. He makes those lines sound great.'

'He's older than you, he's got gravitas. I'm sure younger people spoke differently from their elders, even back in the eighteen hundreds.' She gathered her belongings together. 'Look, I've got a bit of imposter syndrome going on, myself. Working for Magda Franks? And for a named actor on a block-buster series? People all around the world are waiting for the series to come out.'

'That's exactly it! Imposter syndrome.' He stood up and smiled at her, his eyes almost glowing in the afternoon sun. 'Thanks for the pep talk. That's going to really help when Horatio chucks me into the sea. Again.'

'I thought he was a highly trained stunt horse?'

'It turns out he was trained to stop on a sixpence. He responds to my slightest move, he thinks I want him to brake. And I carry on flying forward, unfortunately. We're calling it a personality thing, but I'll keep trying with him.'

As she went to leave, she was caught between giving him a friendly hug or a professional handshake. He solved it for her when he leaned forward, rested a hand at her waist and kissed her cheek again. She knew her cheeks were turning pink, and it felt as though her work glasses were steaming up.

'Bye, Ginge,' he said, laughing at her.

'Bye, Chubby,' she countered with a grin.

12

APRIL 1942

The following day, they had started early. The farmer wanted to take advantage of the brighter mornings to get whole rows of potatoes planted. Nancy was brushing herself down and about to head in for a late breakfast when she saw Ollie. He was walking with a short-haired person with a limp. Ollie said something to his companion, and stopped at the fence.

Nancy had been collecting a few seed potatoes that had lost their shoots for him. 'Hello,' she said to Oliver, raising an eyebrow at his companion, who had stopped on the path. 'Do you still need seed potatoes?'

'Only if you won't get into trouble,' he said. 'This is my cousin, Emma Chancel.'

The woman – it was a woman, even if she was wearing men's clothes – had very short hair and a defensive stare.

'We're supposed to get them to sprout again but I don't think they will mind a few.' She pulled a small bag out of her overalls, made sure no one was watching, and pushed the potatoes, one by one, through the wire.

'This is my friend Nancy, Em,' he said, not looking at her.

'She's going to be growing vegetables, like us. But on all the spare ground of the aerodrome.'

'What happens if the planes fall onto the grass?' Emma asked in a gruff voice.

'Then they will still have somewhere soft to land,' Nancy explained. 'But hopefully most of the spuds will be fine.'

Emma looked sharply at Oliver. 'Dangerous things, planes,' she said, the gruffness not quite covering the anxiety.

'They are as safe as they can be,' he said, putting the seed potatoes into his bag. 'And the anti-aircraft batteries keep the German planes away.'

'I was wondering,' Nancy blurted out, before she'd thought it through, 'are you going to the dance on Saturday?'

'I was invited,' he said, looking down. 'I'm not sure if I'll go.'

Emma snorted. 'That *flibbertigibbet*,' she said, quite clearly, then stomped towards the town.

Nancy couldn't help but smile. Presumably the *flibbertigibbet* was Joy. 'I might see you there, then. I'm chaperoning the girls.'

'Maybe, then,' he said, catching her gaze for a moment. 'Probably.'

Over the course of the day, Nancy looked out for Ollie to come back. The woman who had been with him, Emma, had returned from the town an hour later without meeting Nancy's eyes, but it seemed she was just shy. At the end of her shift, she washed and changed her clothes, but she didn't want to go down to the pub with the girls. She had little money left anyway – unlike a lot of the girls, she didn't get pocket money from home.

One of the girls was trying to darn a stocking by lamplight, another was already asleep under a magazine on her bunk.

Henrietta and Joan had walked down to the pub. They were all excited about moving into their proper accommodation.

At a loose end, Nancy signed out at the guard post at the aerodrome gate and started strolling towards the end of the island, away from the town, before the light went. She didn't expect to walk all the way to Capstan Cottage, but had been drawn there. Part of her just wanted to see Oliver again.

Just as she decided to turn back, she heard a surprised 'Hello.'

He was there, in an open-necked shirt and blue canvas trousers. He looked different out of uniform, maybe a little older.

'I was just going for a walk, to stretch my legs,' she said, aware of the aching in her calves from crouching down planting potatoes all day.

'Have a cup of tea with me,' he said. He was holding a cigarette and she looked at it longingly. 'Would you like a puff?' he said. 'I'm down to one a day.'

'I'm giving up,' she said heroically, and he carefully stubbed the glowing end and put it back in the packet. 'Would your cousin mind me coming in?'

'I doubt it,' he said, his smile so wide it dragged down the skin around his eye. 'She'll be fine if we don't interrupt her radio broadcast. She loves the live music programme. We could sit out here, if you like,' he said, and showed her around the side of the cottage.

She was hit with the huge view of the sea, the changing light, the sun low on the horizon. A seat, cobbled together with driftwood and old ropes, sat overlooking a gap in the coconut-scented gorse. 'My goodness,' she said, and looked back to see him still smiling. 'What a view.'

'I love that reaction,' he said. 'I had it last year, when we moved in. Did I tell you Em used to have a house on Morwen

Island?' The name of that place again, the lurch in her stomach. She turned away from him to hide her reaction.

He disappeared and returned with two mugs of tea, while she watched seabirds come and go, the tide creep up the sand, pushing a lace of bubbles.

'Sorry, these are what we call the gardeners' mugs,' he said. 'Emma's a bit protective over her Crown Derby, or whatever it is.'

'I should think so,' she said, cupping the tea, letting the heat sink into her cold fingers. 'So you haven't been here long?'

'My mother and aunt live over the hardware shop,' he said. 'We were bombed out last year, so we all decamped to cousin Emma's big house on Morwen Island.'

Morwen. Hearing it for the second time that evening, the word was still a shock. When she looked up, he was frowning, as if he'd picked up her discomfort.

'And then you moved back?'

'Emma sold the old house and bought Capstan Cottage. It was a bit of a tight squeeze at the flat with Bernie and my mother, so I moved in here. We get on well. Neither of us is that sociable, to be honest.'

'She looks like... does she struggle a bit?'

'Emma can do anything she wants to. It's just hard persuading her to be sociable. Once a week, she walks to the town, hands over a list and some money, and they pack her bag up for her.' He laughed at the thought. 'The shopkeeper keeps chatting to her, I even think she likes it, but she never answers.' His smile faded and she had to look away. 'What is it, about Morwen?'

'Nothing, really. I haven't even been there.' She wiped her eyes with her handkerchief. 'It's quite windy, isn't it?'

'Would you rather go in?'

And face the strange, silent woman? Nancy shook her head,

sipped her tea. She would rather be outside, with Oliver and the view. 'No, it's lovely out here.'

'I was hoping to see you.'

She turned to stare at him. He had probably been a bit of a plain beanpole before his injuries made him a hero. 'Why?'

'I like you,' he said, simply. 'I'd like to get to know you better.'

'But I'm too old for you,' she stammered, feeling more than a little awkward at his honesty.

'I'm not proposing,' he said, his half-smile crinkling the skin around his good eye. 'It's just that I like talking to you. Even Em liked you.'

'How did you know?' It came out before she could stop it.

He laughed out loud. 'She didn't moan about you, anyway – that's high praise. And does a few years make such a difference?'

She looked into the empty cup. 'It's what I *did* in those years that makes the difference.'

'And you're not going to tell me.' He sighed, finished his tea, reached for her mug. 'Would it help if we went over to Morwen? Then you might be able to tell me more about your terrible and dreadful history.'

She almost folded over the longing, the pain of wanting to travel to the island. 'I wouldn't be very good company,' she said. With a wretchedness that almost hurt, she realised she didn't want him to judge her.

He stood, stared into the now setting sun. The pinks and purples of the clouds reflected off his face. He looked unhappy. 'I'm not sure I'm good company either,' he said. 'But I have a feeling you're one of the only people on the islands I could talk to without worrying it would be in the *Atlantic Island Press* by the end of the week.'

It was the sadness in his voice that echoed in her heart. 'I don't know what we would do over there.'

'Visit my other cousin, Lily,' he said, smiling. 'And then I can bear this stupid dance that I've been almost ordered to attend.'

'Why have you been ordered?'

He made a face. 'They don't want all the men there to be the new American troops.'

'Why not?'

He shrugged. 'I think a lot of our men are a bit threatened. They do seem very confident and alarmingly good-looking. Perfectly friendly to me, but they give the rest of the lads a bit of banter. Competition.'

'For the girls? That's caveman thinking.' She looked down, the last of the light twinkling on grains of sand on her shoes and the grass. She could go to the island, just to catch the lie of the land. Maybe find this house, the address she had been given. If she had Ollie with her, it would look more natural than a woman searching the island by herself.

He touched her hand. 'So, shall we go to Morwen? The first boat will be early – you can't easily land until the tide's halfway up.'

She closed her eyes, tried to calm the jumping heartbeat that seemed so loud she thought he must be able to hear it. 'I will. Let's just have an explore.'

'And then you can tell me what's bothering you, if you want.'

She looked into his kind eyes. 'I wish I could,' she said finally. 'But I can't.'

13

PRESENT DAY, 29 APRIL

Libby returned to St Brannock's on the ferry, then stopped in town to pick up some essentials. She was surprised by the sight of her mother holding Stevie's hand, waiting for her along the coast road.

'Ah, there you are. I saw your boat come in. Let me have one of those bags, we'll walk up with you.'

Libby's mum prised the handle of one of her bags out of her fingers.

'OK.'

'I thought we could have a proper girlie catch up,' her mother said, facing into the breeze.

Libby had a horrible thought, that caught in her throat. 'Oh God, you're not going to tell me there's more wrong with Dad, are you?'

'No!'

They turned past the last row of houses and headed towards the airport. The helicopter overhead made conversation impossible for a couple of minutes. 'Hold onto Stevie,' her mum added as he ran towards the noise.

They were puffing up the hill when it finally landed and powered down. 'You didn't tell me he was ill.'

'He didn't want to tell *me* at first. It felt too personal and private, and he didn't want to worry us. And you know how news goes around the islands.'

'I'm surprised it didn't.' Libby stopped, turned to face her mother. 'What wouldn't he tell me?'

'He started having problems in the bedroom,' she said. 'He wasn't going to tell you *that*. I mean, he's not that old, and having to ask for little blue pills was humiliating for him. He had to go to the mainland to pick them up.'

Libby laughed at the thought of her father sharing *that* detail with her. 'Possibly too much information, Mum. Maybe he wasn't going to go into the personal details. But *cancer*.' She smiled as Stevie handed her a daisy in a handful of grass. 'Thank you, sweetie.'

'He had started having a bit of incontinence by the time the GP persuaded him to be examined, then he was off to Plymouth for a biopsy. Men aren't used to all that private, personal stuff. We get smear tests and examinations and have babies, but your dad – he's a private man.'

'But *cancer*, Mum...'

'From the start they knew it was unlikely to spread. It's stage two, and he's had the necessary treatment. It's back in its box – for now, anyway. If it starts growing again he'll have lots of treatment options, like surgery. But that isn't what I wanted to talk about.'

The shopping bag was cutting into her hand; she released Stevie to run ahead now it was safe, and swapped hands.

'So, what did you want to talk about?'

'It's Jane, love. She's worried about Jory.'

'Why would Aunty Jane be worried about Jory? He seems fine.'

She laughed, a little sadly. 'We all worry about our kids. You think they will leave home and do their own thing, you won't worry about them. But they can get into a lot more trouble than when they were eleven.'

'Well, you don't worry about me, surely?'

'All the time, love. I worry that you haven't met anyone yet, settled down.'

'I'm *twenty-eight*! My generation aren't getting married young like yours did.'

They had reached the turn-off to the cottage. Stevie was picking up gravel from the path. Joanna sighed, and ran her hand over the gatepost. 'Oh, I love coming back to my parents' house. To be honest, I hated renting it out to holidaymakers. They always complained about the lack of dishwasher or the terrible electrics, anyway.'

'But we grew up loving it.' Libby crouched down to receive the best bits of gravel from her nephew, and to plant a kiss on his cheek. '*Thank* you, Stevie.'

'I know, lovey. Me too.' Libby's mum had been a late surprise for her parents. 'It was always crowded, with Grandma and Grandad, your aunt and uncle, and Great-Aunt Emma. And me, when I came along. But we made it work.'

Libby pushed the door open with a shoulder and stepped in, stamping on the mat to get rid of the sand from the path, Stevie copying her. 'How on earth did you all fit in?'

'Your studio used to be two rooms. That's why there are two windows. And the bathroom was another front bedroom for my brother. Mum and Dad shared the big front room, we girls squeezed into the middle room, Aunt Emma had the tiny room up the end.'

'Wow. That was a houseful.'

'None of us had much stuff, and my big brother and sister moved out when I was little, so we all ended up quite comfortable. I loved sleeping in a tiny room with bunk beds. I still find it hard to sleep alone if Dad goes off the island.' She opened the bag, put it in the small fridge which groaned into action. 'Come on, Stevie, let's put the shopping away. The electrician is coming on Monday. You probably remember him, Grant Pullen, from school?'

'I remember.' Her voice came out dry. He had liked to chase the girls and pull their hair, which had not made him popular. He had asked her out, once, and gone quite red when she refused him. 'How's he doing?'

'Married, divorced, married again,' Joanna said, putting the kettle on. 'Now. Jory.'

'I haven't seen much of him. I don't know what's going on.' She put the mugs out. 'Grandma's cup, Charlotte's cup,' she said, out of habit. 'That's what Grandad always said.'

'He got that from Emma,' Joanna said, taking a cup of juice out of her pocket for Stevie. Her voice was strained. Libby turned around to look at her. 'Look, I know something went on between you and Jory at Dorrie's wedding.'

'That was *years* ago. And we were both drunk,' Libby said, turning back and, on impulse, lifting down one of her grandma's many teapots. This one had a film of dust and needed a wash before she could fill it. 'I could have kissed half the eligible, single men there. Even a couple who weren't.'

'Jane said he seems to remember it.'

'Well, that's nice to know.' Libby put the knitted tea cosy over the top. 'There. Grandma would be proud.' She put the pot and the cups on the table and opened a new milk. Stevie climbed onto her lap and rested his head against her shoulder.

'So you *do* remember it.'

'Of course.' Libby didn't want to meet her mother's gaze, smiling at the child instead. 'I had such a crush on him as a kid. It was nice to put a full stop to that. He's just a nice, good-looking old friend. Anyway, isn't he with this Amber?'

'He brought her home a few times, but I can't say his family warmed to her. They're definitely business partners, but I'm not sure it's still romantic, or if it ever was.'

Why did this news make her heart bounce around in her chest for a few beats? She poured the tea with exaggerated care. 'I'm sure they're all busy setting up their new project.'

'Apparently, he was in the dumps after meeting you in the pub the other night.'

'Really? He seemed absolutely fine.' Libby could hear the acid creeping into her voice. 'I probably didn't sit staring *adoringly* at him the whole time.'

'His mum thinks you are unfinished business for him. And now you're going to be swept up by all the glamour of working with movie stars. You can see he might be a bit nostalgic for the past.'

'We don't have a *past*. And my "movie star" is five years younger than me and it's purely business. And he's nothing like a movie star, he's just a nice young actor trying to impress his boss. Like I am.'

'We just wondered—'

'Mum, I've got an important job to do. That's why I'm back, not to impress Jory Trethewey. That's all ancient history.'

Joanna sipped her tea. 'So you won't be surprised if he turns up here.'

'What?'

'He's working with Grant for the week, while he waits for the go-ahead to repair the boats. You know what it's like on the islands, everyone helps everyone.'

Oh, great.

14

APRIL 1942

Nancy sat on the tiny boat. After hours of seasickness on the main ferry, she wasn't hopeful that she would cope with crossing to another island, but Ollie was reassuring.

'No one gets sick on the small ferries,' he said. 'All that fresh air, and it's only a short journey.'

She wasn't so sure; her stomach was already lurching. She didn't want to embarrass herself, but Ollie was a kind person. Maybe it wouldn't be so bad. She sat back into the corner of the boat.

'Tell me about your cousin Lily,' Nancy said, holding on firmly to the side of the boat. It rocked as the boatman cast off, pushed away from the quay with one foot and stepped to the tiller.

'You'll like her. My family is a bit complicated, though.'

He didn't seem inclined to explain but she asked him to, to take her mind off the dark water barely a couple of feet below the edge.

'Well, my great-grandfather was an old seadog, in the worst possible way. He had two wives, one after the other, but also seduced the servants if they were young and pretty.' He cocked an eye at her. 'I mean, *really* young. My grandmother was sixteen when she had my mother, and then her sister, right after each other. He scandalously put his mistress up in a house in the town on Morwen, but eventually he bought them a property on the big island.'

'St Brannock's.'

'It was a small shop and the flat over. Quite humble, but my mum – Cissie – and her sister Bernice had a bit of income from renting the shop out. My mother has had a lot of nervous problems.' He didn't seem inclined to explain at first and she waited. 'Bernie looked after all of us when her mother died. Mam moved over to the mainland when she was about eighteen, and years later came back expecting me. She said she thought she would have me on the ferry; they moved her straight to the hospital when they disembarked. That's Mam, impulsive. Loving, kind, just a bit – impractical.'

'Did she tell you who your dad was?'

He hesitated and she wondered if she'd touched a nerve. A nerve that resonated in her.

'Not really. She was very low after I was born, apparently it happens to some women. But she was more ill than Bernie could handle at home. She was moved to a special hospital on the mainland.' He looked away, his voice so soft she could barely catch it. 'An asylum.' He turned back to her. 'She's been in one or another from time to time. But I don't want you to think I was unhappy – Bernie was a lovely second mother to me. We had a great time, just the two of us, growing up by the beach, me going to the local school, learning about engineering and flying. And Ma would come back for a year here and there, until she got too sad or ran away with some man or other. Carefree, that's Cissie.' He patted her hand, which was clenched onto the edge of the boat. 'It's all right.'

'Nothing like my childhood,' Nancy said, unclenching her fingers where her death grip had marked the palm with white lines. 'My father died in the first war. I was just little, and Mum found religion afterwards. We rented two rooms over a café. At least we always had good food – they gave us anything that was going over. She worked for the post office, I spent a lot of holidays helping weigh parcels and stick stamps.' The words stuck in her throat. 'So, here I am. Mum died last year. Stray incendiary hit her, killed instantly,' she added, matter-of-factly.

'Sorry.' And she could tell he really was as his eyes focused sympathetically on hers.

'So, who is your cousin Lily?'

'The old captain married twice. With his first wife he had two sons, and when she died, he married another young bride. Lily is her daughter, but she grew up away from the old man and Chancel Hall.'

'Chancel Hall sounds very grand,' she said.

'You'll see it in a minute, once we clear St Piran's. Are we stopping, George?'

'Just to drop off some mail,' the boatman replied. He pulled alongside a quay on the low, sandy island, and threw a mailbag expertly onto the side without stopping. He turned the boat and motored off again.

'The captain's first son died in Jamaica, where the family had holdings, but his younger son was in the church. He moved to the islands after his father died. Strange, no one wanted to share the house with the old man. Emma is that son's daughter. She was a twin but they were both caught in a terrible accident, run over with a delivery van. Charlotte died. Emma talks about her a lot, but always in the present tense. You get used to it.'

'So, why is Lily here?'

He turned back to her and smiled, his eyes sky blue. 'Emma inherited the hall but also the old cottage next door. It was just a wreck really, but Emma gave it to Lily and her husband to do up. You'll like it. The hall is going to be a hotel or holiday flats, they're working on shoring it up at the moment.'

They rounded the end of the island, long strands of under-water plants brushing and flowing around the boat. The flash of silver fish zigged and zagged between the fronds, scattered by the boat and reforming into shoals behind it.

He pointed. 'There!'

Nancy looked up and saw, in a shaft of sunshine, the green corner of the furthest island. It was far steeper that St Piran's, rockier, a low town huddled along the eastern edge. In the northernmost corner was a large house, windows staring out to sea. Beyond it, tucked further into the corner, was a white-washed cottage, a sloping lawn just visible through a gap in the hedge. Ollie pointed it out as Lily's cottage, although it was bigger than any house Nancy had ever lived in, then Chancel Hall beside it. She could see the scaffolding around one end of the large building, areas of new slates on the roof around the chimneys. The boat carried on to the quayside and a slipway by the town.

'There you go, maid,' the boatman said, holding out a hand. 'Not seasick, then?

'No, not this time, thank you,' she said, wobbling a bit until he steadied her and she could step onto solid ground. 'What time do we need to be here to go back?'

'I'm taking a party about four-thirty, but the Ellises will be going back around six if you miss me. Bye, Ollie. Good to see you.'

The two men shook hands and chatted for a moment – she gathered George hadn't seen Ollie since he moved away. Then Ollie walked forward, crooked his arm. 'Ready?'

The truth crashed in on her.

They were here.

She stopped, her heart skipping in her chest. 'Do you... do you know anyone else here? In the town?'

'A lot of people. I went to school with some, others I know from work on the big island.'

'Do you know some people called Pascoe?'

'I know Daniel Pascoe. He's about my age, married a girl on West Island and went into the navy. There are a couple of younger girls at home, I think.'

A family with children. That was good.

'Are you going to tell me your dark secret now, Nancy?' he asked, but his tone was sombre. 'I can see you're upset even coming here.'

She took a deep breath, took his arm. It had been so long since she had spoken about it with anyone who wasn't a solicitor or – worse – a police officer. She felt like she could trust Ollie, and she couldn't imagine him looking at her as her mother had. Her gaze had been hard, judgemental, rejecting.

She started, her voice coming out low and quiet. 'When I was seventeen I fell in love with a man. He said he had a business, he had his own little flat overlooking the river.'

He didn't answer, just waited. She could see Richard now, dark hair flopping over his forehead, driving her mother mad. *Why doesn't he get a proper haircut?* she used to say.

'I was head over heels. He seemed so grown-up and sophisticated. He was ten years older than me, he used to take me out for meals and to dances.'

'Did your mother approve?'

Nancy shook her head, not able to put into words what her mother had actually said. 'She thought I was too young. I *was* too young.'

He squeezed her hand encouragingly. His fingers were warm and she felt cold. 'Go on. If you want to.'

She did. She desperately wanted to say something to someone. The secret was bubbling up inside her, making her gasp awake at night, or cry in her sleep.

'I married him on my eighteenth birthday. My mother insisted we got married in a church. It was strange, he didn't want any of his friends or family there, nor mine.'

'Are you still married?'

She stared down at the stones of the quayside, which gave way to a wide path of grey gravel. 'No.'

'Divorced?' That was scandalous enough, although he didn't sound like he was judging.

'It was annulled.'

He didn't answer, nor ask why. 'So, you're free of him.'

She shook her head, tears swimming across her vision.

I'll never be free...

15

PRESENT DAY, 1 MAY

Libby was already cutting out pattern pieces for breeches when a voice shouted up the stairs.

'Libs! It's just us, come to start the rewire.'

She found herself smiling. All that worrying about how Jory would be, and he had slipped straight back into the easy familiarity of childhood.

'Better put the kettle on before you cut the power off,' she called down the stairs. She had dressed carefully, though – new jeans and a new top she had made of leftovers from a BBC job. 'Mine's a decaf coffee,' she added.

By the time she got downstairs he was standing by the coffee maker, head on one side. 'There's a knack to this, right?'

'Some electrician,' she said, plugging it in and switching it on.

'Grant's the electrician,' he said, and for the first time looked her straight in the eyes. The shock was as if he'd touched her. He looked away. 'I'm just the monkey. I'll grab my tools.'

After he left, Grant walked in, his bulk and height blocking out the light from the doorway. 'Hi, Libby,' he said. 'This is going to take a few days. We'll try and leave you with power somewhere in the house each night.' He looked over the kitchen area with its cheap units. 'Got any biscuits?'

She opened a cupboard. 'Mum said you would need them.'

He patted his substantial belly. 'There's a lot of me to keep up,' he said, smiling, the hint of awkwardness fading. 'Malory is such a good cook.'

One problem with growing up on the islands was that there was only one high school. Libby knew everyone around her own age on the islands. She had always been a bit intimidated by the confident, loud Malory Bishop. 'How long has she been cooking for you?'

'We've been together for four years, married for two,' he said. 'We have a baby due in October.'

'I'm so glad!' Libby found she really was thrilled for him. He was, in her mind, morphing back into the funny, kind bear he had been in her childhood.

He winked at her. 'So, I'll just be the one that got away, huh?'

She laughed. 'You'd be a lot skinnier if you hadn't,' she said. 'I can't cook for toffee.'

Jory walked back into the kitchen. 'You used to make fantastic firepit pizzas,' he said.

She waited until the coffee maker beeped and poured out two coffees, and then she made Grant a cup of tea. 'It's a very specific culinary area,' she said. But there was an awkwardness there again. 'I'll be upstairs, working. What exactly are you going to do?'

Grant explained how they would isolate the electrical outlets and lights downstairs and start running new wires. Her parents had specified some minor changes, more sockets and some downlighters in the low ceiling. 'We'll have to cut you off upstairs in a couple of days, but I'll try and rig up an extension for lights and your – sewing machine?'

'Thank you.' She looked at the kitchen with new eyes. 'But no kettle, no cooker?'

'You could take the kettle and toaster upstairs,' he said. 'But not the cooker. But you were just saying you don't like to cook.'

'I don't mind cooking,' she said, gathering up the warm kettle and lead. 'I'm just not very good at it. I like eating, though. Is the power on up in the summer house?'

'It's a separate supply,' Grant said.

'Your mum will be thrilled if she has you visiting every day,' Jory said.

'Worse. She'll want me to stay over,' Libby said, visions of her teenage bedroom coming to mind. 'I'll feel like a kid again. No, I'll take them up the summer house.'

'Sure,' Jory said, then started unscrewing the cover to the cooker supply. 'Hey, Grant, is this really off?'

'Always assume it isn't until proved otherwise,' Grant called back. 'Leave it to the expert. Libby, you probably need this lounge furniture moved or covered. When we start chipping into the plaster it's going to make a bit of a mess. I'm not sure the old plaster's going to cope with us cutting into it.'

After covering up the sofa and armchair downstairs, Libby tried to concentrate on marking and cutting cloth. Unlike modern trousers, nineteenth-century breeches had a lot of pieces and a complicated fly fastening called a flap. Getting the fit right would make it easier to make the fitted pantaloons later.

The noise from downstairs ate into her concentration, and when something heavy clattered to the ground, she slipped with her cutting wheel, carving into the seam allowance.

She swore under her breath and moved the pattern piece to cut the curved line again. She hadn't even started when there was another huge bang. She jumped off her stool and stormed halfway down the stairs, suddenly afraid one of them had been hurt.

'What are you...? Oh.'

Both men were covered in black dust. Every surface was coated, and the air was grey with it. She dived through the room to get into the garden, holding her breath, and they followed her out, choking.

'What have you done?' she said, coughing.

Jory walked over to the quad bike he had parked in the garden and retrieved a bottle of cola. He drank deeply then passed it to Grant, who was hacking and spitting. 'Ceiling,' he said. 'Fell down.'

'I can *see* that! I meant, *why* did it fall down?'

Jory shrugged, took the bottle back and finished it. 'It's very, *very* old?' he suggested. 'Anyway, it will make it easier to run wires under the boards upstairs.'

'I can't even vacuum it up without power,' she said, her hands shaking as she clenched them by her side.

Did I shut the bedroom door? Has the dust got onto my clean cloth?

Jory lifted a heavy box with a grunt. 'You can use this. It's a power station, you can do your cleaning, at least.'

Anger poured into her, partly fed by the panic that the bangs had caused. 'Me? You made the mess, you clean it up!'

Jory raised an eyebrow as Grant started laughing amid coughs. 'You want to spend your parents' money getting two electricians to do *housework*?'

'Grant's the electrician,' she said, turning around with a flounce. 'And Jory, you're just the monkey.'

Libby had remembered to shut the door to the workroom, and better still, the box with the stash of fabrics had been secured. Everything had a faint dusting of grey on it, but nothing like the chaos of downstairs. Jory had dragged the armchair and small sofa outside and vacuumed them thoroughly. Any attempt to sweep the floor made it worse, so most of the furniture ended up in the front garden, and even on the path.

She went backwards and forwards emptying the vacuum cleaner into a rotting old compost bin her grandad had made. By the time she had cleaned the furniture, damp-dusted her work-room and checked the power was still on for her machine, she was almost as hot and dirty as Jory was.

She walked out to sit on the garden wall; Jory was slumped in the old armchair. She noticed how ragged the upholstery fabric was at the back, probably courtesy of their old cat. Or maybe just age. She had always loved it, loved how it was so close to the ground.

'A proper nursing chair,' her grandmother had called it. Libby loved the idea that her grandma had nursed her mother there, rocked her to sleep as a baby. When her grandma died, her grandad had taken the chair for his own, as if wanting to be close to her.

'How's it going?' she asked Jory.

'We got the rest of the ceiling down. It was going to fall down when we started trying to put spotlights in it, anyway. Which reminds me, why would anyone put modern spotlights in a cute little cottage?'

'Tourists expect to be able to see what they're doing,' Libby said. 'The ceiling's too low to hang a centre light.'

He laughed. 'It is now. You could have table lamps, or those tall lights, anything other than something out of the twenty-first century. Have a look, those beams are *old*.'

She got up and stuck her head around the door. He was right – deep beams crossed the ceiling, showing the undersides of the upstairs floorboards, crisscrossed with dangling wires and modern pipes to the bathroom.

'They are quite cool.' She sat down again in a small cloud of dust.

'That dust was there from before,' he said, rolling his head on the back of the armchair. 'This housework stuff is exhausting.' He managed a lazy smile that somehow ignited a heat inside her chest.

'Well, I'm not paying you to loll about in the garden,' she said, looking up at the clouds racing across the china-blue sky. 'Keep an eye out for rain,' she said. 'You'll have to help me move the furniture up to the summer house if it does.'

'I could. But you'd better listen out, too – I'll probably have my head under the downstairs floorboards.'

When she walked back in, she could see how much plaster had cracked off the walls when the ceiling had come down.

'Grant?' she called, and he stuck his head around the kitchen door. He must have been under the ceiling when it fell – white gravel filled his wiry hair and the dust had left him looking like a panda with rings of white around his eyes. She pointed up at the beams in the room behind her. 'Do you think it would be possible to leave the beams exposed? I mean, it would give more headroom and I think they look lovely.'

'Possible. But what are you going to do for lights? I suppose I could run some angled lights along the beams and then some uplighters on the walls...' he said enthusiastically, and Libby could tell he knew what he was doing. 'All of which will cost more money than whacking up a new ceiling with half a dozen spotlights.'

'I'll talk to Mum,' she said. 'Thanks, Grant.'

'While you're talking to your mum, can you warn her that all the wires in the outside kitchen wall – which is horribly damp – are corroded? To get them off, we're going to have to take the tiles off and at least one cupboard. Oh, and the sink. It's a bit more complicated than just putting in a couple more sockets. You may as well put in a new kitchen.'

'Oh...' She peered to the dark space where the washing machine had sat. The wall was black and gleaming with moisture. 'How much is that going to cost?'

'And I think you're also going to have to look at the back wall.' He pointed at the small window, the sill cracked and split. 'Does the sea reach up this high?'

'Big waves in the winter spray the back of the house. A couple of times they've broken a window because they've thrown pebbles up from the beach.'

'Jory, take Libby around the back, have a look at the wall,' Grant shouted through the door.

She headed outside. Beside the house, the low garden wall was crumbling, and part of it had fallen onto the narrowest part by the corner of the house. The ground at the back fell away sharply in a tangle of brambles and leggy shrubs.

She stared at the house wall and sighed.

The painted render had worn or cracked away, and some chunks lay embedded in the blown sand. The house wall was constructed of irregular stones packed in with what looked like mud and some old fibre, a few bits of wood and even rusted chicken wire filled with dirt. The kitchen window was barely supported by a cracked and eroded frame, riddled with worm holes. No wonder it was so damp.

Grant pushed the window open amid a scraping sound and a shower of paint chips. 'How's it looking out there?' he said, pushing his head out the small opening. 'Ugh. Spiders.'

'The wall looks like it's falling to bits,' Libby said, mentally scouring the budget for renovations her parents had suggested.

'The plaster inside is full of salt,' Grant said. 'It's soft, like damp sand. It needs rendering and plastering from scratch.'

'The sea spray's been getting in,' Jory said, touching the wall under the window frame. 'It's soaked in, rotted the old cob and plaster. And woodworm love salty timbers. Let's have a look further round...' He disappeared along the back wall, stamping and pushing through chest-high vegetation to the other corner of the wall facing the sea. 'Sorry, Libs. It's all like that.'

The sand was eighteen inches up the back wall; when she

scooped it aside she could see the damage, including a giant crack she could have fitted her hand in. 'It needs a lot of work,' she said.

'It's so close to the sea,' he said, shrugging off leaves and twigs. 'I guess the sand has moved in the last couple of hundred years, letting the sea come closer. The other corner has been eroded away, too; it's hanging over the cliff. It's global warming, whatever you want to call it, the tide's coming up higher every year. You might not be able to save it.'

'We can't lose it,' she said. 'I can't lose it. It's part of my history.'

'Whatever you do – at great expense and by hand, because you'd never get big machinery down here – won't last long. The sea is moving the dunes west.' Jory seemed to sense her distress and moved closer. 'It's going to need a lot of work, Libs.'

She dashed away tears she didn't even know had been creeping down her face until they reached her jawline.

'OK. Well, we'll do our best, then,' Jory said, reaching for her hand, his warm fingers against hers making her catch her breath. 'But you'd better talk to your parents about what they want to do, and how much they've got to spend.'

'I'll find a way,' she said, sniffing back more tears and wiping her face with her dusty sleeve. 'I'm not giving up on this cottage.'

16

APRIL 1942

Ollie didn't look disgusted at Nancy's revelation of her failed marriage. He just squeezed her hand gently, and they walked on.

'We've both been injured in this war,' he said simply. A few steps further on, he stumbled on the loose slate path.

'Careful,' she said, tucking her hand more firmly into his arm.

'Wonky leg,' he said, smiling at her. 'It's still recovering. Everything gets better over time.'

She took a deep breath, pulled her cheerful mask onto her face. 'So,' she said, 'who does your cousin Lily live with?'

'Her husband James when he's home. He does something with maps and photographs for the War Office, very hush-hush. He was an architect in civvy street. Her mother is staying, to help with the baby. He's just gone back to work.'

That word stung. '*Baby?*'

'Catherine. You'll love her, she's the sweetest child. She even lets funny old Uncle Oliver hold her, doesn't mind the scars at all.' They walked through a gate, past what looked like a small factory which stank of fish. 'Look,' Ollie said, and she peered over the low sea wall. Just on the edge of the sea, three fat seals lay on the sand. 'They come for the scraps the cannery gets rid of every day. Most of it gets spread on the fields, but the whole fish get thrown back.'

'Whole fish?'

'Occasionally the boats catch things people don't like to eat. Mostly mullet and small sharks, too small for rock salmon. Odd things.'

They walked up to two gateposts, one leaning slightly into the hedge. 'That's where Emma lived until last year,' he said.

The dilapidated building towered over them, a broad terrace covered with grasses and weeds sticking out between limestone slabs. A path ran along the sea wall to a smaller pair of gateposts with a five-bar gate in it. Stone pavers wound their way beyond the terrace to a handsome cottage, a small portico over a low door, with wild roses tied into it. Windows looked out either side of the door, and the cottage looked a good size. On the side, two more windows peered over the side garden, where several rectangles had been dug. One had a ragged row of leeks at one end, another had some leaning towers of some sort of brassicas. Despite being a budding farmer, Nancy couldn't recognise anything that wasn't on a barrow at the market. She pushed the gate open and they walked up to the porch.

Ollie disengaged his arm gently, then tapped on the door. A ginger and white cat walked around his feet, rubbing its head on his knee.

The door opened, and a slim fair-haired woman around her own age was smiling, reaching up to kiss Ollie's cheek.

'It's lovely to see you,' she said, turning to smile at Nancy. 'Hello, I'm Lily Granville.' Nancy shook hands, then Lily beckoned at them to come in. 'My mother's just having a nap. That blasted baby kept us up half the night, just awake.' Her words held no anger, just warmth. 'Come into the living room. Mind the mess, the house is a work in progress.'

The stairs were bare, rubbed down ready for painting, Nancy imagined. The living room was lovely and looked over the garden. The furniture was old, with velvet curtains and overlapping carpets. Lily saw her looking. 'We took a lot of stuff from the hall when Emma sold it,' she said. 'She took some, too, for Capstan Cottage.'

'Which was helpful,' Ollie added, 'when I came to stay.'

'It's lovely,' Nancy said sincerely. It was homely, warm, with a stunning view out of the low window.

'I'm going to make a cushion for a window seat,' Lily said, walking over to a perambulator in the corner. 'Oh, she's finally asleep.'

Nancy walked over, leaned in, getting it over with. The baby had creamy blonde curls over a lacy collar of a little dress, a handknitted jacket, and looked very new.

'She's adorable,' she whispered realising too late that her eyes were already full of tears. Lily didn't say anything about Nancy's reaction, just smiled and walked away. A kettle started hissing then whistling in another room. Nancy discreetly wiped her tears away as she gazed down at the baby.

Ollie sat down on one end of the sofa and waved at the other end. 'Do you want to sit down?'

She perched instead on an armchair by a small coal fire, which trickled a little heat into the room. 'Did you say her name is Catherine?'

Ollie smiled immediately. 'Catherine, Cathy, Catty-cat.' He stretched the arm on the scarred side. 'I ought to do my exercises more often.'

'Have you got scars down your arm, too?' For a moment she thought she was being rudely nosy.

His smile was more of a wince. 'Arm, shoulder, hands, part

of my chest, and a bit on my thigh. I'm lucky to still be here. Most people with more than thirty per cent burns don't make it.'

'Well, I'm glad you did.' It just popped out, heartfelt.

Lily came in with a tea tray and put it down on a small side table. 'While that brews, would you like to see the house?'

'I'd love to,' Nancy said, while Ollie settled back onto his seat.

'I'll keep an ear out for the baby,' he said.

On the large landing, Lily pointed to a shut door and put her finger to her lips. *Mum's room*, she mouthed, walking towards another door. 'This is the main bedroom. We're just stripping the window frame and the old shutters,' she explained. The room was quite bare except for a large bed and a cot, a huge chest of drawers and a couple of old rugs.

'It's lovely,' Nancy murmured, drawn to the low, wide windowsill, bigger than the ones below.

The view was uplifting, she thought, the house perched above the garden, looking over the hedge to the sea, the islands and rock stacks beyond. Here she could hold her history without shame.

'I'm so glad Ollie brought you,' Lily said. The springs squeaked as she sat on the edge of the bed. 'He seems to really like you.'

'It's not like that,' Nancy said, tearing her gaze from the view. 'We're just friends. We've both been in trouble, we both have scars from the war.'

'Is that what puts you off?'

Nancy was startled into exclaiming, 'No, of course not!' before she remembered to speak quieter. 'No. It's just he's so young, he deserves to start out brand new.'

'But he's not brand new himself,' Lily said thoughtfully. 'Girls might be attracted to him for the wrong reasons.'

Like Joy. Who just sees a hero.

'Maybe,' Nancy murmured, her heart beating a little harder in her chest.

17

PRESENT DAY, 7 MAY

Libby woke up in the cottage, feeling relaxed, and rested. The only thing that had haunted her dreams was the odd bird call across the sand. Maybe it was a curlew, she thought. She would have to brush up on her wildlife.

She took her coffee beans and croissants around the cottage and up half a dozen irregular stone steps to the summer house. Her grandparents had built it the first year they had married, mixing bits of driftwood with scraps of second-hand timber donated by friends. It became a labour of love, apparently, and Libby suspected it had been a private nook for the young couple, a retreat from their busy and full cottage. They were living with an older relative when they married, and they had children from the start. The bottom and top steps were both wobbly, some of the sand that used to support them having been blown or washed away.

She opened the summer house door to the morning breeze, already warming in the sun, and took a few minutes to enjoy it while the coffee brewed and the croissants warmed in the toaster. The cabin had a large sofa built in to one end that pulled out as a bed, with storage underneath for beach toys. She had a quick look, pulling out memories from her childhood. The first kite she had sewn with her grandmother, lovingly repaired with stitches and patches. Buckets and spades, a deflated old paddling pool they used when the sea was too rough to play in, a couple of folding garden chairs. Even at the end, her grandparents had loved to walk up here to sit out on the small veranda and catch the evening sun.

She finished her breakfast, and rinsed the plates in the tiny enamel sink that hung on the timber wall. The brass tap gurgled and spluttered, but then worked. Perhaps no one had used it since her grandad died. As she walked back down to the house, she resolved to fix the stone steps that rocked perilously in the loose sand. When she had time.

Upstairs, she laid her pattern pieces at the big table in the back bedroom of the cottage, while watching the boats come and go. The tabletop was scratched with generations of people's drawing and sewing and eating. There was a line in the varnish made by a pen when Libby had traced a purple dinosaur with her grandmother twenty years ago. All the polish in the world hadn't got that out, nor the memory.

Libby immersed herself in her work, cutting out the paper pattern as the scents and sounds flowed in through the windows. She was jolted back to reality by the timer on her phone. Time to get ready for the big Sunday dinner that her parents were so looking forward to. She just hoped Jory was as relaxed as he had been at her grandfather's cottage.

As usual, the roast dinner was at Jane and Nick's, Jory's parents, at the house next door to Libby's mum and dad's. Joanna would bring dessert and wash up. Jory's sister Dorrie was already there, looking well.

It was as if the time apart hadn't passed. The childhood best friends asked insincerely if they could do anything to help, then made a complete hash of laying the table, talking and laughing.

'Jory's on his way,' Dorrie said. 'Do you want wine?'

Libby's heart still skipped a beat at his name, which she told herself off for. 'I did bring some, but it's just from the shop.' Libby rolled her eyes. 'The flavour of my misspent youth.'

Dorrie laughed. 'We thought we were such rebels. Sharing a can of sweet cider on the beach, watching the boys row a gig up and down.'

Libby opened the French doors. The sun had warmed up the garden, and Stevie was already riding a toy tractor around on the grass. 'And playing in your garden, or ours. And badminton over the hedge.'

'Dad still finds old shuttlecocks when he trims it back,' Dorrie said, plonking herself in one of the garden chairs, shutting her eyes against the sunlight. 'Oh, this is magic.'

'So, you're teaching now?' Libby sat next to her. 'I thought you were going to train to be an education psychologist.'

'I had to do a teaching qualification first,' Dorrie said. 'I just fell in love with it. But enough about me, how about you? How did you end up doing costumes for the biggest series on television?'

'Honestly, it just happened gradually. You work your way up in costuming.'

Something plastic in the corner of the garden caught Libby's eye.

'Is that our old sandpit?' She walked over to it, a faded green shell with a lopsidedly-grinning turtle on it.

'Mum babysits Stevie sometimes.' Dorrie smiled sadly. 'She's pretty keen for a grandchild. She's thinking of getting a trampoline to lure him from next door.'

'Do you want a child?'

'It's not really happening,' Dorrie said, and wiped a tear away from one eye. 'Oh, Libby...' She started to cry, and stood up to receive Libby's hug.

'I'm sorry,' Libby said, holding her tight. 'Are you getting help?'

'We are. I'm trying to stay positive.'

'I've got my fingers crossed for you. You'd make a brilliant mum.'

Dorrie wiped her eyes. 'How about you? Anyone special?'

'I haven't had time,' Libby said, finding a clean tissue in her jeans pocket and handing it over. 'Here. Don't worry the olds.'

'There must have been a few handsome actors, surely?' Dorrie said, sniffing.

Just the one so far.

'Hi, baby brother!' Dorrie called, as Kris sauntered into the garden.

'Hi, old and wrinkled sister,' Kris answered, lifting Dorrie off the ground.

He smiled at Libby. 'Do you need a hug, too?'

She reached for him. She had always loved Kris, little Kris, who ran along after them and let them try hair and make-up ideas on him. Now he was taller than Jory. She stepped back. 'How's the business? Are you both about to set the racing yacht world alight with new designs?'

He shrugged, put his hands in his pockets. 'That's Jory. I repair and polish things.'

Libby's mum put her head around the door. 'Come and sit up at the table. We're almost ready. Jory will be a few minutes, he's just at the quay tying up.'

It had been a standing joke through their shared childhood that Libby's mother, Joanna, couldn't cook. Sunday lunch was always cooked by Nick and Jane, with Joanna doing the pudding. It was as engrained in Libby as her DNA. She kissed Jane as she passed. 'It's lovely to be here.'

'Maybe you can cheer Dorrie up,' she said.

'I'll try.' Libby smiled as she passed to get a huge hug from Jane's husband, Nick.

'Libs! Look at you, amazing!'

'I wish,' Libby said. 'Dorrie seems well.'

He made a little face, drawing the corners of his mouth down. 'She's been a bit stressed for a while, now.'

Jory came in, smiled a hello at Libby, and went to sit next to Stevie's high chair.

The meal, as always, was brilliant. The lamb melted off the bone, grazed off the field by the airport, so local that Libby's dad joked he could tell which one it was by its baa.

Kris sat next to her, and between applying himself to a heap of roast potatoes, asked her questions. How did she like the mainland? Did she miss the islands? Would she ever move back?

'How about you? Would you ever move away for good?'

'I don't know. Would you?'

She reached for more mint sauce. 'I would for the right person. Or the right job, I suppose. But not yet, I'm enjoying life on the move, and this way I can do both.'

'Right person,' he said, glancing at Jory. 'Not that easy, though, is it?'

'How do you meet people on the islands?' She couldn't imagine that being stuck on an isolated boatyard most of the year would give him much time to socialise, let alone travel.

'You know what it's like. You grew up with almost everyone you know.'

'That's true,' Libby said, looking around the table. 'It would be like dating your sister or cousin.'

'Is that how you feel about Jory?' Kris's voice carried a little bite in it.

She kept her own words light. 'Well, can you imagine dating someone who's known you since childhood?' She firmly suppressed the thought. 'I do recommend a few years away, Kris. How about university, like Jory? You'll meet all sorts of different people, maybe travel a bit more widely.'

'Mum's not keen on her baby boy going away for too long,'

Dorrie interrupted. 'Libs, if you're not after that last potato, I will steal it.'

'I'll share it with you,' Libby said.

'I'd love to see Kris get as much out of a degree as Jory did,' Kris's mother suddenly intervened, and Libby realised most people were now listening to the conversation.

Kris mumbled something about the loo and got down from the table, his tanned face brick red as he went back into the house.

'I'm sorry,' Jane said. 'He's had a bit of a crush on you, Libby. You know how uncomfortable that is.'

The whole table fell quiet for one horrible moment; Dorrie dropped half a potato on her plate, her mother winced sympathetically and even Libby's dad raised his eyebrows in alarm.

The spell was broken by Uncle Nick, who had obviously missed the whole conversation. 'So, Libby, what's it like dressing half-naked movie stars?'

18

APRIL 1942

Ollie had been the perfect companion. They had enjoyed tea with Lily, and met her mother, who wasn't even fifty but looked frail and lined beyond her years. And they met the baby once she woke up.

After the first few awkward moments, holding Cathy was heaven. She sneezed, squirmed and waved little fists around, gazing up at Nancy.

'You're good with babies,' Lily's mother, Elizabeth, said.

'I like them,' Nancy said, her heart aching behind the smile. 'I know some people prefer older children, but babies are like puppies, they are just adorable. Even when they're loud.'

Lily reached for the baby, whose expression had changed. 'If I leave her feed any longer, she'll sound like an air-raid warning. Do you mind keeping me company, Nancy?'

They climbed the stairs, and Lily sat in a low chair, perfect for feeding the now grizzly baby. Cathy was nuzzling Lily's blouse, and Nancy could almost feel it herself, feel the sharp pain and release of her milk coming down. She stood in the window, glancing down at her cotton blouse, half expecting to see a milk stain. Finally, Cathy gulped that first rush of milk, then fell quiet.

'She always sounds like she's drinking a pint of ale,' Lily said, looking down as Nancy turned from the window, from the long view between the islands. Nancy sat on the edge of the bed as Lily started to rock the baby a little. 'My first baby wasn't any better. I remember travelling by train with her, trying to juggle a shawl over my shoulder, hold the baby and still keep her latched on. She swallowed so loudly everyone knew what I was doing.'

'You have another child?'

'*Had.*' Lily looked down at the baby, eyes closed, little hands loosening on her lacy blouse. 'Grace. She died when she was six, soon after the war started.'

Tears jumped easily into Nancy's eyes. 'I'm so sorry. I didn't know, Ollie never said...'

'It's what it is,' Lily said, brushing her lips over the baby's hand. 'You either learn to live with it or it consumes you. That bond with a child, it's unbreakable.' She glanced up at Nancy, then looked away as if she found it too painful. 'This war has torn lots of families apart.'

Nancy stared at the woman, watching the two connected into one. 'I was married before the war,' she said, her voice cracked like she was a hundred years old. 'We had two children. They were evacuated.'

Lily's voice was almost a whisper. 'I had no idea. Oliver never said anything to me.'

'I didn't tell him.'

'Why on earth not? Nancy, what's wrong?'

'I had to give them up. I couldn't work, or pay rent when they were so little. My mother took them, but she sent them to be evacuated in the country.' There, it was out. 'I was so ashamed.'

'Why?'

Nancy hugged herself, suddenly cold in the small draught

from the top window, open an inch. Gulls flew past, their cries mournful and otherworldly. 'I couldn't provide for them by myself, without a job or a place to live.'

'Where was your husband?'

Nancy shook her head. It was all too much, it was too easy to fall into the pain in Lily's face because Nancy knew that agony.

Lily stood up, her chair creaking. 'I'd better change her before she gets too comfortable,' she said, sliding the baby onto a folded towel on a chest of drawers. 'Would you get me some water, please, Nancy?'

There was a small bowl by the towel, and the bathroom was right next door.

'Thank you,' Lily said. 'Perfect.' The baby was awake, but only just, lazily squirming as Lily unpinned her napkin, washed her. Nancy folded a nappy into a kite for her, and Lily smiled. 'I can't do that one handed,' she said.

'I always folded them up, ready, straight off the line,' Nancy said, mechanically, and walked back to the window.

By the time the baby was redressed and ready for the rest of her milk, Nancy's eyes were sore with unshed tears. The stack of folded linens on the windowsill, the cot at her side of the bed, Richard's pyjamas under his pillow. Edmund's tiny, rosebud pout when he stretched out of a nap; his dark, dark eyes, like pools of ink. Her mother always said Richard must have some Spanish in him somewhere, but he was Irish out of Liverpool; she adored his accent. He was only ten years older than her, he said, probably another lie. When he held their children, he was as wobbly and clumsy as if he'd never held a baby before. She'd believed him, every day, for years, until the police came...

'Maybe I'll do that from now on,' Lily's soft voice came from behind her, sounding sad, and a little confused.

'Let me.' Nancy fixed a smile on her face. 'I'm sorry. I just can't talk about it yet.' She started folding the nappies into a stack of perfect kites.

'Then don't,' Lily said. 'I can't always talk about Grace, even now.' They sat in silence, then Lily looked up as if startled by a thought. 'But Ollie doesn't know?'

Nancy shook her head. 'No. I did mention I was married. And it was annulled.'

'Poor you.' Lily didn't say anything else, just rocked the now drowsing baby against her breast. 'So painful for you.'

Yes, it was. Nancy allowed the moment to wash over her, the memory of Edmund's little fingers twined in her hair, Louisa singing as she jumped in puddles. 'I'm going to try and get them back,' she said, hardly daring to imagine how that would be possible. As an unmarried mother she had less standing in the community, and no home or livelihood to sustain them. 'I'll find a way.'

'I believe you will,' Lily said, looking deep into her eyes. 'And if I can help, please will you let me?'

Nancy couldn't say anything more, and just nodded.

19

PRESENT DAY, 12 MAY

Libby had discovered that she could keep most of the dust out of her bedroom by taping the door shut with duct tape. The work-room was more difficult, but Jory came up with a thick plastic curtain that kept most of it out, and she left the windows open. Grant and Jory had taken it in turns to chop off old plaster and complain about the corroded and dangerous wiring underneath. She was absorbed in stitching over machined seams by hand – to make the soft, linen shirt look more authentic – when she heard her father calling up the stairs.

'Libs? I sorted out your hotel booking.' She scampered to the top of the stairs, but before she could stop him, he was already boasting to the men downstairs. 'She's got her *movie star* coming over, no less. Double room en suite with bath and sea views. How the rich live, eh?'

Libby had flushed to her hairline by the time she walked downstairs. 'Dad!'

'Well, I've got to boast about my *famous* daughter enter-taining a TV star!'

'Shoo. Mum won't thank you for getting covered in dust.'

But he wasn't smiling any more, looking into what was left of the kitchen.

'You'd better come and stay with us, Libs. This place is shot to pieces.'

'It's OK. I'm going to sleep in the summer house. It's still got power and cold water.'

He walked in to talk to Grant, while Libby went outside to find Jory sitting on the low garden wall, drinking a cola. They had cut off the water for the day to expose the leaking pipe under the kitchen floor.

He waved the can at her, and she took it just to allow the heat to fade from her face. The bubbly sweetness was good, she handed it back to see him looking quizzically at her.

'So, we'll meet him, then?' he asked. 'The film star?'

'He's coming over for a fitting,' she said. 'I must have talked the islands up, he wants to see them. But he's staying on Morwen, not here.'

'The hotel has got good rooms,' he said, then took a long drink. Catching Libby looking at the can longingly, he reached over and took another from his bag. 'Help yourself. You look parched.'

'I was concentrating on a long seam,' she said, taking it with a smile. 'It's a bit hypnotic, sitting in the light off the sea, just stitching.'

'So, what's he like?' Jory asked suddenly, and for a moment Libby didn't realise he was talking about Callum.

A spark of something ignited in Libby. 'What's Amber like?'

Her counter made him smile, grin a little even. 'You want to know about *Amber*?'

'Her name came up, that's all.' Libby said, blushing at how jealous she sounded. 'Kris said she's part of your business.'

'She is our financial adviser. She's brokering finance deals so we can deliver on our promises to design an award-winning, race-winning hull for Sabre and Quick to finish out.'

'So, she's really important to you, then?' Libby realised she was holding her breath, waiting for his reply.

'She was, for a few months. We met sailing. We had a little fling but she's way too much for an island boy. Wants to be a millionaire by the time she's thirty, which is in about three months. She slapped me and Kris into shape, I delivered plans and she got the deal a few weeks after I graduated.'

'Wow.' It was hard to imagine the scruffy, dusty Jory as a designer. 'And in the meantime...?'

'Kris and I have just finished working on a damaged yacht, and we have a trimaran coming in next month for repairs.'

'Had that one hit a whale, too?'

'No, they hit the jetty too hard, in New York. They were celebrating a cross-Atlantic race win, got drunk and crashed their boat. I preferred the other one, the whale story was better.'

She laughed. 'I hope the whale was all right.'

'By all accounts, it was fine, swam alongside and around the boat for an hour afterwards. Sometimes they like to rub their skin against yachts, you can get capsized easily, but this one kept its distance. It was quite a knock, the lone sailor spent all day putting temporary patches on, baling like mad and getting ice off his beard.'

'Didn't he have an electric pump?' She remembered sailing with Kris and her school friends. Most of the children her age learned as part of their school curriculum. Rowing, sailing, swimming. Essentials for living on a group of islands.

'The battery went flat. The problem of relying on solar.' He looked up as her father walked out of the house, his face thoughtful.

'You'd better show me the back wall, maid,' he said to Libby, and she did. He hummed and hawed, feeling his way along the wall. When they returned, Jory offered him a soda, too, but he rejected it. 'I can't see how we can fix all that damage. The foundations need rebuilding.' He made a face at Libby. 'I'm sorry, love. I'm glad it lasted long enough for Grandad to live there, and die there. But it's not really viable financially.'

'Can't we save it?' she said, her voice coming out louder than she expected. 'Dad, it's such a lovely cottage.'

'You probably could, if you could afford to get all the equipment here, rebuild the foundations, completely replace the inside.' He shook his head. 'It's a dead loss to your mum and me. We were hoping to sell it, maybe retire a bit early.'

Jory pointed to the side of the house. 'You might be able to develop the site, even rebuild up the hill. The summer house is on rock, isn't it? Higher, anyway. Is it your land?'

'All the scrub comes with the cottage,' Paul said. 'It used to have a proper back garden, they had a few shrubs and roses out there. Up the hill they had a few veggie beds, and they kept chickens. Your grandad said he never wanted to go without eggs again after the war.' He smiled at Libby. 'Maybe the site would go for development.'

Libby turned away, struggling to hold back her tears.

'Would you get planning permission?' Jory said, dubiously. 'Even to knock it down? They let the Griffins' cottage just fall into the sea. They said it was a sea mark, useful for navigation.'

Libby remembered the angle of two walls, sitting forlornly on the shore at the other end of the island, finally swept down in a huge storm a few years ago. And Mr Griffin, wizened and sad, wheeled down to the pub from his care home every Friday.

'There has to be a way to save it,' she said, looking at Jory. 'I'm going to do some research. Don't do anything straight away, Dad. Please.'

'Well, if you say so. But I don't like the idea of you being in that bedroom, right over the edge. The whole house could come down.'

'You could get the council surveyor to have a look,' Libby said. 'Before we put any wiring in. The house would need replastering, anyway. Jory says the walls are so soft they are falling to bits.'

'Good money after bad,' her dad grumbled, as he sat next to Libby and put his arm around her. 'I've paid the boys to get the ground floor ripped out, anyway. Why don't you come and stay at home? And then you're off with this actor for the weekend. We'll make sure the place is safe enough for you before you come back, if we can.'

'Notice he's happy for us to carry on risking our lives,' Jory said, standing and stretching.

'It's stood up this long,' Libby said. 'No, Dad. It's OK, I need to do as much work as I can before he gets here. I expect I'll be showing Callum around a bit, but I'm not staying with him.'

'You love going to Morwen,' her father said, looking at her out of the corner of his eye until she smiled, nudged him.

'I'll get a room, too, until the cottage has been checked. Separate rooms,' she said primly. 'That ought to subdue the gossips. Which, let's face it, is just you and Mum and Jory's entire family.'

'Me too!' Grant shouted through the open door. 'I'm going to gossip about you as well.'

'Honestly.' Libby laughed. 'No one in my block even knows my name in London! Let alone who I'm seeing.'

'Aha!' Jory said. 'So you *are* seeing him.'

For a moment, their eyes met, and she felt the sizzle of the connection she remembered from her teens, and from his sister's wedding. She couldn't look away, she couldn't breathe either, until he glanced down at the sea. She looked at his profile, his strong jaw.

She turned to her dad. 'He's just a nice young man, a bit insecure, who needs help getting his costumes finished before they start filming,' she said. 'But I love showing the islands off anyway.'

'But you will sleep at ours tonight?' he said, and she made a face.

'I'll sleep in the summer house. That way I can work as long as I need to before I fit his costumes.'

'Your mum would want to put the first series of that *Polzeath Manor* on,' he conceded.

'Dad, I've seen both series back to back. Several times. I'd come as long as you watch it with us,' she said, giggling at his changed expression.

He smiled. 'Sorry,' he said. 'I'd love to, but I have a prior engagement.'

'Would that be with my dad and his skittles' mates down the Bargeman's Rest?' Jory said, laughing as he looked over at Libby.

Their eyes met for another incendiary moment, causing her to catch her breath. She broke his gaze as a heat crept up her neck.

She just couldn't understand why he still had such an effect on her...

20

MAY 1942

They had planted and earthed up the potatoes, now they were trying to get the ground ready for vegetable crops. Nancy had argued persuasively that they could do better if they had access to one of the only two tractors on the island; one was out of commission and awaiting parts, the other was in heavy demand at a farm on the south coast. She had learned to drive agricultural vehicles and had done a week's course on maintenance at the agricultural college.

Nancy got ready for the dance. Supposedly it was to welcome the new American troops stationed on the island. The ferry had brought over a proper band from Truro, and the hall had been decorated with the flags of all the Allies. She hadn't wanted to go but Henrietta was desperate to, and now several more land girls had moved out to their farms, there was a diminished group of six left at the aerodrome.

She twisted her hair onto the top of her head, fixed it with a few pins and wound a colourful scarf around it. It would hide the fact she hadn't been able to wash it, but it also made her look older. She really wasn't interested in attracting the young men from the base, and was feeling a hundred years old anyway.

She put on her best cardigan – the weather was finally warm enough not to need a thick coat. Maybe she would meet Ollie walking down. Even as she thought it, her heart raced a little.

They didn't run into him, although they did meet up with several American trainees on the way down. One was older, and seemed in charge. He walked with Nancy, asking her questions in a quiet drawl.

His name was Walter and he came from some place called Ohio, not one of the states she knew anything about. He seemed less gung-ho and excited than his young colleagues; it turned out he had lost a brother at Pearl Harbor and was more realistic about the consequences of the conflict. There was something about him that she also saw in Ollie, some hurt, and she was happy to slip her hand through his arm when he offered.

He bought her a drink, a white wine. They hadn't seen much wine since the war started, but the base had contributed a case, along with some whiskey. There was still plenty of the local beer, although most of the barley fields were now growing wheat and oats.

She was finishing the wine and chatting to him when she saw Ollie walk in with Joy on his arm. He was laughing and chatting with a couple of lads and a small group of girls. She turned away.

He's young. He deserves to find a girl right for him.

She drained the last of her wine and Walter bought her another.

'So,' she asked, boldly. 'Are you married?'

'Divorced,' he said, over the rim of his beer. He sipped, made a face. 'I should never have got married.'

'Oh?'

He took a larger sip, smiled at her. 'She was pretty gorgeous. But she was high maintenance, if you know what I mean?'

Nancy had never been difficult with Richard. She deferred

to him for the first couple of years of her marriage. Then she started to suspect he was seeing someone else...

'What did she want?'

He snorted a laugh. 'Much more money than I was ever going to make,' he said. He was very tall, she liked that. 'What about you?'

She took a deep breath and looked away, across the smoke-filled room, where the band was starting to play. 'Same. Married the wrong man, got rid of him.'

'So we're both free.'

She didn't answer, just smiled. When he nodded towards the dance floor, she tossed back the last of the wine and let him take her hand.

He was a good dancer, and hard work had made her both fitter and slimmer. It was lovely just to have an arm around her, an admiring glance here and there and to enjoy the music. She caught sight of Ollie at a table, holding a beer, Joy hanging on his arm. He was listening to Joy and didn't see Nancy looking at him.

'Friend of yours?' he asked.

'Oliver? Yes, he's my friend.'

'He's been through it,' he said, looking at him. 'But he's got a good girl there.'

Nancy carried on dancing and pretended not to hear. By the time they sat down her muscles were beginning to ache. He waved to the bar for more drinks.

'I ought to get back soon,' she said, scanning the room for Henrietta. She was quite shocked to see her locked in an embrace with some stranger, at the back of the room. 'I came with a friend,' she explained.

'I'd like to see you again,' he said, taking her hand and tracing the lines on her palm with his thumb. 'We're both free and both adults.'

'Yes, we are,' she said, turning to him. 'But what do you mean?'

He smiled, the curve of his lips suddenly very attractive. 'I mean we're both grown-up enough to enjoy adult company.'

'Are you asking me to have an *affair* with you?' she asked, quite startled. The last time she had been in this position she had been eighteen and they had ended up in a church.

'Would that be so dreadful?' he asked, then lifted her hand to his lips, kissing the base of her thumb. An electric shock went straight through her. Richard had never made her feel like that.

'No,' she whispered, but he looked questioningly at her, as if he hadn't heard her in the crowded room. She shook her head. 'But I'm not that sort of girl.'

'You have days off, I have days off. There are hotels in Penzance. I can afford a decent room and some room service.'

That made her laugh. 'Very flattering. But the answer is no.' She looked down at her drink, which suddenly seemed sour. 'We're here to help the war effort, just like you. Not to entertain the troops.'

He raised his half-empty glass to her. 'A guy can try.'

She was impressed that he didn't push. 'In different circumstances,' she said slowly, 'I might be interested. But now is not a good time.'

'I'll walk you back,' he offered, but she refused firmly.

'I have to take my friend home,' she explained. 'But it was lovely to meet you, and dance. And thank you for the wine.' Which was hitting her system as she stood up, waved goodbye and walked around the dance floor to get to Henrietta.

Henrietta was drunk, her lipstick smudged from kissing the young man who was holding her. 'Time to go, Hen,' she said, giving the boy a stern look. 'Come on, sweetheart.'

After some argument, she managed to get Henrietta to her feet, eyes tragic and running with tears.

'Is she all right?' said a soft voice over her shoulder.

'Oh, Ollie, hello. She will be,' Nancy said, dabbing a hand-kerchief over Hen's face. 'Don't worry, she'll be fine tomorrow. Lots of double digging in the fresh air.'

'She'll be hungover,' he said, laughter in his voice but sympathy on his face.

She smiled at him, noticing a glare from the young woman on his table. 'Aren't you with Joy?'

'She's badgering me to dance. Well, to try to. But I think it might be beyond my dodgy leg.' He smiled back at her, waved, his expression that of an adult appeasing a child. 'I saw you on the dance floor with that American. You're a good dancer, Nancy.'

She didn't know how to reply to that. 'Joy is a lovely girl.'

'She is. And she doesn't know me at all if she thinks I want to get up and dance in public.'

Acrid blue smoke filled the air, and the room was heaving with couples, alcohol having disinhibited some of the young dancers. 'She knows about your injuries...'

'She ought to know I'm not that sort of chap. I'm more likely to go for a walk or sail around the island, or to walk someone's dog. I don't think I've ever danced – not sober, anyway.'

Despite Joy's disapproval, Nancy felt an urge to talk about the conversation with the American, but she couldn't, not in a crowded place. 'I'll get Henrietta back to her camp bed. We move into our new barracks tomorrow.'

'Well, good luck with that.' Before he turned away he leaned forward and said in a low voice, 'Maybe you could come to tea at the cottage on Sunday? We could sit and watch the sea and cousin Emma is a great cook. She makes a cake every weekend.'

She was touched, but could see Joy's face growing more twisted. 'Go! You'll get into trouble.'

He did turn back towards Joy for a moment but still added: 'Well?'

'I'll come if I can,' she offered as a compromise, and lifted Hen's arm over her shoulder to direct her footsteps towards the door.

She stepped out into the cool air and the sound of crashing waves. She wondered why Walter had such an effect on her, and yet she was still drawn to Oliver. His invitation to go to tea kept her warm along the aerodrome road as the storm picked up.

21

PRESENT DAY, 13 MAY

Libby slept well in the summer house, the sound of the sea and the mournful cries of the birds lulling her to sleep. During the evening, she had been filled with speculation about whether they could save the cottage, but had ended up determined.

There must be a way.

She was already up and dressed by seven, walking down the steps from the summer house to the cottage to work on the alterations she needed to finish before she met Callum.

A bang on the door made her jump – she must have fallen into the concentration of counting threads and placing tacking stitches. *Maybe it's Jory?* She ran downstairs. 'Hi!' she shouted, her voice catching in her throat, making the words squeak.

'Hello, darling.' An older man, short, broad, with sandy hair was smiling at her.

It was her uncle Ed, her father's youngest brother, who worked for the council in various capacities. 'Have you come about the foundations?'

He waved a fat folder of papers. 'I have. Put the kettle on, maid, and I'll show you. Tea, two sugars.'

'I'll make it in the cabin,' she said, taking the kettle up the stone steps to fill it from the brass tap. When she came down the wobbly steps with two mugs, he was looking around the wrecked living room: furniture was piled into a mountain covered with sheets in the middle, and the kitchen was down to a sink unit and a packet of biscuits perched on the windowsill where the frame had once been.

'More than a bit of redecoration, then?' he said, staring up at the sagging kitchen ceiling as she handed him a mug.

'Come upstairs; I have kept it reasonably clean. I'm working up there.' She led the way.

'That is a great view,' he said, nodding his thanks and sipping his tea.

'I'd like to keep it that way,' she said, sitting on her work stool.

'After your grandma died, your grandad had the place looked at. We did a survey then,' he said, unfolding a piece of paper and laying it on the table. 'We got a geologist in to have a proper look.'

'Oh.' She warmed her fingers on the cup, blew steam off the top. 'What were his conclusions?'

'The cottage is built off solid rock foundations, all right. But they were surrounded by the sand dunes, the storms have pushed the beach back quite a few metres back since then. The dunes have been walking for hundreds of years.'

'But that corner almost looks like it's hanging in mid-air...'

'It was extended about a hundred years ago. They built partly over the sand. The surveyor and the geologist recommended underpinning the corner with deep piling to get right down to the bedrock.'

Libby looked out at the wheeling sea birds, the wave tops like snow, racing towards the shore. 'Would that be possible? Or too expensive?'

He spread out another set of plans. 'Your grandparents were going to do the work but then she took ill and died suddenly. He never really got over it. Said he'd be happy if the place fell down with him in it.'

'And you let him?' It seemed odd to Libby that anyone could let a loved one live somewhere that was unsafe.

'We couldn't stop him. And we were reasonably certain it wouldn't fall down,' he reassured her. 'But it's deteriorated since. Your parents would love to save it, if they can. But it might not be economically sensible.'

Her father had never shown much interest in it, but it was her mother's childhood home. Libby had found that she really cared about it now she was staying there.

'Do you think he will pay for the underpinning?'

'He's already asked me to recommend a builder, to get a quote, at least.'

She laid a muslin cloth over her work to protect it. 'What would it involve?'

'You moving out, for a start. It's going to be less stable once we start rooting underneath to see how bad it is.'

She shook her head. 'Do I have to?'

'Well, if you can give us a few days to get under there and get some props in, maybe you could come back once it's safe.'

'That soon?' She smiled at him. 'I'm going over to Morwen for a couple of nights, then going to location on the ferry.'

'Say by Thursday, then,' he said, and finished his tea. 'We'll start Monday if I can consult with the surveyor today. You might have to bribe him with a bottle of whiskey.'

The council surveyor was her dad's cousin. 'That would be amazing.'

'But underpinning will mean ripping out the inside of the cottage, replastering, rewiring, and probably building a sea wall around the edge of that dune. I don't know if your dad is up to all that.'

'That sounds expensive.'

'Not as expensive as knocking it down and losing it, but you have to understand, this will be its last big refurb. With global warming, it will go eventually. Unless you move it up the hill.'

She folded her arms, looking over at him as he gathered up his papers. 'Would moving it even be possible?'

'This is the plot plan,' he said, flattening the paper out. The cottage sat in the pointy corner of a triangle, the rest of the land collapsed sand and scrubland, but it had an edge that ran up towards the road. 'The geologist suggested that this high point would look straight over the current location but four hundred metres further back. You could recycle the stone to rebuild it up the slope, or planning might let you build something modern and eco-friendly. But my feeling is the cottage might be listed as soon as anyone has a proper look at it. It's possibly of historical importance.' He folded the site plan back up. 'Think about it, talk to your dad.'

'I doubt if he could afford all this. He's got a lot on his mind.'

'He does,' he said, his mouth downturned. 'He didn't tell me about the cancer, but your mum did.'

'He's a bit shy about it,' she said, looking back out at the view.

'Well, he shouldn't be. I got tested a few years ago, I was all clear but I'll have regular checks.' He mimicked snapping on a glove. 'You can't be squeamish when they're going to save your life. But I think he feels a bit mortal at the moment.'

'Thanks, Uncle Ed.'

'Let's go and look at that whole site from the top of the hill, then I ought to call Joe.' He put an arm around her shoulders and hugged her. 'I promise, this place isn't going to fall down on you.'

'I know,' she said, feeling relief as she swallowed the lump in her throat.

He led the way to the corner of the plot, up the hill, a rocky high point that was about level with the cottage's lopsided chimney pot. Libby cautiously climbed along a rabbit path down to a sloping rock platform that was about equal height with the roof, into a relatively bramble-free area. She could see the back of the building, tucked into a rocky cliff a dozen feet high. 'There's a huge hole back there,' she said. Ed climbed in after her and leaned over to see where she pointed. 'Down the dune, where the summer house is. What's caused that?'

'The sand's getting blown out all along there,' he said.

A piece of something curved caught her eye and she picked it up. A curl of wrought metal, which fitted around her thumb. 'What's this?'

He took it and inspected it. 'You'll laugh at me, but this looks like shrapnel. I only know because my dad used to collect it from bomb sites when he was in London. Maybe someone found it in the town.'

'But there weren't any bombs dropped on the island, were they?'

'Well, there were a few dropped in the town, two girls were even killed. But there were also a few near misses, and I suppose some fragments might have washed up. We had lots of mines come ashore when I was a kid.' He laughed. 'We still get the odd one.'

She slipped it into her pocket. It had a pleasing smoothness and shell-like curve on it. 'What do you think? Is there enough room to move the cottage up here, if we got planning permission?'

He looked around at the ground. 'I think there would be room for a small dwelling here, but I doubt the council would go for it. It's historical, there are all sorts of stories about it being a smuggler's haunt, for example.'

'Couldn't we literally move the stones uphill and rebuild exactly the same? We'd be conserving it.'

'It would cost a fortune, you'd never get heavy machinery here.' He looked at her. 'So we'd better shore up the old house for you. You can find out about the history of the cottage at the museum, they have something on it. Maybe you can get it listed, get a conservation grant.'

'Will the renovation be very expensive?'

'I'll talk to your dad. If we can get enough people out over the next few days we can at least excavate for some better permanent foundations. We can repair the cob and stone then.'

'I'd like that.'

'Perfect. But we have to get you out for a few days. Pack up anything fragile, I'd take it to your mum and dad's.'

She thought of the heavy, industrial sewing machines. 'I think I'd better put my machines back in their cases, then I can put them in the summer house.'

'I'll call in some favours to give me a hand. The place is part of the island's history, and it's survived some terrible storms. Once it's stable, you can get Grant back to start the rewire. Will you be able to carry on working?'

She couldn't see why not. 'I've got power and water in the summer house. I do need a good light and occasional power to run the sewing machine.'

'But you can't move back into the cottage until I say so. OK?'

Libby agreed, then ran upstairs to start packing to go to Morwen with Callum, relieved and excited. All she had to do was persuade her dad to save the cottage...

22

MAY 1942

Nancy was just moving into her tiny cubicle in the wooden hut they had erected for the land army, when she heard someone call her name.

'Baldwin?'

'Yes, ma'am?' she replied smartly, and walked into the shared living space with its sink, tiny stove and wooden settle and table.

Miss Westacott was overseeing the heating of a battered field kettle, blackened with use. 'I have had a call from the farm at the eastern edge of the island. Plover Acres, do you know it?'

Nancy remembered exploring the island with Henrietta, when they first arrived. Taking only a flask of tea, they had walked around the coastal path.

'I think I've seen a sign to it. Of course, the signpost might have been switched to confuse any German invasion.'

Miss Westacott smiled. 'You can walk to it from Lowertown – ask for directions from the corner by the post office.'

'More planting?'

'Actually, no. A farmer has hurt his back, quite severely by the sound of it. His wife and son have a Case CC tractor, only about eight years old. But it was driven into a ditch and needs a lot of work. I know you have some skills in automobile repairs.'

'My grandfather owned a garage,' she said. 'I trained on an older model at agricultural college, and I've also worked on buses.'

'Perhaps you could look at it? The only mechanic left on the island has just joined the marines.' She rolled her eyes. 'Leaving the British people to starve, no less. I believe he did order a part or two before he went. The family will tell you more.'

'I'd be glad to.' *And no double digging or ploughing, at least for half a day.*

'Can you tell me...' Miss Westacott looked away. 'Henrietta Penhale looks very peaky. Is she homesick, do you know? Being bullied?'

Nancy shook her head. 'I think she enjoys the work. She has troubles at home.'

'Well, keep an eye on her. We're responsible for her, you know.'

'Yes, ma'am.'

She changed into her uniform coat and walked over to the edge of the field where the girls were standing around smoking or talking. 'Come on, you lot, we need all that done by this evening!' she snapped out in a fairly good facsimile of Westacott's tone.

Hen jumped. 'That's not funny. Anyway, we were waiting for you.'

'I'm off to look at a tractor,' she said. 'Who knows? If I get it working we might be able to borrow it.'

'Yes, please,' one of the older girls, Rosie, said, winding her arm through Hen's. 'Come on, lovey, we need to make a start. We'll leave some digging for you, Nancy!' she called after her with a grin.

. . .

The farm looked neglected and poor, a few stringy-looking chickens dodging about in the gateway, one nervous-looking cob in a stable. A woman walked out at Nancy's shout, as thin and unkempt as the horse.

'I'm here to look at the tractor,' she said cheerily.

The bundle of washing the woman was carrying turned out to be a grubby-faced sleeping baby. 'You're welcome to it,' the woman said, without anger. 'It nearly killed my husband.'

'I'm sorry. Where is it?'

The woman showed her to the end of an open-sided barn, where the wrecked tractor had been left. The engine cover had been torn off, and part of the side was caved in.

'What sort of farming do you do?' she said, peering into the blackened, oily depths of the engine.

'Mostly animal feed and sheep,' the farmer's wife answered. 'But we haven't sown any mangel-wurzels this year, the fields are just weeds. My husband isn't well enough to plough.'

'We can possibly get some land girls up to help,' Nancy said, pulling out a couple of rags. 'I can see the whole side of the carburettor is damaged.'

'The mechanic looked at it and put in an order for a new one,' the farmer's wife said, jiggling the bundle as a thin cry came from it. 'There's no promise they can get one.'

'I can see what to do,' Nancy said. 'Do you mind if I have a good look at it?' It wasn't too bad, the welded join gaping and deformed. 'Can I take this with me? We have mechanics up at the airfield who might be able to bash this back into shape and weld it up.' She reached into her overalls for some spanners. 'I should be able to get it off.'

The woman shrugged, but with a spark of interest said, 'If you like. I'll get you a bag for it.'

Nancy worked the bolts loose. A hessian sack accommodated it but it was still heavy. At least the bag might keep the oil off her trousers.

'I noticed you have a horse.'

'Poor old thing, he's either stuck indoors or out in the cold,' she said, walking back towards the farmhouse. 'My son's only nine, he's too small to hold him. I used to ride him, and he used to pull the pony trap, but not since I had the baby and it needs a new wheel. And obviously, with Tom hurt so bad...'

'Do you think he would let me ride him?'

'Maybe. But it's been a long time since he's had a saddle on his back.'

'Let me groom him and at least saddle him up. I could borrow him to get this back, and maybe the farmer we work with at the aerodrome will be able to use him. Stop him sitting idle.'

'Well, we're out of feed for him, he's been living on grass,' she said, but she did let Nancy into the stable and indicated the dusty old tack and brushes. 'My boy does what he can. Old Minty is quite gentle, but he can't reach his back.'

'Well, check with your husband and I'll ask at the farm. Maybe he can be off your hands and useful at the same time.'

An hour later, Nancy was slowly riding the horse back to the base, the sack tied to the saddle. He seemed pathetically glad to be brushed but was less impressed by Nancy climbing onto his back from the top of a crate.

She was no rider, and he wasn't a riding horse, but he soon settled down to a walk, occasionally trying a few bone-jarring trots. She talked to him, which made his ears flick forward, and he seemed less twitchy. When she sang to him, he relaxed and they turned into the high street without incident. Nancy had expected to have to dismount and lead him, but he was unbothered by the odd bike sidling around him, and just snorted at a delivery van.

She headed onto the aerodrome road, and apart from a bit

of banter from the guards at the gate, rode him in without difficulty. A hundred yards on, he saw the lush grass by the fence and she was powerless to stop him. He put down his head and started eating; she barely held on, clutching the carburettor to stop it sliding forward, and clambered down.

Shouts alerted her to the girls, racing across the grass, to join her and pat the horse. At a slower pace Miss Westacott walked over. Nancy quickly explained that if she could get the mechanics to have a look at the part, she might at least be able to get the tractor working again.

'It's a good one,' she explained. 'Just ten years old. We could really use it, and there is growing land being wasted at the farm too.'

'That's good to know. Go over to the hangar and ask for Leading Aircraftman Peters. He's in charge of the apprentices, he'll know if they can help or not.'

Nancy walked over, smiling at a couple of servicemen in uniform that she recognised. There were several small planes behind the hangar. She recognised them as Bristol Blenheims, small bombers, but once she could see in the giant doors she also recognised a Hurricane, a fighter plane. Inside, in overalls with black grease down one arm, was a familiar face.

'Nancy! It's nice to see you,' Oliver said, his warm smile causing her heart rate to increase. A few friendly whistles and comments came from the other mechanics. 'Ignore them, they're jealous. Pretty women never turn up for them.'

She laughed but could feel herself going red. It had been a few years since she thought of herself as pretty. 'We have a problem with a tractor carburettor. It's not old, but the farmer crashed the tractor and the side has split. I was wondering if someone could fix it.'

'Probably. We weld things together all the time, stick them back on and they work fine. For a while, anyway.'

'They've ordered a new one but who knows when it will

come?' she said, looking up at the huge shiny nose of the plane. Individual scars covered hundreds of tiny marks – bullet holes, she realised.

'I'll come and have a look,' he said, wiping his hands on a rag. He limped still – his shoe was a little worn down on one side – but he looked much more relaxed in his own environment.

'You look well,' she said, as she walked out of the hangar.

'So do you. The uniform is very fetching.'

She laughed, pulling out the wide flares of her trousers. 'Well, these helped me this morning. I had to ride a horse back. I wouldn't have been able to lug the carburettor back by myself.'

'Was this from Plover Acres?'

She fell into step with him as they crossed the runway. 'Yes. Why?'

'I know him. He crashed the tractor after he got drunk, after he found out his brother had been killed in action in Greece.'

'Oh.' It seemed the war followed them everywhere, even across the sunny grass. 'He's hurt his back really badly, he can't get out of bed, apparently.'

'I'm sure that's part of it. But my grandma Bertha would have said he has turned his face to the wall. Given up.'

'The part's over there, by the horse.' She steadied the cob and patted him as Ollie unwrapped the machinery and had a good look.

'It will be a funny shape,' he said, 'but I think it might be serviceable. I'm not sure it will go back in the engine space, though. Maybe we can modify the door.'

'Oh, that's OK,' she said. 'The door's already modified. It's probably still in the ditch.'

He grinned. 'Well, we'll need something to keep the rain out, at least. Can you give me a hand moving it? Unless your noble steed would like to help.'

'He's in horse heaven right now,' she said, unable to stop

him putting his nose back in the grass. 'I'll have to move him, take him over to see if our farmer can use him. At least give him a proper rub down. He's been so helpful.'

'All that green grass isn't good for him anyway,' Ollie said, pulling at his halter. 'Come on, lad, up you go. We'll take him over to the girls, they can look after him.'

It took both of them to chivvy and persuade Minty to walk over to the other women.

Ollie picked up one side of the sack, Nancy the other.

'It's heavy,' he said.

'Which is why I brought the horse,' she said, laughing.

He waved goodbye to the girls with his spare hand.

'They all seem to know you,' Nancy said.

'I'm very distinctive,' he said. 'I'm scarred for life. It will always be like this, which is uncomfortable for a shy person.'

'You're very kind to them, that's why they know you,' she said. 'I don't see you as a shy person, just a quiet one.'

He smiled at her with genuine warmth in his eyes.

23

PRESENT DAY, 13 MAY

Libby had been surprised when Callum had opted to travel by ferry rather than fly. Apparently, he wanted the 'full island experience'. Hopefully that hadn't included seasickness – there was a strong wind blowing from the north, enough for Libby to wrap up in a coat she had made herself out of hand-dyed wool. As soon as she saw him she waved and he grinned back, carrying two large bags.

'That was *amazing*,' he said, as he reached her. 'We saw dolphins. And terns. The captain gave us a running commentary every time we saw an animal. And there were *seals* on a rock.'

'You might see more on the way to Morwen,' she said, giving him a proper showbiz hug and double kiss.

'I'm glad to see you. You look different here. Your hair all whipped about in the wind, like a Cornish heroine.'

She shushed him, laughing. 'Don't even *say* the word Cornish on the islands. Come on. That's the little boat that goes straight to Morwen.'

The pilot, a tall woman in waterproof leggings, waved them over. 'Off to Morwen? I know you, don't I? You're Libby Elliott.'

'And this is Callum Michaels. Who is about to become very famous as a lead on *Polzeath Manor*.'

'Not that trashy, sexy Sunday night series?' She leaned forward to shake his hand. 'I *love* it, I've seen every episode. I'm Corinne, I'm off home to Morwen so this will be my last trip today. Perhaps I should get your autograph before you get famous.'

Callum blushed as Corinne helped two more people on and lifted a baby in a buggy.

'We've booked him in at the hotel,' Libby said.

'Ooh. Fancy rooms, the views are great. How about you, Libby, are you staying too?'

There it was. The kind but nosy questions that you got on the islands.

'I'm busy working,' Libby said. 'I'm making Callum's costumes. Well – some of them, anyway. The special ones.'

'That's right. I remember your dad saying you'd got a job with the BBC at one point. Well done, you.'

She deftly steered around a few ripples in the water where the rocks were close to the surface. The Sound was full of hazards and currents.

'So, Callum, how are you coping with all the bodice ripping?' Corinne asked.

When Libby looked at him, he was already scarlet with embarrassment. 'I haven't filmed anything like that yet. Just a few action scenes. I've met my horse, he's been very kind so far.'

'Have you fallen off yet?' Corinne asked.

'Repeatedly, and I can't get him above a canter. I get nervous and he senses it and slows down.'

Libby leaned back against the gunwale as the current speeded the boat up. 'We'll have to ride out together, it's easier along the sand. St Petroc's used to have a riding stables.'

'It still does,' Corinne said, peering over their heads at the water ahead. 'Hold on, guys, it's going to get a bit bumpy here!'

Waves lifted the bows and dropped them down three or four times, then spray spun over the boat and hit everyone before the water calmed down. 'It's just where the tide runs over the current,' Corinne said, drying herself with a towel.

Libby dabbed her scarf over her face, laughing, and handed it to the still startled-looking Callum. 'Quite different from just jumping in a taxi in London,' she said.

'I haven't really got used to that either,' he said. 'I grew up outside of Bristol, in the countryside.'

Libby supposed she had lots of preconceptions about him that she shouldn't rely on. 'You'll have to tell me more,' she said, as Corinne waved at the shore. 'We're nearly there.'

Corinne tied up alongside the quay then swarmed up the rusted ladder a few feet and jumped to land. She turned back to reach down for the bags, two of his and a smaller one of Libby's. 'Up you come,' she said to Callum.

He looked at Libby. 'I'm scared of heights.'

'It's a few feet. And if you fall, you'll hit the water. Look, it's easy.' She followed Corinne up the ladder, past the zone of seaweed and onto the cobbles of the quay.

He reached up for one rung, his mouth tightened enough to make his skin white around it. With a lot of encouragement, he managed it, but crawled onto the wet stones and sat there. 'I want to kiss the ground,' he said. 'It won't be that bad going back, will it?'

'Catch the big ferry back,' Corinne reassured him. 'It calls at the slipway. I just need to moor up here for the night. We live in the town, Tink's babysitting.'

'How is Tink? I went to school with Corinne's partner,' she explained to Callum.

'Tink's fine, but your friend doesn't look too good.' She was right – Callum looked a bit green.

He staggered to his feet, breathing rapidly. 'Honestly, I'm

scared of heights, I always have been. It doesn't make riding any easier.'

'Poor you,' Libby said. 'Come on, let's get you onto dry land and checked in at the hotel.'

As they walked, he paused to admire the church in its yard, filled with the gravestones of some of her ancestors. 'The captain's buried over there,' she said. 'My great – well, loads of greats – grandfather, Captain Steadfast Chancel. He built the hotel as his private home, and had a plantation in Jamaica as well.'

He stared over at the mausoleum. 'We haven't got anyone like that in our family. Was he involved in the slave trade?'

'His predecessors probably were,' she said. 'He was known as a bit of a bluebeard, couldn't be trusted with the maids.'

He looked back at the sea. They were standing shoulder to shoulder and she was very conscious of him, his arm occasionally brushing hers, the fresh smell of his cologne. They walked past the low sea wall, at the scrubby grass at the top of the beach, the sand running down to decent waves.

'My mother's cousin has a cottage up by the hotel. Well, they say cottage, but it's a four bedroomed house. If we have time, I should pop in and say hello to my great-aunt Catherine.'

'Everyone seems to know you.'

She shrugged. 'There's only one high school, so I know anyone around my age. So, yes, I probably know a lot of people.'

He paused, sat on the wall looking over the water. 'Our village was a bit like that,' he said, as she sat beside him. 'There were farming families. My dad was in charge of milking at a big dairy farm. Then there was the vicar's family, he retired to the village after working there for thirty-odd years. He's my mother's dad so they were posher.'

'So, are you local royalty then?'

He laughed.

'Come on,' she said, reaching a hand out to him as she stood.

His fingers in hers were warm, and lingered for a moment as they resumed walking on the path. 'The hotel's further down the path.' Someone had cut down the worst of the nettles either side of the path, new shoots were glowing lime green. The two gateposts had also been recently repaired and repointed, each one having a stone lion snarling from the top. As they turned to the left the hotel came into view.

Standing on a platform of rock, it loomed overhead. The portico was wide, and neatly stacked with logs either side. The door had a sign on it: *Private*, but Libby pushed it open anyway. Callum followed, looking confused.

She walked through a door at the front to a large room with beautifully upholstered sofas and chairs, and a desk with a man tapping on a computer keyboard. 'Libby!'

'Hi, Rob,' she said, and kissed his cheek when he hugged her. 'This is Callum, the actor I'm making costumes for.'

He shook Callum's hand. 'Welcome. I heard all about it from Catherine,' he said. 'We've put you in the front room. Fortunately we aren't too busy.'

'And me?' Libby asked.

He looked at her, eyebrows raised. 'Ah. We weren't certain... Your dad didn't sound sure if you wanted another room.'

'We're just friends. And colleagues,' she said, embarrassment warming her cheeks. 'Honestly, that's Dad's idea of a joke.'

'That's OK. Just a misunderstanding. You could ask Cathy...?'

That was a brilliant idea. There would be no misunderstanding if she stayed with a relative. 'If she doesn't mind.'

'You know she loves visitors.'

'I'll pop around and find out. You get settled in, Callum. I'll be back in a minute. We'll get some food, then you've got to be introduced to the islands properly.'

She headed out through the French doors onto the terrace, half full of people enjoying high tea, and walked down the small path to the side of the building, towards the corner of the island. The little gate was half obscured by climbing rose stems, bursting with buds already. She remembered coming over as a small child, helping Catherine and her mother, known to everyone as Grandma Lily, picking the soft petals to make potpourri. The house always smelled of it, and banks of lavender flowers already sprawled over the stone path to the front door.

She knocked on the door and was surprised to see it opened by a man in his forties, so tall he had to stoop in the doorway.

'Oh. Josh!'

'Hi, Libs. Good grief, how old are you now? I remember you going off to university.'

She punched his arm lightly. 'That was eleven years ago, you've seen me lots since then. I was just wondering if Auntie Catherine was around?'

'In the garden. She says she's meditating but I reckon she's asleep. Do you want to come back later?'

She hesitated. 'I was wondering if I might stay? I have a friend staying at the hotel and you know what the gossip's like...'

Josh smiled. 'I'll help you make up the bed. Maybe you could eat at the hotel, though? She'll wear herself out cooking a three-course meal for you otherwise.'

Libby laughed. 'Of course.'

He handed her a stack of clean bedding from the big cupboard at the foot of the stairs. She followed him upstairs, catching a glimpse through the window on the half landing of the hillside behind the house. A few rabbits nibbled the grass between brambles and gorse and a profusion of wild roses that flourished there. He walked down the hallway, past Auntie Catherine's room to the room beyond.

'This used to be the old nursery,' he said, and she walked

over to the window. It had bars across the low windowsill. 'The bed's original, it sounds creaky but it's very comfortable.'

'How is Nicole?'

'We're both working on converting the old aquarium into a research centre,' he said. 'But we had to get out, we found some asbestos in one of the walls.'

'Wow. Where are you living, then?'

He smiled as he joined her at the window, staring out to sea and the stacks full of seabirds that he was responsible for as wildlife ranger. 'We've bought a house in the town, right on the quay.'

'I was wondering,' she said, trying to remember the exact sound that caught her attention at night, 'is there a kind of seabird that sounds like a baby crying?'

'Some of the waders have a high pitched cry. Can you imitate it?'

She couldn't, but her attempts made him laugh. 'Maybe a redshank,' he guessed. 'There's a few visiting at the moment. Or just a few oystercatchers.'

He helped her shake out and tuck in sheets and put on a duvet cover. The fresh sheets smelled like the house, like the garden, like lavender and roses.

'I'd better get back,' she said. 'Callum doesn't know anyone. Yet. Once they air his first episode, everyone will know him.'

'Why's that? Is this the actor everyone's talking about?'

'He is. He has a very dramatic entrance into the TV series, and his costume will be fabulous. Gets ripped off at the right moment.' She laughed at the memory of reading the first two episodes. 'But you can't tell anyone that. It's top secret.'

She knew he would look wonderful in that scene.

24

MAY 1942

Nancy was helping the farrier at the farm by the airfield, as Minty's feet were long neglected and needed a good trim. His shoes were barely hanging on with a few nails, and he looked grateful for the attention. The stench of burning hoof as the farrier fitted a new shoe sent her away from the malodorous smoke just as Rosemary, one of the new recruits, shouted her name.

'Miss Westacott wants you to come quickly,' she panted.

A bolt of terror ripped through her and she grabbed her chest. *The children. Have they tracked me down to tell me terrible news?* 'Do you know what it's about?' she stammered, her pulse racing.

'No. But someone's come up to the gate, and Miss Westacott wants you to go down.'

Nancy started running, slowed by her heavy boots and the mud in the lane outside the farmyard. She let herself through the farm gate to the aerodrome, which was normally forbidden, but she had taken the horse through it and it was unlocked. Her mind was running in a dozen directions at once. Maybe it was something to do with her work, the horse or Henrietta. Or was it something to do with the children? Surely they wouldn't know how to contact her if it was, she wasn't on their paperwork anywhere.

She couldn't keep up the pace, her heart hammering uncomfortably in her chest with panic, her face hot. Miss Westacott was walking towards her, her face grim. As she strode closer, Nancy saw that she looked angry rather than upset; Nancy breathed deeply with relief.

Miss Westacott stood in front of Nancy, hands behind her back. 'We had a most surprising – and unwelcome – visitor half an hour ago.'

Nancy's breathing was resuming its normal rhythm, and her eyes were less blurry. 'Visitor?'

'A Mr Richard Shore. He says he is your husband. As you know, we don't take married ladies in the Women's Land Army.'

'I'm not married,' Nancy said.

'He has a very convincing marriage certificate and a wedding photograph to say you are.'

'The marriage was annulled,' Nancy said as calmly as she could, her face heating up with the humiliation of it. 'Mr Shore was imprisoned for bigamy. He... he had another wife, in Bristol.'

Miss Westacott's face softened. 'I've heard of this happening to other women,' she said, more gently. 'But why didn't you tell us?'

'I just filled in the form and joined,' Nancy explained. 'It was all very anonymous. I didn't want to be excluded.'

'He *insists* on talking to you,' Miss Westacott said. 'I told him you are doing valuable war work and can only be spared for a few minutes.' She looked closely at Nancy. 'Is there still – uh – any affection there?'

'None,' Nancy said, unable to prevent herself frowning. 'He lied to me, left me homeless and penniless. I could even have been charged with wrongdoing if the police thought I knew that he was already married.'

'Goodness. I still think you should hear what he wants before you dismiss him. If he becomes a nuisance, just call for me, I'll be in the base. They took him up to the offices.'

'Thank you,' Nancy said.

Richard was standing with his back to the door when she walked in. He turned, smiled broadly, and looked as if he was about to walk over and kiss her, before he saw her scowl.

'What do you want, Richard?' she said coldly. He looked as he usually had, just a little paler and thinner. Prison, she assumed, had done that. Despite her anger, she could still see the charming, genial man she had fallen for, although he looked older.

'It's lovely to see you, Nancy. You look – wonderful. Brown and happy.'

'I am. I'm too busy to waste any time on you.'

He took one step towards her and she shrank back. 'Please, Nancy. Barbara is divorcing me. I'll be free.'

'You must be mad to come here,' she spat, glaring at him. His eyes were too close together, she decided. 'I wonder what I ever saw in you.'

'I don't blame you for being angry,' he admitted. 'But my marriage was over, I'd almost forgotten she was even my wife. Then I fell in love with you. You were the love of my life.'

'Had you forgotten the two children you had with her, as well? The house payments you kept up, the lies about working overseas you told her?' He looked surprised. 'My solicitor interviewed her, Richard. You kept her while you made a... *tart* out of me.' Her chest heaved.

'I loved you.'

'You made our children *bastards*; my mother took them into her home and refused to let me see them. I *lost* my *children*.'

'*Our* children,' he said, a harder note in his voice. 'Who you aren't caring for.'

'I couldn't earn a living and pay for somewhere to live,' she stammered, overcome with rage, with hurt. 'Your wife took everything we had. The courts decided it was all hers, we barely walked away with a suitcase of clothes. I wasn't eligible for any relief because I wasn't married. What could I do, hand them to an orphanage? They took them to my mother's place.'

'They aren't with her now, are they? I went to her house and the neighbours told me she was killed last year.'

Nancy couldn't speak. Could he claim them, could he get custody?

'They are safe.' She was dizzy with tension now.

'I will apply to the authorities to tell me where they are,' he said. 'At least to visit them.'

'Their bigamous, *jailbird* father?' she snapped. 'Over my dead body.'

'You never used to be like this,' he said. She noticed the smart suit, the groomed moustache and hair. He had never been short of money, and his arrest had uncovered some of his shady dealings, adding to his sentence. 'Why haven't you been called up?'

'Didn't pass the medical,' he said, tapping the side of his nose. 'It's all about who you know.'

'Just go,' she said. 'I would never take you back, and the children are lost to you now. They are mine, do you hear me? They are safe and well. That's all you need to know.'

'Does that officious lady know you have two illegitimate children?' he asked, an unpleasant smile on his face.

'That was your fault,' she spat, her breath short in her chest. She had loved this man so much. Had he always had that mean look in his eyes? And he looked so old. More than the ten years older he had always claimed to be. She supposed he'd lied about that, too. She'd been dazzled by his sophistication, at eighteen. 'Just leave me alone.'

'All I have to do is show you are an unfit mother,' he said, coming closer. 'Do you think the government want to take on more orphans in the middle of the war? They'll let me have them if I can house and feed them.'

'What do you want from me?' she whispered.

'I want you back. I really do love you, even if you're being very tedious right now. I know I should have got a divorce but that's coming. We could be happy, Nancy.'

'I can't *ever* trust you again,' she said, looking into his face for a trace of the man she'd fallen in love with. 'I don't even like you any more. The trial killed any affection I'd ever had for you. The police interviews. The threat of being charged. Losing the children.'

'We could be good together,' he said, shrugging, like her love wasn't that important. 'We'd both be respectable; we could put this all behind us.'

She heard a sharp tap on the door. 'Don't mention the children to anyone. I'll think about what you've said,' she said, sidling past him to open the door. 'Thank you, Miss Westacott. Mr Shore is going now.'

'So, I assume you're not leaving our employment?' she said to Nancy. 'Good. Your work is excellent, you are very welcome here.' She turned to Richard. 'You, sir, are not. Please make a proper appointment before asking to see Miss Baldwin again.'

After he left, Nancy collapsed into a chair. *What is he really after?*

25

PRESENT DAY, 13 MAY

Libby dumped her bags on the spare bed at her great-aunt's cottage on Morwen, and ran a brush through her straight hair until it shone, fell like a curtain. She ran out through the open front door, through the garden and across the hotel terrace before she caught sight of Callum sat on the low sea wall.

'How's your room?'

'Amazing.' He smiled as he turned to look at her. 'And your family owned all this?'

'Well, going back about six generations. I'm definitely from the junior branch. It's the best location, though. Do you need anything to eat? You must have missed lunch.'

'They're bringing me a sandwich,' he said, standing. 'Do you want to sit at a table?'

When the waitress brought him a steak sandwich oozing with crispy, oily onions, her mouth started to water. She ordered a sparkling water with some bread and olives.

'So, what do you need to do?' he mumbled around a bite of food. 'Oh, my. You should taste this.'

She took a dainty bite of the proffered food and rolled her

COMING HOME TO THE COTTAGE BY THE SEA

eyes. 'Don't eat all that, or you won't fit your new breeches,' she joked.

'It's OK. I won't eat again for a few days,' he said, laughing, as he tucked in. 'So, what do we need to do?'

'I've packed the things I've cut out and tacked together. The production needs me to hand-sew for the look but reinforce with extra seams inside just along crucial areas. Which will make the items a little smaller, so they have to fit.'

'Then I can try them on?'

'The costume designer is looking for what she calls a romantic fit. A bit flowy in places but showing off the muscles in your shoulders.'

'I have literally spent two months in the gym getting these bad boys,' he said, flexing one arm to show off the definition.

'Which is why you can't get nervous and hit the carbs,' she reminded him.

He made a face. 'You're supposed to be secretly impressed and excited by my masculinity,' he said, sipping his beer and eyeing her.

'Oh, I am,' she said. 'I'm just concealing it really well.' Actually, he did have a nice body. Although a colourful bruise on his forearm stood out. 'What happened there?'

'Horse-related,' he said, and took another bite as if trying to change the subject.

'You fell off at a full gallop?'

'Not *quite* a gallop,' he admitted.

She started laughing. 'Are you too embarrassed to tell me?'

'I was just about to get on—'

'Mount,' she added, helpfully.

'Mount the horse, when he was startled.'

'Did he bolt with you?'

He sighed, pushed back his empty plate. 'If you must know, I was half on when I sneezed; he panicked and knocked me off into a wall in the yard.'

She couldn't help laughing, and the more offended he tried to look, the funnier it became until they were both chuckling. 'I wish I'd been there,' she said, and drank some water.

'So do I,' he said, sitting back, a big grin on his face. 'You could have broken my fall.'

'Do you want to go riding? I could book an hour or two tomorrow. I haven't been on a horse since I was a teenager, though.'

'Let's do this fitting nonsense later,' he said. 'Because the manager said the tide's coming in, and he recommended Seal Cove for a swim.'

'It will be freezing,' she said, watching his features change as he looked around. 'But I'll come swimming if you come riding tomorrow.'

'Done,' he said.

She led the way up the footpath to the very corner of the island, a flat area where a lighthouse had once stood, then south along the ridge past a series of tiny coves. One was more of a rocky inlet, with sailing dinghies already pulled up on the beach ready to take people out at the weekend.

'I can sail,' he said, puffing a little up the steep part of the path. 'I did a course when I was at school.'

'They have canoes as well,' she said, pointing at the sailing school shed. 'But we're going to the next cove.' The wind whipped her long hair around her face as she stopped at the top of the steps. 'This is better for swimming, but don't go out deep. The currents curl around the coast with the tide and I don't want to have to rescue you.'

'I might like that,' he said, grinning and taking the steps two at a time.

'Or we would both drown and your career would be over before it starts,' she said. 'What a tragedy that would be.'

He snorted with laughter, his eyes sparkling. 'They'd get some other reasonably tall, reasonably good-looking actor to fill my riding boots in a heartbeat.'

She laughed as her feet hit the sand. 'He wouldn't fit the costumes and he definitely wouldn't have spent two months in the gym,' she said, walking to the side of the steps to find a level bit of dry sand. 'How about we just get you back in one piece instead?'

'What's that?' he said, standing over her, looking left to the end of the cove to a shelter made of stone.

'Oh. That's the hermit house,' she said. 'This old guy built it and lived here until he died. A bit of a recluse. They did an article on him last year. He was a decorated war hero.'

'There's a good story, if someone wanted to make a film.' He was already slipping out of his shoes and jeans, brightly coloured swimming trunks underneath.

Libby had to resort to undressing under a towel and dancing her swimsuit up to her waist.

'Good moves,' he said, shucking his T-shirt.

'Shut up,' she said, as she took in his youthful body. He was very nice to look at, she had to admit. He headed for the edge of the water, and while he tiptoed in and out of the freezing waves, she managed to pull up her one-piece swimsuit. She hadn't expected to be trying to impress anyone – it was the costume she'd had since high school. She squinted down the top. Yep. Still had all her swimming and lifesaving badges on it.

'It's like ice,' he said, still only up to his ankles, teeth chattering. 'This is a terrible idea. Why didn't you say it was a terrible idea?'

'I did,' she said, set her teeth and ploughed in. 'It's OK once you get past your...' Her thighs stung as the water crawled up, hit her swimsuit, made her squeal. By the time she was up to her waist, she could splash her arms and chest, shaking with cold. 'It gets better,' she called back to Callum, who was up to his knees.

'Right. After it gets past your – crotch. *Ow!*' he shouted, wading in behind her. '*Ow, ow, ow.*'

She sank into the water, started swimming, a swift front crawl. He was still shivering, but he managed a doggy paddle that was slow but kept him moving forward.

'Stay parallel to the shore,' she shouted. The water was becoming bearable, if still cold. By the time she reached the end of the cove, by the hut, he had caught up with her. He shook his hair back like a shampoo model, then caught her looking at him as they stood in waist-high water.

'You look like a mermaid,' he said, and stepped towards her. 'With blue lips,' he murmured.

She allowed him to step closer, even wrapped her arms around his body. She looked up at him, glanced at his lips. 'I'm just getting warm.'

'Me too,' he said, and then kissed her.

For a moment another face intruded, a memory of that look in Jory's eyes. She pulled away quickly, but smiled at him. 'Race you back to the towels,' she said, and splashed away. She won. The tide was against them and he was quite out of breath by the time he paced up the sand.

He sat down, dried his face, wrapped the towel around his shoulders. Little beads of sea water reflected off his arms, like jewels. She looked away, her chest tight.

'Libby, in the water, did I do something wrong?'

'No! Of course not. It's just, we work together.' She dabbed the water out of her eyes with a corner of the towel. 'I shouldn't have kissed you, I'm sorry.'

'I'm not.' He bumped his shoulder into hers. 'No harm done.'

'Of course not. I just don't want to be that cliché of the costume girl who falls in love with the star.'

He laughed then. 'I won't be the star.' She studied his profile as he gazed out to sea.

'I think you will be,' she said. 'If the costumes are good, anyway.' He half smiled but didn't look convinced. 'Sam Worthing wasn't a star before *Polzeath Manor*,' she added.

'He was much better known than me,' he said, finally looking at her. His beautiful hazel eyes were filled with warmth. He looked at her as if he really wanted her. Jory had never done that.

'He was in his thirties when he landed the role. He had so much more time to do sitcoms and soaps, build his profile.'

'Maybe.' He looked away again. 'When the job is over, I'd like to ask you out. On a date, I mean, not to nearly drown in ice water and kiss to stay warm.'

She smiled. At the end of the job, at the end of the summer... Anything could happen by then. 'Maybe,' she said.

'Will you say yes, do you think?'

She impulsively leaned forward and kissed him. 'I might,' she whispered. 'But now we have to get back to work.'

'OK. OK,' he said, shaking his hair. 'But tell me something first.'

'What?' she said, rubbing her goosepimply arms dry.

'Do you do that wiggly little dance to get your swimsuit off, too?'

She swatted him with the end of the towel and the moment was lost.

26

JUNE 1942

Nancy couldn't sleep, knowing Richard had finally found her.

He might still be on the island – she was too fraught to wander into the town to find out. Maybe he'd be able to track down the children... She shut her eyes with the agony of it. For the first time, the rage at what he had done was giving way to despair at losing the children. The anger had been holding her up, she thought, miserably curled up on her camp bed in the small cubicle in the new bunkhouse.

Henrietta was just as upset; the date for her visit home was approaching. She couldn't explain it to Miss Westacott. Hen's eyes were ringed in smudges, like she wasn't sleeping either. When she put her head around the open door, Nancy could see how thin she had become.

'Are you all right?' she asked.

'I'm going for a walk.' The attempt at a smile looked like a grimace of pain. 'Just along the beach.'

'I'll see you later.' Henrietta disappeared, leaving Nancy brooding on her own woes. But Hen's demeanour and words bothered her.

She slipped on her light jacket and walking shoes and

headed for the guard post. They had seen Hen, not walking towards the town and the beach, but heading north towards the cove at the end of the island, by Oliver's cottage.

The breeze was so mild she was able to tie the jacket around her waist by its arms. Working in agriculture had melted the extra pounds of her complaisant married life off her, and made her fitter and faster. She picked up speed, still not seeing Hen.

She'd neglected her, she realised. The girl couldn't solve her difficulties, or she would have already. How could her parents be so blind to what was going on? But her own mother had loved Richard, had accepted all his stories about being an orphan, which she now knew to be lies.

She broke into a jog as the road dropped a little. She was more than halfway to the cottage when she saw a flash of blue over the sea wall.

Henrietta was sitting on a timber groyne that led up to the sea wall, dangling her feet in the water every time a wave lapped the vanishing sand. She was oblivious to Nancy jumping down, and started when she touched her shoulder.

'What are you doing, Hen?' she asked gently.

'Nothing. I'm... too scared,' Henrietta said. Nancy guided her up to the sea wall, away from the water, and held her close. Henrietta wailed with distress, sobbing in her arms. Nancy could feel the bones of her back through her summer dress.

'Look, we have to tell someone,' Nancy said. 'I got caught by a man like him, I couldn't bear it if you did too.'

'What do you mean?' Hen looked at her, her eyes red and puffy.

Nancy guided her to sit above the wall on the grass verge, and stared out across the water. She took in a painfully deep breath.

'I was married at eighteen. I thought everything was wonderful, lovely. He had two rooms above a shop. He said he part-owned the business, but that wasn't true. When I caught him out in that lie, he said he just wanted to impress me. I thought he was twenty-seven, I thought he was unmarried, that he had a business.' She sighed. 'I loved him. Richard went away a lot, for work, and he didn't want a baby. He always came back with money and we ended up renting a nice little flat. And then I found out I was pregnant. Eventually we had a baby girl. She was the love of my life.' Her eyes filled with tears.

'But it wasn't all true?'

Nancy's hands were cold. She wiped her eyes and shoved them under her arms inside her jacket. 'It was all lies. I found out after I had our second baby. Richard was dealing in stolen goods, he was already married and had two boys already. He would visit them and hand over some of the money to her, but he kept her very short. When the police came to arrest him, she was entitled to anything he had in the flat.' She was shivering now.

'Where did you go? Where are the children?'

Nancy couldn't speak for a moment, then forced the words out. 'They went to my mother's. I was humiliated. I couldn't believe it at first, I was naïve.'

Henrietta reached over and hugged Nancy. They clung together for a long moment.

'So, you see, you must call off this engagement or whatever your parents think it is.'

'I'm not as brave as you are,' Hen whispered. 'I just dream sometimes of being somewhere else, starting my life again, alone.'

'That's not the solution,' Nancy said. 'My mother died in a raid, a direct hit to the shelter. I know she was terribly ashamed to have a fallen woman as a daughter, but I do miss her. And she kept my children safe.'

Henrietta turned, distress on her face. 'Tell me *they* were safe?'

'They had already been evacuated, thank goodness.'

'Where are they? How old are they?'

'Two and a half, and four and a half,' Nancy said. 'They were evacuated to the islands.'

'*These* islands?'

Nancy nodded, feeling as if something was tearing in her chest.

'Have you been to see them?'

'No. They've been placed with a kind family, that's all I know. My mother was their proper guardian, and all the papers went up in the bombing. I'd have to get new certificates just to prove who I am, then prove I'm the best person to look after them.'

'Of course you are!' Hen said, her hands clenched together in front of her. 'Nancy—'

'I gave them up, Hen. I had no money, nowhere to live, I was grieving for the marriage and life I had. And I felt so guilty. They didn't ask to be brought into the world, the illegitimate children of a bigamist crook and a penniless, homeless young woman.'

Hen sighed, tucked her hankie into her pocket. 'What a mess for everyone,' she said. 'Was that the man who came to visit you?'

'It was. I thought everyone would know by now.'

The light was fading, the sky a darkening blue. The water on this part of the island was deeper, a sullen navy that looked even colder now the sun was dropping.

'It doesn't look very inviting now,' Hen said. 'Funny, isn't it? At first it was this beautiful turquoise colour, like the municipal baths.'

'Hen, there are people who will help you. Like me. Let me get my hands on the man who's confused your parents and I'll soon see him off.'

That made Hen laugh. 'I believe you would. No, I need to stand up for myself.'

'Do you still want me to visit them with you? I could probably get a couple of days' leave.'

Hen smiled back. 'Thank you,' she said, nodding. 'And if
you want to go and visit your children, I'd be happy to come
with you.'

Nancy had contacted the department of child welfare in the
islands, a man who was a social worker with special responsibility for evacuated children. He arranged for her to be interviewed at his office on St Brannock's, and she was shown in by a
motherly lady who turned out to be his aunt.

'We are very pressed for staff,' the social worker explained,
his own withered arm making it clear why he hadn't been called
up. 'You were enquiring about some children you are related
to?'

'My *own* children,' she said. She brought out her wedding
certificate and the certificate of annulment and he made
copious notes. Where and when the children had been born,
where and with whom they had been living when evacuated. 'I
was informed by the borough that the children had been registered as orphans.' She folded her hands in her lap, squeezing
them tight.

'Goodness, well, they are not, are they?' he said, staring over
his spectacles at her. 'They have both a living mother, and a
living father.'

'Their father is a convicted criminal,' she reminded him.
'Who had no right to marry me under false pretences.'

'Indeed. Nevertheless, if he wishes to claim them, he *might*
have a case.'

'Better than mine?' she said, struggling to keep the strident
note out of her voice. She moderated her tone. 'He is married to
another woman, he has other children by her. She's divorcing
him.'

'But you can see the problem,' he said, patting the notes in front of him. 'You are presently engaged by the Women's Land Army. You have no home to offer the children, no income. And the children are *very* young.'

'I know they are...' she began, but tears thickened her voice.

He waited for a moment while she wrestled with her emotions. 'Their present foster parents have registered an interest in adopting them.'

Nancy reeled under the weight of the disclosure. Her heart stuttered in her chest, she felt faint. '*Adopt* them?'

'They are a kind and caring couple, they have older children of their own, who apparently love the little ones dearly. The latest report shows the children settling down and that Louisa is doing well at nursery school.'

'They couldn't adopt without me agreeing, surely?'

He looked over his notes and the thin file beside him that Nancy longed to reach for. 'They have been declared in need of adoption,' he said, 'although, of course, they are not orphaned.' He smiled at her kindly. 'Let me make further enquiries, Mrs Shore.'

'Miss Baldwin,' she corrected. 'I was wondering,' she added, taking a deep breath. Maybe she had been holding her breath as she felt dizzy. 'I was wondering if I could visit them?' *Please say yes.*

'Oh, I see.' He pushed his glasses further up his nose. 'With the children so settled, it might not be in their best interests to disturb them.'

'If I was introduced as a relative only?' She held her breath again.

'Well, possibly. I'll talk to my counterpart back in London, and then write to the foster family. But I'm not sure...' He seemed to consider as he stared at her for a long moment. 'I will do my best.'

'My... the children's father has also talked about trying to claim them,' she said, clutching her handbag. 'Would his claim be considered?'

'Every claim must be ruled out before an adoption is carried out. We will contact him, in due course, now we know he is alive.'

'Please don't tell him,' she said, her voice wobbling. 'Not before I have seen them. He's been pressuring me. He came to the island. He wanted to pick up where we left off, he wants to take the children on.'

'Does he have a domicile and regular income?'

'He's a criminal,' she said, the words coming in a rush. 'He can probably pretend he has all those things. He's a cheat and a liar.'

After a long moment, the only sound the scratch of his pen on the notepaper, he looked up. 'I believe you,' he said. 'But I must act in the best interests of the children. How long has it been since you saw them?'

'Just under two years,' she whispered, tears now creeping over her eyelids. 'I used to be allowed to see them, once a fortnight, but never at her home. She thought it was better if they weren't associated with an unmarried mother. She is – was – very religious. So I was called to factory work. I never thought the war would drag on like it has.'

'None of us did,' he said drily. 'We thought that last time,' he added, waving his damaged arm. 'Arras, 1917.'

'Exactly,' she said, in a low voice. 'If I can get my children back, I'll work something out, find somewhere to live.'

'It won't be easy,' he warned. He hit a little bell on the desk and the tinkling chime made her jump. 'But I'll be in touch.'

Nancy stood, shook his good hand and walked out, still tearstained, into the street.

Maybe there is a chance.

27

PRESENT DAY, 13 MAY

Callum had been the perfect guest all evening. He enjoyed a walk around the island, loved his seafood dinner and hadn't been pushy although he was very attentive. She returned to her aunt Catherine's house happy and slightly tipsy, to enjoy a good catch-up before going to bed late. She did lie awake for a while wondering how he was, before sleep overcame her.

After breakfast, which they ate together, they went up to Callum's room for the fitting. He was co-operative, as keen as she was to get the costumes perfect, and very professional. She measured him for hats, and emailed the measurements to the milliner. She found a little tight spot under his arms which made it hard for him to stretch right over his head, and eased the seam of his shirt a little.

'I'm not going to do yoga,' he said.

'No,' she mumbled, several pins sticking out of her lips. 'Just fencing.'

'It's not exactly fencing,' he said, 'more slashing with long swords.'

She imagined the scene. The two men, loose shirts open at the neck, maybe a little oil as fake sweat to make them gleam in the low light. That would catch the viewers' attention. Libby found the idea a bit distracting.

'Does your character ever win a fight?' she said, crouching to pin a hem a little higher.

'Not in my first two episodes,' he said, fidgeting from one foot to the other. 'Sorry. You said stand still. I imagine Sam has to come out on top most of the time. I mean, he's the star.'

'For the more mature lady, maybe,' she said, laughing up at him. 'But you are the star for a younger audience. There, you can come down off that stool now.'

'These shirts are more like nighties,' he said, twisting to see the back.

'Women wore much the same,' she said, helping him slide the long shirt off. 'No pants and bras.'

'Just corsets.'

She couldn't help noticing how warm his skin was as she helped him slip out of one arm without disturbing the pins. 'You can put your shirt back on,' she said, deliberately turning away from the smooth, toned torso, even as her breath caught a little in her throat.

She could hear him rustling as he got dressed. 'I'm just going to get changed into riding gear at the cottage,' she said, fixing a bright smile on her face as she turned back. 'Then we can catch the boat over to the stables.'

'I'll get ready,' he said, moving a step closer. 'Although horse-riding sounds a lot like work now.'

'This will be fun. And it's all around the beaches and across the moorland, with lovely views across the islands.' She packed up her box of scissors and pins and the rolled-up fabric and headed towards the door. 'See you in a minute.'

'Libby?'

He was holding out a hand. 'I was wondering if you've had any second thoughts about us getting involved, even though we're working together.'

She stared at his smooth, brown hand. 'Sorry. It's still a terrible idea,' she said, shutting the door behind her.

I should stop kissing him, then.

In the hotel foyer she walked straight into someone coming through the door. A deep voice stopped her. 'Libby.'

She closed her eyes in sheer frustration. This was going to be such an easy, uncomplicated Saturday, but Jory was standing in the doorway, almost blocking the light out with his wide shoulders, staring. His eyes looked almost black with the sunlight behind him.

'Hello, Jory,' she said, her heart skipping a few beats.

'We're picking up a pilot to bring in a boat.'

Despite herself, a little spark of interest caught her attention. 'A yacht to repair?'

'And modify,' he said. 'So, I hoped I would catch up with you.'

'I'm just off to the cottage to get changed. We're going riding.'

His face was a picture. 'I can't think of anything worse than climbing onto a horse.'

'Other people would hate to go sailing.'

He shook off the idea with a shudder. 'I know you're staying here with your movie star.'

Let him think that, if he likes.

'I am working with the new actor of a very popular television show, yes.'

He stepped closer and she started to feel indignant. What was this caveman instinct men had to invade her personal space?

'I wanted to ask you...' He shuffled from one foot to another. 'I wondered if you'd like dinner sometime? When you're not working.'

Libby had fantasised about this moment since she was a

teenager. Now it was here, it felt like a cup of cold water down her back. 'What?'

He looked away. 'If you're too busy—'

'I am, but that's not—' She took a deep breath. Looking into his face meant looking into those eyes... 'Why, exactly, do you want to go to dinner with me?'

It made her heart jump just to speak directly to him, challenge him.

Why did you kiss me years ago? Twice?

'Well,' he said, looking down, off to the side, anything other than right at her. 'I thought we'd catch up. Old friends, that sort of thing.'

She could feel her resolve softening.

'I thought we caught up at Sunday lunch. And I'm quite busy,' she said briskly. 'I'm working on location in Cornwall next week. And Callum is here to get his final costume fittings.' He turned to look directly at her. His dark eyes had glints of gold around the pupil. She could feel her breath sighing out of her, involuntarily. 'Sure. I could. I'd like to,' she said, aware that her voice had gone softer. 'For old time's sake. Grant has my number.'

She smiled as he left, loping out of the lobby and waving to someone out of view. Then she realised almost everyone in the lobby had heard their conversation.

It will be all over the islands in no time.

'Jory is helping rewire my grandad's cottage,' she told the girl at reception, in a bright tone.

The girl gave her an awed look. 'And you're going out with Callum Michaels? I saw him in *Green Acres*, he was amazing.'

'Well, I'm just helping him with his costumes,' Libby said. 'Tell him I won't be a minute, I'm just getting changed.'

. . .

Callum met her outside the hotel, and he offered to carry her soft leather satchel. 'What's even in here?' he asked, putting it over his shoulder.

'Just a bit of work I'm doing. In case we're stuck waiting for anything.' It was her habit, always having something to hand.

'Tell me about this new island we're going to?'

'St Petroc's is the second biggest island,' she said, sounding like she was reading from a tourist brochure. 'It's got a manor house and the family own most of the properties on the island. Including the riding stables.'

'So you've been there before.'

She laughed. 'Everyone has! I mean, anyone from here. The manor house has the most amazing gardens, with a gorgeous al fresco restaurant.'

'Maybe we could have lunch there,' he said. 'Purely a business lunch, if you insist.' There was a little snippiness in his voice that made her smile.

'Don't be like that! This is my first big gig, and yours too. We don't want to get a reputation for being unprofessional on our first starring outing.'

'I suppose not.' As they walked past the old cannery he flashed her a cheeky smile. 'So I guess you ought to pay your own way, then.'

She laughed. 'I doubt if we'll get a table,' she said. 'They're booked up months in advance. People make a booking when they secure their holiday cottage. It's that prestigious. It's the only other island with a helipad.'

'When I'm rich and famous, then.'

Despite Callum sitting right next to her, and the fact she was having a lovely day, Libby found her mind kept wandering back to Jory.

28

Nancy finished the work day rubbing down all the horses. It filled the time before they ate, and she could settle down with a book. Having better lighting and facilities in the bunkhouse made life so much easier, and it stayed cooler than a tent in the sunshine.

She sensed someone was watching before she saw him, and turned around to see Ollie standing in the stable doorway.

'Henrietta said I would find you here,' he said. 'I needed to talk you.'

'Did they tell you?' she said turning back to the dried mud in Storm's mane.

'Tell me what?'

'I'm sorry,' she said, patting the animal's back and putting the brushes in the bucket. 'I just thought everyone would know by now. My hus— *ex*-husband turned up early this week.'

'Oh, I'm sorry. What did he want?'

She hung up the harness and put the grooming tackle away. 'He thought I might like to forgive him and move back in with him,' she said. 'Now he's out of prison.'

'Prison?'

'He was convicted of bigamy. And theft, but I didn't care about that.' She swallowed hard, dust from the hay sticking in her throat. 'I need a cup of tea. Come over to our new quarters.'

'If no one minds,' he said.

She glanced over at him as they walked across the grass. 'You came over to talk to me about something?'

'It's much less important than your situation,' he said, after a long pause.

'Please,' she croaked. 'I can listen.'

'Very well,' he said, smiling at her. 'You know I was trying to get assessed for air crew?'

She nodded, but she had a leaden feeling in her stomach.

'They kept refusing me the assessment, and I didn't want to push too hard in case they took me off my role now. I love tinkering with planes, it's very satisfying, but I think I'd be more useful in the air.'

They reached the barracks and Nancy got herself a cup of water and put the kettle on to boil. As she sipped the water, she could feel her shoulders tightening at the thought of him back in a plane, maybe on fire...

'Please don't!' It burst out of her. 'I'm sorry, Ollie, but you've done your bit for the war.'

He stood close to her, staring at her with those china-blue eyes. *So young, so kind.*

'I wouldn't be going on bombing missions like before,' he explained with a soft voice. 'I would be teaching new gunners on training flights, we'd be relatively safe.'

'Relatively?' she snapped, thinking of all the patched-up bullet holes in the planes he repaired. 'Listen to yourself, Ollie. You'll still be on a plane, in a war.'

'You can't understand,' he said, turning away, his shoulders hunched.

'No, I'm sorry. You're right, I don't understand.' She sat on one of the barrels the girls had placed under the wall of the barracks. 'Explain it to me.'

'All I could think about when we were shot down was to keep the co-pilot alive. He was in the plane with me when it crashed into the sea. Honestly, I think he got me out of the plane before it sank.'

There was a soft ache in Nancy's chest that she couldn't identify. 'What happened to him?'

'The fishermen rescued both of us, but the co-pilot passed away the next day. They all died.' He smiled wryly. 'I nearly died. I didn't remember much until we got to the Breton coast, waiting for the boat to take me back to England. Those hours on the beach – I don't think I was ever more scared. For the first time, I cared if I lived or died. Before that I was just waiting to join the boys. My crew.'

Nancy's heart ached for him, for the agony in his voice, the way he bent over as if in pain, talking about them. 'Poor you.'

'No. Poor *them*.' When he looked up, his eyes were brimming with tears. 'Now I have a life, my family, my friends. I get to walk away. I want to make a difference; I want to contribute.'

She took a deep breath; it made her head spin. 'You have people who care about you, who just want you to get better.'

'This *is* better,' he said, raising his scarred hand. 'I think I'd do a good job preparing boys for the war.'

'What about that girl? Think how she would feel if you were killed or hurt some more.'

'Joy?' His mouth drooped. 'She's a *child*, Nancy. She should find some nice, undamaged boy and settle down with him.'

'But she seems very fond of you.'

'She's impressed by my war record, by my apparent heroism. She doesn't really know me, and if she did, she wouldn't want me.'

'Why on earth not?' The kettle stared to sing in the hut. 'Put some tea in the pot, will you?' she called back into the doorway.

He stared at Nancy angrily, then stood and pulled up his shirt, revealing a patch of scar tissue crisscrossing his chest and stomach like the threads of a sack. 'My shirt and webbing burned into my skin,' he said, snapping out his words. 'Do you think any girl – any sweet girl like Joy – wants to look at that?'

Nancy stood too, and placed her fingers lightly on the burnt skin. 'She will if she loves you,' she said, then realised what she had said and dropped her hand. 'Please, Ollie, you have a long life ahead of you. Don't risk that.'

He tucked the shirt back in, his breath coming fast, and stared at her as if surprised by her words, or her touch.

'Your husband came here... So, are you going back to him?'

'Absolutely not. Never,' Nancy said. 'It was the worst mistake I ever made.'

He turned away from her, his body hunched over. 'Don't make another one,' he said, his voice hard as he walked away.

29

PRESENT DAY, 14 MAY

The stables were run by a young woman Libby immediately recognised from school.

'Frankie!' They hugged, although as she did so Libby was aware they had often fallen out as teenagers. She looked different, though, her face rounder, her cheeks red.

'Hi Libs. I saw the booking and couldn't believe it was really you.'

Libby stepped back. 'You look great.'

'So do you,' she said, looking critically at Libby. 'I'm not sure about the dark hair, though.'

'It's the only way anyone takes me seriously,' she answered. 'This is my friend, Callum. He's learning to ride for a role on *Polzeath Manor*, he's an actor.'

'I heard. Hi, I'm Francesca. Frankie.'

He stepped forward to shake hands. 'Hello.'

It was then that Libby realised Frankie had a rounded belly, sticking above her waistline. 'Oh, wow! I didn't know you were pregnant.'

'You've been away too long. This is baby number two, the first one's at nursery.'

'That's brilliant.' She wondered what the rest of their class were doing now. 'We ought to catch up properly at some point,' she said, suddenly full of affection for them all, for the past.

'We will. Let me introduce you to your horses. You said he was intermediate, Libs, so I chose this monster for him.' She patted a patchwork piebald, who towered over Callum and had just a suspicion of shire horse feathering around his hooves. 'Blue's mother was a cob, but he's a lovely ride and he's got an easy gallop if he needs it.'

Callum's hand was already raised to the horse's nose. It stalled. 'Monster?'

'Blue has one bad habit. He can't resist an ice cream, no matter whose it is. We'll go north, get a bit of a canter over the headland and then come back around the beach once the tide's gone out far enough.'

'Hopefully avoiding ice creams...' His voice tailed off as she walked over to a roan mare and ran a hand down her neck.

'I saved Elsa for you, Libby,' she said, testing the girths. 'You'll love her. Do you remember Peanut? How many times did he throw you?'

Libby laughed. 'He only ever tried when we were on sand so I generally had a soft landing.'

'Excuse me, what happens if he sees an ice cream?' Callum looked thoroughly spooked.

'Honestly, it's best if you don't know,' Frankie said, with a sly smile at Libby.

'I'm worried already,' he said, as Frankie led him to a mounting block and held the bridle while he climbed up.

'You might need to adjust the stirrup length,' she said, looking critically at him as he clambered onto Blue's back. 'You're taller than I thought.'

'Long legs,' he said, gathering up the reins and allowing her to lengthen the stirrup leathers.

She waved at a young stable hand. 'I'm coming with you. He's already saddled up.'

By the time both women were sat on their horses, and Callum had relaxed his death grip on the reins, they were ready to go. A stable girl ran out to open the gate and shut it behind them.

Libby could see Callum was a lot better than he thought he was. Blue was fairly relaxed anyway, but she watched him pick up as they walked along the bridle path to the few acres of 'moorland' that ran along one side of the island, crisscrossed with footpaths, a stream and a few nice open areas.

It was a pleasure to give the horse her head and feel her respond; Libby was loving the freedom of riding again. She hardly gave a thought to Callum as Elsa began to canter easily up the low hill, building to a full gallop for a few hundred yards before Libby slowed her down. She was enthusiastic, sidling a bit as if she would have carried on over the hill down to the sea, but Libby looked around to see Callum's horse also powering up the slope, something like surprise and pleasure on Callum's face. He pulled him up a bit sharp and wobbled, but kept his seat.

'That was *amazing*,' Callum said, his face flushed. 'I mean, it was a bit like flying, and a bit like being beaten with sticks, but *wow*.'

'You haven't had that from the stunt horse?'

Blue pulled ahead to start down a steep path cut through sandy grass.

'I think I could have had, but I've always been too chicken.'

Libby and Frankie followed Blue, just stuttering a bit at the steep incline, then picking his way through tussocks of the stiff marram grass. Libby's horse followed easily.

By the time they reached the hard-packed sand, they were ready for a long canter, over a mile from the rocky cliff at one end of the beach right down to the far end, with the small village and a few boats below a rocky promontory. This time, Libby gave the mare her head, the horse knowing what sand was hard enough for a bit of pace.

Callum followed; she could see him out of the corner of her eye, her horse coquettishly keeping ahead of his. By the end of the beach both horses slowed to a walk as they saw the houses.

'There's a pub at this end that will serve riders,' Frankie said, trotting up behind them. 'They do fantastic hot chocolates if you're in the mood.' She tied up the horses next to a trough by the beach.

They ordered drinks and settled on the stone wall over-looking the sand.

'This is beautiful,' Callum said, staring out to sea and the distant islands beyond.

'There's a gorgeous rocky harbour around the corner,' Libby said, pointing beyond the village. 'There was a secret base there during the war. They used to send fishing boats out to rescue people from occupied France.'

'I'd love to see it,' he said.

'I think it's better approached from the sea,' she said, finishing her drink, swirling the remaining ice cubes around the glass. 'We used to sail in there, tie up at the old submarine landing, and drink lemonade at the museum. It's fantastic.'

He gurgled the last of his drink up his straw. 'It sounds fantastic.'

Libby was tempted too. 'We've got to ride back, though, and help Frankie put these lovelies away.'

Frankie looked up from her huge bowl of hot chocolate. 'Mm?'

'Callum wants to see the old harbour,' she said, smiling at Frankie's whipped-cream moustache.

'Well, you're paying. Me and the horses will chill out here in the sun, wait for you if you want to walk up. I don't have to be back until two thirty.'

So Libby and Callum walked up through the narrow, stone corridor of the main street, admiring the tiny cottages with their windows set deep against the Atlantic storms. A shop advertised a window full of everything from milk to magazines, and the other window was packed with varieties of fudge and toffee. They bought a packet, arguing over the flavours like children and settling on sea salt. As they walked, their hands brushed against each other, and at some point one of them – Libby wasn't sure who – slid their hand into the other's fingers.

Just helping each other up the hill. Just friends.

When they got right to the top of the street, the view opened into the curve of the natural harbour, like a crab embracing the water with two rocky claws. Libby let go.

'That's the museum.' She pointed at the low building almost tucked into the cliff. It had a narrow lookout tower on top. 'The Special Operations Executive used to send spies over to occupied France. They rescued all sorts of people in disguised fishing boats. They gathered a lot of important intelligence that way. They even prepared the French Resistance for D-Day.'

In the harbour was a stone jetty with a permanent display of one of the trawlers that had gone backwards and forwards across the dangerous channel, dodging U-boats and German patrols. She explained that the ship, *Talisman*, was an old favourite from a school visit she had done years ago. It was a Breton deep-water fishing boat, a malamok. It had changed colour so many times the paint was inches thick in places.

'Do you want to see the museum?'

He did, so they walked around the two simple rooms, looking at old radio sets that had to be smuggled across, and memorabilia from the men and women who risked their lives to travel in and out of France under pain of death if they were caught.

The curator, an elderly woman who walked around with

them, quizzed Libby about her family history. She already knew Libby was the costume designer on the new series of *Polzeath Manor*, and Libby dragged Callum forward to explain he was going to play Sam Worthing's half-brother on the show.

Libby checked the time on her phone. 'We'd better get back.'

By the time they'd walked back up the rocky steps to the ridge again, Libby was ready to ride back. They found Frankie asleep in the quiet taproom, stretched out on one of the padded benches.

'Hi, Frankie,' Libby said, as she sat up and stretched. 'We're back,' she said, unnecessarily. 'Sorry if we were a long time.'

Frankie yawned. 'I was glad of a break, to be honest. Pregnancy is a lot harder when your first child wants to read stories in the middle of the night.'

They ambled back, the horses relaxed and content to walk, enjoying the sand. Frankie led them into the water for a horsey paddle. Then, finally, they walked up the beach and climbed the steep path.

'Last canter?' Libby said to Callum, and set off across the open ground. Well-rested, Elsa ate up the ground, and Libby let her find her gallop for a while, before dropping back into a trot. She turned around to see Callum following, his horse seeming to enjoy the run as much as he had.

'That's amazing,' he said. 'I don't know why I don't feel more confident on the horse I'm learning on.'

'Ask to try another one,' she suggested, waiting for Frankie. 'Horses are like people, sometimes there's chemistry, sometimes there's tension. You know enough about riding now to at least ask to try a different one.'

'He's the right size and colour for the role,' Callum explained. 'He goes well with Sam's horse.'

She laughed out loud. 'They can make any horse any

colour. If the role demanded a turquoise pony, they'd spray-paint one with dye. Horses get colour-matched all the time.'

He smiled, waved at Frankie who was just coming up the last rise. 'I did not know that.'

The three of them walked back to the stables and Libby helped Frankie with the heavy saddles. After a bit of tuition, Callum managed to unsaddle his own horse.

'You two lovebirds go,' Frankie said. 'I'll brush them down. That was a lovely ride, though.'

'Wonderful. Where do I pay?'

'Oh, Callum's already done that.' She grinned at Libby. 'He's very cute, too.'

'We're *so* not lovebirds,' Libby said, dropping her voice.

'Well, no. You're Jory Trethewey's, aren't you? Through and through like a stick of rock.'

Libby was frozen to the spot. 'Who said that? It's not true.'

'You adored him when we were at school.'

'When I was a child. Now I'm a grown-up and have a mind of my own.' She fished about for a strong argument. 'Jory's not even my type.'

'Jory's everybody's type,' Frankie said, taking off Elsa's bridle. 'Even me, and I prefer skinny intellectual types. But a girl can dream.'

'Not me,' Libby said, firmly. 'I'm not fourteen any more.'

'But not Callum either?'

'He's younger than me, he's...' *Kind, intelligent, sexy.*

'Right,' Frankie said, watching the teenaged stable hand start rubbing Blue down. 'He's got salt and sand in his feet,' she warned. 'Could do with a rinse.' She turned to Libby. 'The islands are buzzing about you and Jory. Now they'll be gossiping about you and Callum. Your reputation as a book-worm and seamstress are over.'

Libby half smiled. 'I was never just a bookworm, you know.'

As she walked out of the stables, carrying her bag, Callum was waiting.

'So, who's Jory?' he asked, his gaze intense.

'He's just an old friend. A childhood friend, really.'

Callum nodded and held out his hand, but she pretended not to see it. Somehow it felt wrong to take it when they were talking about Jory.

'We missed the one fifteen,' she said as easily as she could. 'We'll catch the two fifteen easily. Then maybe we could get some lunch?'

'Sounds good,' Callum replied, but there was a note of tension in his voice.

30

Nancy had to wait another few days before she received the letter from the social worker. He had referred her request to amend the children's records, and listed her as their next of kin to the social worker in charge of evacuated children in the county. He had also recorded and returned her birth certificate with Edmund's and Louisa's, which had thankfully been copied at the time they were evacuated.

She didn't see Ollie, except very early in the morning walking to work. He didn't look at her, or respond to her waving. She was a long way away, she could pretend that he didn't see her, but it felt like she had lost a friend. *Well, you'll have lost a friend if he gets shot down and killed.* It was a pragmatic attitude, but it left her empty inside, and she thought about him in the long evenings.

The airfield was as ploughed up and planted as it could be without impinging on the increasing use of the extended airstrip and the planes taxiing up and down it. A couple of planes, flown by pilot trainees from the American contingent, skidded off the tarmac and bounced onto the grass that had been left for that emergency, but no one had been injured.

She checked her bag for the last time. Gas mask, tickets, handbag, some cash. Her trip to Henrietta's home was to support her while she talked to her parents. Henrietta didn't expect them to be sympathetic, and she was terrified they wouldn't believe her. Miss Westacott had given permission for the two to go off the island at the same time.

It was a relief to get away from her worries. Nancy was surprised to see Ollie's cousin Emma queueing for the ferry, looking completely lost, frowning at anyone who tried to help her. She walked over.

'Miss Chancel? I don't know if you remember me, but I came to tea with Oliver?'

'Of course I remembers you,' Emma snapped crossly, but she looked relieved. 'You went to see Lily and the baby, too.'

'I did. Are you travelling to Penzance today?' The absurdity of the question immediately struck her, even as Emma's eyebrows stretched up. 'Of course you are. Here, shall we get on, find good seats? This is my friend, Henrietta. We're going to see her mother and father in Truro.'

Although Emma didn't offer any information, she did copy Nancy when she showed her ticket and stayed close to them while they found a table and seats by a window in the saloon.

'I haven't been on the boat for years,' she volunteered once they sat down, huffing. 'I hate travelling.'

'I'm not partial to the boat, myself,' Nancy admitted. 'I felt awfully sick when we came over here. Not like Henrietta, she's an excellent sailor.'

'I wanted to see you,' Emma said, staring at Nancy in a disconcerting way, ignoring Henrietta. 'But you never came again.'

'Oh. But I wasn't invited,' Nancy blurted out, surprised by Emma's words.

'Well, you is invited now. Any time you are passing, you can call. I won't always have cake but I'd be grateful of someone to share a pot of tea.' She nodded, once, like the subject was closed. 'Have you talked to Ollie?'

'I did a few days ago. I'm afraid he got quite cross with me. I didn't think he should go flying any more.'

Henrietta leaned in, her interest caught. 'Nancy, I didn't know he was hoping to fly again. Surely they wouldn't take him?'

'I did ask that nice captain,' Nancy said. 'He seemed to think experienced air crew might be needed. They have—' She swallowed the sudden lump in her throat. 'The RAF have lost quite a few recently. But he probably won't pass the medical.'

'Can they afford to be that fussy?' Henrietta said, and Nancy was pleased to see her interested in someone else.

'The new American servicemen are filling more and more roles. Maybe he won't even be needed.'

Emma looked from one to the other as Henrietta said, slowly, 'You really like him, don't you?'

'He's a nice young man,' Nancy said. 'That's all.' But her heart raced at the idea of him being shipped off to die.

'He likes *you*,' Emma said, then sat back in her chair as if the conversation was over. She pulled out a small bag of boiled sweets and put one in her mouth, looking out as the sailors cast off.

Nancy was welcomed into the sweet shop in Truro. Despite rationing, and there being a shortage of sweets, the shop had been adapted to sell other treats. Cigarettes, pipe and chewing tobacco, and newspapers filled up the shelves. The glass jars full of rationed treats sat behind the counter, in the position of highest security, glowing in unlikely colours. Just walking past them made Nancy's mouth water. Mrs Penhale was welcoming, fluttering anxiously around them, offering tea and immediately saying George was already here. She was a thin woman, in a shabby flowered dress and an overall.

'I want to talk to you and Daddy on your own,' Henrietta said. 'Outside if necessary. *Not* George.'

Mrs Penhale muttered 'oh, dear,' but clumped up the narrow stairs behind the counter to fetch her husband. There was some conversation with male voices, then an older man, stout and balding, came down behind his wife.

He gathered Hen in his arms, hugging her against his Fair Isle jumper. 'Dearest girl,' he said, his eyes wet. 'We missed you so much, and then you stopped writing.'

'I did write, Dad,' Hen said, her eyes streaming, too. 'But I couldn't post the letters. Please, can we talk somewhere else? Maybe in the park?'

'Just those postcards, no proper news,' her mother said, taking off her overall and putting her hat on.

'I'll wait here,' Nancy said.

'George can mind the shop,' Mrs Penhale said, stepping from one foot to the other.

'I'll make sure he does,' Nancy said grimly, hearing the shuffle of feet upstairs and seeing Henrietta flinch.

They were gone twenty minutes, enough time for George to walk up and down the stairs a couple of times, peer around the corner shelves to see Nancy, arms folded, and recoil.

Eventually, Nancy walked to the bottom of the stairs. 'The game's up,' she called to him. 'You may as well pack your bags.'

He walked to the top step. He looked young for his age, with a long, floppy fringe that looked more like the fashion of the American airmen. His face was very pale, making his hair look almost black. 'I don't know what you mean,' he said.

'What you did to Henrietta. She told me.'

His face twisted into an ugly sneer. 'I don't know what *lies* she told you, but it would be her word against mine. She's always been a bit hysterical, fragile. She never should have gone to the land army, it's too much for her.'

'She joined to get away from *you*,' Nancy growled. 'And for your information, she's an excellent land girl. Popular with the men on the airbase, too. She has many admirers.'

'Mr Penhale will believe me,' he said, but something of his certainty had gone.

'I'd pack your bags and be off, before he gets back, just in case,' Nancy said. 'Henrietta's grown up now, she'll tell them everything.'

The word hung in the air and he whirled around, and before Henrietta and her parents came in the shop's front door, the back door had banged behind him.

Mr Penhale's round face was grimly set, his face was red. 'Where is he?'

'Gone,' Nancy said, and Henrietta lifted her tear-stained face from her mother's shoulder. She mouthed, *Thank you.*

'I can hardly believe it,' her mother said, sitting on a small set of steps up to the top shelves, fanning herself with a motoring magazine. 'Taking advantage right under our noses...'

'Why didn't you tell us, maid?' her father asked Hen.

She looked down. 'He told me you would be angry, really angry.'

'Well, I am.' Hen shrank back close to Nancy. 'Not at *you*, my lovely.' He looked down at his fingers. 'I know where to place the blame.'

'Daddy, please,' Hen wailed, her face running with tears. 'Can't we just forget him, and move forward?'

'No, we can't,' he said, grinding his jaws. 'I'm going to report him to the police.'

'Dad!' Hen stepped forward, her shoulders back. 'It's *my* story to tell. Everyone in the town will know, everyone will see me as – spoiled, ruined. I just want to move on.'

He sagged against the counter and her mother stood, put

her arm around him. 'I hate the idea of him getting away with this, too,' she said.

Mr Penhale drew a deep breath in, looked at Henrietta. 'He's been using every trick possible to avoid conscription. I'm going to make sure he gets called up.'

Nancy smiled at the determination in his voice. 'They'd take him if he's got two arms and legs right now,' she said. Mr Penhale looked up at her.

'You've been a good friend to our Henrietta,' he said. 'We won't forget your kindness.'

'She's a dear girl,' Nancy said. 'Look, she's got a week's leave, but I have to be back on Monday so I'll be on the ferry tomorrow. I would just ask you not to let that man talk to you. He sounds very persuasive and what Hen needs now is someone who believes her.'

He sniffed his tears back. 'Honestly, we always thought we would hand the shop on to our daughter's husband, and he just seemed perfect.'

'When the time comes,' Nancy said, squeezing his hand for a moment. 'You will pass the shop on to *Henrietta*.'

He looked at her. 'I suppose we will. She's changed. Grown up.' His face creased again, tears squeezed out from his shut eyes. 'We've failed her.'

Nancy stepped towards the door. 'You were all his victims.' She recognised the mixture of rage, hurt and shock in their faces. She'd felt the same when Richard was arrested.

Henrietta flew towards her, hugged her. 'Thank you so much, Nancy.' She looked radiant with relief. 'I'll be back at the end of the week.'

'If not, let Miss Westacott know,' Nancy said. 'I think she'd give you extra leave if you need it.'

'I'm looking forward to putting the baby leeks out,' Hen said, and kissed Nancy's cheek, smearing her with tears. 'What will you do tonight? We have a spare room.'

'No, I'll head back for Penzance. There's a little hostel there, I reserved a bed before we left.'

'The Waterside? It's not very nice, I'm afraid.'

'Good enough for me,' Nancy said. 'Now, go, talk to them, help them understand.'

She let herself out of the shop, the bell tinkling over her head, as Hen's father turned the sign on the door and clicked the lock shut.

As she walked away, Nancy wished her own situation was as easy to solve. Her heart was so heavy, and it was hard to see a way forward. She knew she needed some outside perspective, but more than anything she longed to talk to Oliver.

31

PRESENT DAY, 15 MAY

After a good evening with her great-aunt Catherine and a pleasant night's sleep, Libby and Callum met up for breakfast in the hotel before he caught his flight back. She felt a bit self-conscious, not least because she couldn't forget the kiss they had shared.

'I'd love to see this cottage by the beach,' he said, through a mouthful of toast. 'On St Brannock's.'

'It was my grandparents',' she explained. 'My family bought it during the war. But it's falling down at the moment.'

'I'd love to see it, anyway.' So they caught the tourist boat – thankfully less vertiginous for Callum – to the big island.

She led the way to the cottage, opened the door and invited him in. The house was worse downstairs than when she left it: the plaster was half off the walls now. But up the dusty stairs, through a tarpaulin curtain Grant and Jory had rigged up, the studio was still workable. He stood in front of the window, mouth open as he stared over the water.

'I'm going to have to move out soon,' she said. 'The rewire has turned into a whole replaster, major repairs and even underpinning.' She sat on her work chair, enjoying watching the expression changing on his face as he looked across the bay.

'It will be worth it,' he said. 'I've never seen a view like it. The water is almost the same colour as the sky. It's like the Mediterranean.'

'Yes, but as an investment it's not really working. It will take years of holiday lets to pay back the investment, maybe decades.'

'I'd buy it,' he said. 'If I could afford it.'

'And that's the other problem. We're all really attached to the place, we don't want to sell it to someone outside the family.' She could feel a lump in her throat strangling her voice. 'We all really love it.' She wondered if her parents needed the money. Her dad was only working in the chandler's part time now, although he hadn't really explained why. She found she couldn't talk about her dad's cancer to Callum. He wasn't part of her island family, even if everyone else on St Brannock's knew. 'My grandparents lived here, my mother was born here.'

'My grandparents live in a town-centre council flat,' he said, smiling over at her. 'They love it, they're lucky to have some-where to rent for life. But it has a view over an off-licence and a chip shop.'

'Very handy. I'm guessing they are quite a bit younger than my grandparents. I think my grandmother was in her forties when she had *my* mother.'

'They're in their seventies.' He looked around. 'So this is most of the top floor?'

'There's a bedroom for me at the front and a tiny bathroom, but that's it. The main outhouse was outside at one point. There was just a tub and a sink upstairs when I was little. I remember doing my teeth overlooking the sea then having to walk outside to go to the loo. Then the family rearranged upstairs, created two large bedrooms and a proper bathroom as my grandparents got older.' She walked to the end of the room, pointed out the small window next to the corner. 'This looks over the outhouse, which is down there. And up the hill is the summer house, which is where I'm currently sleeping because of the dust...'

He leaned disturbingly close to peer over her shoulder. His warm breath tickled her ear, started a cascade of speculation. If she turned around, she would be in his arms...

'What's that next to it?'

'Just a hollow in the ground. The dunes fall away all along here, the sand moves all the time. The steps are just stones stuck in the slope.'

'So, how do you plan to save the house?' The moment was gone. Jory's intense gaze popped into her mind.

'They are going to put some props under the corner of the house. They are hoping to build underneath it, support the corner of the house at least. But we don't know where the bedrock is under this end.'

He laughed. 'Perhaps we ought to stay up *this* end in case it falls.'

'You'll be OK. And you have to go, anyway, you mustn't miss your helicopter.'

'You're right. Will you see me off?'

'I don't need to. I'll see you Tuesday. I should be back in the sewing room, working on whatever is needed.'

'I'd like you to.' He reached for her hand for a moment. 'You can't blame me for trying. Maybe you'll get the impulse to give me a big kiss at the airport.'

'I won't,' she said, even as her heart quickened at the thought. 'I can't. I have some... unfinished business with someone else.'

'This Jory?' He picked up his bags, slung one over his shoulder.

'Yes. Jory, I suppose. My childhood crush. I used to adore him.'

'But not now?' He stepped closer to her. 'I know you think I'm too young for you, Libs.'

'Well, you are—' His kiss took her breath away. It was everything she'd wanted from him: sexy, complicated, disturbing. She put her hands onto his chest, maybe to push him away but ended up holding him closer.

'Not that young,' he said, his breathing uneven. He slowly took his hands off her waist. 'I really like you, Libby.'

'I really like you too.' When she was that close, she could be honest.

Jory. The past collided with her when Callum stood back. 'I'm going to go. You can get this old history out of your system, and we'll meet up on the job.'

'But we're still working together...'

He shrugged. 'As long as we behave completely professionally, why does it matter? We're grown-ups.' He smiled at her. 'I'd better go.'

She escorted him to the door, where he gave her a peck on the cheek. *Professional.* She clenched her fists and kept them by her sides. Despite her best intentions, she wanted to be *very* unprofessional.

'See you soon,' she managed, and stepped back into the doorway.

After Callum left, Libby wandered around the garden, letting the sounds of the sea and the birds soothe her. She sat on the old lobster pot that overlooked the sand. She could see where the builders had put temporary metal struts under both corners of the house.

A curlew set up its trilling call, and although she couldn't see it, it took her straight back to walking along the sand with her grandad. Terns would dive overhead as she built sandcastles within reach of the smell of her grandma's baking. He called them sea swallows, while turnstones piped along the shore at low tide. He had lots of local names for birds and animals: the turnstones were 'shippies', the jackdaws were 'chogha'. He didn't speak Cornish, he just loved the old names. Her favourites were chaffinches, 'tinks', which Libby called tinkies as a child and hung feeders for. She still couldn't identify the birds that were calling at night.

She shut her eyes, listening to the waves bubbling in on the returning tide. It had been a long time since she had felt at home anywhere; now she felt a longing to stay, make bread and biscuits in the kitchen like her grandma had. She had died when Libby was nine, and her grandfather hung on for another decade. They had loved the house, they had fought for it. She couldn't imagine how hard their lives had been. Both had been damaged by the war.

She put a finger to her lips, and she could almost feel Callum's kiss. She hadn't expected to be so affected, it had always seemed like he was just a slice of fabulous cake in a shop window; she hadn't thought he would live up to expectations.

She hadn't thought anything could match the kiss with Jory at Dorrie's wedding, but now she was way past seeing Callum as just a lovely-looking movie star.

32

JUNE 1942

Next morning, Nancy was more than halfway back on the ferry before she saw Emma Chancel, looking at her from a bench seat outside the saloon. Perhaps she felt sick too. Nancy walked into the fresh air, leaning on the railing to watch the rolling waves cut by the ship's prow. White horses showed on every wave – even in the late spring the Atlantic was rough.

She looked back at Emma, who didn't look away, so she inferred she might not mind if she joined her.

'May I sit here?'

'You are Oliver's friend,' Emma said, as if in explanation.

'I hope you had a good visit?'

Emma nodded and looked out to sea. 'I went to see my aunt Elizabeth. I only met her for the first time when the baby was born. She is Lily's mother. She's gone back home now.'

'I'm glad you met her,' was all Nancy could say.

'I like Lily,' Emma said, in a statement of fact. 'I like Oliver, too. And my cousin Bernie. I don't know her sister, Clarissa, but she has moved in with Bernie so I'll meet her soon.'

'I hope you like her, too.'

Emma glanced at her, her mouth downturned. 'Mr Ellis in the post office says she is mad.'

Nancy nodded. 'We don't call people mad any more. We just say they have been ill, and they come home when they are better.'

'People used to call me mad,' Emma volunteered. 'But I'm not.'

Nancy didn't know what to say to that. For several minutes they sat side by side, lifted and dropped by the ship, holding fast to the armrests at each end of the bench. A fellow passenger lurched past them to fold himself over the rails to be sick. Emma made a face.

'I don't usually go on the boat,' she said. 'Just a few times in my whole life.'

'It is a bit of a challenge,' Nancy said, feeling even worse. 'It was better when we were talking.'

Emma nodded. 'Ollie has a girlfriend. The people in the shop said so.'

Nancy felt a pang somewhere in her chest. 'I know there's a very nice girl who likes him. They go out sometimes.'

'He never talks about her.'

Nancy sensed Emma's anxiety, noticed the skin crinkling around her eyes. 'She's a very nice young woman,' she said, with certainty.

'He only talks about *you*.'

'Oh.' Nancy felt warmth spreading through her. 'Well, I like him too.'

'I don't want him to fly in an aeroplane,' Emma concluded, and now there was definitely a tear in her eye. 'He helps me. He gets the coal in. You could tell him not to.'

'I don't think he would listen to me. I did try.'

A shadow of anguish passed over Emma's face. Another passenger walked by, clinging to the rail, but at least he wasn't ill. Emma reached into her pocket, took out a sweet and put it in her mouth. Before she put the bag back, she hesitated, then offered Nancy the bag. 'You can have one.'

'Thank you, but I'm fine,' Nancy said, certain that anything she ate would come back. 'But that was very kind to offer.'

'You should come for tea tomorrow evening,' Emma said. 'And see Oliver. Maybe you can talk him into staying safe.'

Nancy nodded. 'Thank you. That would be lovely.'

'I might not be able to make dumplings, though,' Emma warned. 'The butchers haven't had suet for *three weeks*.' She sounded outraged.

'I understand,' Nancy said, smiling into the scarf around her mouth.

Back on the island, Nancy was walking back to the aerodrome when a huge plane rumbled overhead, starting its long approach. It wasn't German, but she hadn't seen this type before. As she shaded her eyes against the late afternoon sun, she could see it had American colours, so she concluded that it must be a new Liberator, a heavy bomber. The runway had been hastily extended only recently, and she could see it would need all of it to land safely. She watched it land, then walked across to the hangar to join a couple of the land army girls and one of the guards.

As it came to a halt, a couple of aviators jumped down, followed by several of the men she recognised from the dance last month. One of them was Walter, the serviceman she had met there. He smiled, waved, and after helping another man carry equipment out of the plane and shifting his own pack onto the ground, he walked over.

'I had hoped to see you around,' he said, lighting up a cigarette. 'What do you think of her, then? Fresh delivery from Canada. Not quite like your boys' Hurricanes.'

'No,' she said, looking at it. 'It's huge!'

'We'll be using it against U-boats,' he said, 'as well as German ships.' He offered her a cigarette, and when she didn't take one, he put the packet in his breast pocket. 'I wanted to say sorry,' he said, before she could walk off. 'I was very forward, asking you out like that.'

'No. You were quite honest,' she said. 'I'm sorry, but I'm not interested.'

'You like that young fly boy, the burnt one.'

Nancy didn't answer, but didn't deny it either.

'Well, if you ever want a drink, no strings, let me know.' He grinned around the cigarette clenched between his teeth. 'We could all do with someone to talk to in this crazy war.'

'What do you do?' she asked, pointing at the plane.

'Train your boys to fly them,' he said.

'So you're the pilot?'

'Flight Officer Walter Baker,' he said, offering a sloppy salute. 'At your service.'

'Will you be training my friend?'

He looked surprised. 'Is he able to be flight crew? I know he was a rear gunner.'

Nancy looked over at the group of British ground crew and staff from the offices who had come over to look at the plane. 'He's applying for the medical.'

'Well, it's a great ship, he'd be safe with us,' he said, waving to one of his colleagues. 'Excuse me, we have to debrief. If you ever change your mind about that drink, you can leave a message at the base.'

'Thank you,' she called over to him, but he was already jogging back to the plane.

With a lurch in her stomach, she recognised Ollie talking animatedly to one of the other crew. She turned and trudged back to the wooden shack.

33

When Libby got back from Cornwall, her dad had already moved the basic furniture up to the summer house and put the big table in, although it took up a third of the space. She swapped the bedding onto the built-in bunk and carried up a few plates and cups. Kris and Jory had installed her equipment but couldn't fit the nursing chair or the wing chair in, so they had taken them to her parents' house. She missed the chairs; the house seemed very empty without them, like the last thread back to her grandparents was gone. She set up the dressmaker's mannequin and adjusted it to Callum's measurements. The hardest pieces by far were the tailored coats. They needed to be very close-fitting to give an elegant outline in close shots in the indoor settings.

Cutting the hand-dyed, superfine worsted was a responsibility. She had printed off pattern pieces on the specialist machine in Cornwall, so she could now place them exactly parallel to the grainline. Twenty-eight pieces for an elegant tail coat, in a rich golden brown that would look good against the lead actor's blue.

She was talking as she worked. 'Left pocket lining, right pocket...'

'Libby?' Jory was leaning in the open door. She started, her heart jumped and, strangely, she felt guilty about her kiss with Callum.

She pushed her glasses back onto her head. 'Yes?'

'Kris and I are going for a swim before lunch. Do you want to come?'

'I have so much to do...' She looked down at the pattern pieces spread out. 'I don't really have time.'

'We're starting to knock the plaster off upstairs, if you want to have a look.' A breeze from the door curled around the summer house, lifting up the delicate paper. Outside, she could hear the waves washing the shore.

She sat back, frustrated. 'No, you're right. I'm getting confused anyway.' She folded a sheet over the top of the whole thing.

'It looks as complicated as a CAD drawing of a boat design,' he said.

She slipped on her canvas shoes and grabbed a beach towel and her swimsuit. 'Have you found any more cracks in the walls?'

'Not too many upstairs, but the joists in the roof are a bit tatty. I think the woodworm are actually holding it together. It's better if you don't sleep up there, anyway.'

'No, I'm staying up here in the cabin.' She threw her swimming stuff in a canvas bag, filled a water bottle from the enamel sink and walked out onto the small veranda. The first step wobbled and she lost her balance.

Jory caught her under the elbow, steadying her. 'I almost did that on the step at the bottom,' he warned. 'Maybe I should spend some time fixing the steps before my boat arrives to work on? It would be safer at night, going down to the bathroom.'

'Maybe,' she said, breathless and very conscious of the

warmth of his hand on her elbow. 'Thank you, I'll be OK now. I'll be careful.'

He let go and stepped away, down the steps. 'I'll get some crisps and cans.'

She stepped over to the door of the cottage, almost scared to look at the damage. The side of the stairs was just timber framing, the lath and plaster had all been taken out. She crunched her way up the steps, over a drift of old grit and dust, to push open the bedroom door.

Kris was there, wearing a visor and holding a hammer. He looked up, pulled off the visor and grinned at her. 'What do you think?'

The room was trashed. Not only was most of the plaster on the floor, but bits of ceiling, too. 'Are we saving anything of the original?' she said weakly. It made her want to cry.

'Not much to save,' he said. 'There might be some old stuff in the attic.'

'I suppose so.' She coughed in the dust. 'Let's get some fresh air, we can have a look later.' She stepped out into the slight breeze, already hot in the morning sun.

By the time they got outside the tide was high, just nudging at the roll of dried seaweed at the top of the beach. Getting changed was easier with Jory and Kris, because it evoked childhood. And because they were busy stripping down to their boxers and then trying to outdo each other racing into the sea. She wriggled the top up, still embarrassed by the unglamorous teenage costume. *Why didn't I pack a bikini?*

The water was stinging and sharp. She waded halfway in, took a deep breath and dived forward, the water pale blue-green like sea glass, rippling with sunlight over the sand.

'Oh, that's good!' she said, when she stood back up, a hundred yards further down, next to the brothers, pushing her hair out of her eyes.

Jory was still huffing and puffing, his shoulders still dry. Kris caught her eye and nodded towards Jory, and she couldn't resist it. They splashed him until he dived in and swam away, laughing and swearing at them.

From the water, Libby could see the cottage, gazing serenely out to sea, beyond the boys chasing each other in the surf like – well, boys. It pulled at something in her heart, tied as it was to her past, her mother and grandparents, but also this bit of sea, this bit of land. Even Jory.

The place was in her DNA. She had to find a way to save it.

Libby swam up and down, loving the feeling of the water passing over her shoulders, fanning out her hair. When she started to feel cold again, she headed up to the beach, to wrap up in the old towel.

'That was great,' she said.

Jory looked at her critically. 'We were just wondering. Why did you dye your hair?'

'I like it dark,' she said. 'My friend says it makes my eyes look good.'

'It does. But it was just such a pretty colour when you were younger.'

Kris lay back on his towel. 'Wake me up before I burn,' he said lazily, and Libby could feel the same lassitude in her own muscles as she warmed up, the sun replacing the heat and energy that the cold water had sucked out.

'It was ginger,' she said, pulling her T-shirt back on over her suit and straightening the towel out so she could lie on it. Something sounded in the distance, like a loudhailer. 'What's that?'

'I don't know,' Jory said, looking back towards the town. 'Is it another public announcement? We had a dead whale wash up on Windmill Bay last year. They managed to get chains on it and tow it out to the reef.'

'No,' she said, sitting up and shading her eyes. 'Something's going on. They want people off the beach.'

'Hard to see why,' Kris said lazily.

A few minutes later, the coastguard's car reached the end of the lane. A man in uniform got out and walked towards them.

'Please leave the beach... Oh, hello, Jory. I thought you were tourists.'

'What's the problem?'

'See that mass of seaweed over there, floating past the town beach?'

Libby covered her eyes. 'I can see it. Not a dead whale, then?'

'We're not sure. It could be another wartime mine, we get the odd one in our waters.'

She could see something black now, a curve rolling back and forth in the water. 'Could they still be dangerous?'

'They can be. Also, after eighty years in seawater, they are pretty unstable. So get your things and move back to the road.' He stared at her. 'Libby? Someone said you were back.' She recognised him as one of Jory's old rowing mates.

'Hi, Nick. Just for a few months. I'm staying at the cottage. Will it be OK?'

'I don't know. I doubt any explosion would do much damage beyond breaking a few windows. But hopefully we can safely net it, tow it out to sea and blow it up there.'

They grabbed all their belongings and walked up the sand.

'It's nice to see you. I almost didn't recognise you with your hair so dark,' Nick said.

'I fancied a change.'

'Are you really working on a film?'

'TV series, but yes.'

He smiled at her. 'Try not to make the extras look like complete yokels, will you? Just because we've got an accent doesn't mean we're stupid.'

'I make costumes,' she explained, laughing. 'I'll try and make sure the extras are all dressed in clothes that make them look clever.'

'At least stop them chewing straws,' he said, climbing back into his car and starting the engine.

She trudged back up to the cottage and flopped onto the driftwood bench, enjoying the blissful sun. Jory appeared with an open can for her and sat next to her. 'I miss this,' she said, sadness sinking into her. 'I really miss this in London. Although there are lots of things I love about the city, but the summers are too hot and dry.'

'The beach will still be here, you'll still be able to sit on the wall and look over the sea.'

'With holidaymakers in our new and improved cottage?' she scoffed, unable to look at him. 'This feels like our ancestral home.'

'Your great-aunt, or whatever Miss Chancel was, only bought it during the war,' he reminded her. 'It was owned by all sorts of people before that. It's even supposed to be haunted.'

'Old houses are always thought to be haunted. I suppose any house this old will have had people die here,' she said, looking along the rough water on the rocks beyond the end of the beach. 'When I was sleeping in the cottage, I kept hearing a crying noise. I thought it could be a curlew but Josh suggested a redshank. But I don't think it is a bird.' She turned to him, and he was looking at her with those eyes. She dropped her gaze, her pulse jumping. *He should wear dark glasses*, she thought crossly.

'Well, a ghost can't hurt you.'

'My grandparents always claimed Great-Aunt Emma left Morwen because she was haunted,' she said, looking away. 'By her dead sister.'

'I heard that story way back, when I was a kid. Only I heard it was the sea captain.'

'Possibly,' she conceded. 'Did you ever hear about the Morwen witch legend?'

'Everyone did,' he said. 'Didn't you have to do a school project on her? We did.'

She smiled at that. 'I remember doing some very horrible designs for her prison outfit. But she was reprieved, so it was less of a story.'

'I thought she was hanged,' he said, idly. 'Or it's just a local legend.'

She shook her head. 'I'm going to look up the history of the cottage. Maybe if it's got historical value I can help get it protected, or get some funding for the restoration.'

'You could try. But the story of its past might make it seem more haunted...' he said.

34

Nancy trudged up the small incline to Capstan Cottage after Emma Chancel's invitation. She had found a two-ounce bar of fruit and nut chocolate to take as a gift.

She just hoped Ollie wouldn't be upset with her after their argument the last time they met. *Well*, she told herself. *He doesn't have to stay and talk, does he?*

'Nancy!' She turned to see him jogging up the hill, more lopsided than usual. 'Emma said you would come to supper.'

'I hope that's OK,' she said stiffly.

'I'm sorry. I've been a bit standoffish, I know. I've had a lot on my mind.'

She softened when she saw how much he was favouring his bad leg. 'Don't blame me for hating the idea of you going back up in the air.'

'I don't.' He shrugged. 'I've been thinking what you said. Honestly, I have. I can't explain the pull, it's something I can't talk about. I just feel it.'

'Well, that's out in the open, then,' she said. 'Did Lily tell you about... my children?'

'Your what? No!'

She walked towards the gate. 'You know I was married to a bigamist?'

'You told me.'

'Well, what I couldn't talk about – *explain* – was that I have two children. They were given to my mother when I was chucked out of my home.' She clenched her teeth for a moment against a wave of emotion. 'Fortunately, they were evacuated before my mother's home was bombed. They were sent here to the islands, to Morwen.'

'Morwen.' He whistled. 'So, *that's* why you were so drawn to the island, but you seemed so scared. You didn't want to bump into them?'

'I doubt if they would even remember me,' she said. 'My mother let me see them at a canteen, every other week, for tea. Edmund was just a baby when they were sent here. Louisa was just two and a half. She's not even five yet.'

He paused in front of the door. 'You poor thing. You must long to see them.'

'I do.' She looked up at him. He was slim, and comfortably three or four inches taller than her. 'Their foster family want to adopt them.'

He pushed the door open, shouted through a door to Emma. 'It's just us, Em. We'll get washed up for supper.'

'Ten minutes,' she shouted back, and a wave of savoury smells rolled through the door.

'The bathroom's out here,' he said, showing her the outhouse down the side of the cottage.

He left her to wash her hands in private then went in to wash his.

'What are you going to do?' he asked, shutting the front door behind them. 'What do you even want to do?' His voice was soft, kind, and her eyes welled with tears.

'I want them back. I just have no idea how I will support them. Married women aren't allowed in the land army, let alone mothers. If they find out, I'll lose my job, with a censure.'

'You could look for work on the islands. We're desperate for workers.'

'But how would I look after them while I was working? Where would I live?'

He opened the door for her, waved at a cosy living room with too many chairs, including a rocker. 'Do sit down. Here, next to the fireplace. You can see the sea.'

'This is lovely,' she said, staring out of the window before sitting next to him. 'You are so lucky.'

'I am,' he said. 'Someone has always looked after me. I don't know what I'd do on my own.'

'You won't be on your own.' She smiled through sudden tears. 'You'll marry, and then there will be children.'

He stared at her until she dropped her gaze. 'Maybe,' he admitted. 'If I could find someone that I really liked, who wasn't repelled by me.'

'Joy isn't repelled.'

'All she sees is the uniform. But I notice she always sits on my good side, and tries to hold my better hand. It's starting to dawn on her that I'm probably scarred over my body, too.'

'Oh, Ollie.'

He reached over and held out one reddened, contracted hand. After a moment staring at it, she put her own in it. 'You're going to say I'm too young for you, aren't you?' he said softly.

'You know you are.' She looked up at him, really saw him. Whatever he had been through had aged him, put a weary, wise look in his gaze. 'I'm six years older than you.'

'I'm not a boy any more,' he said softly. 'And I think I could solve your problem.'

'How?' But in truth, she knew what he was trying to say; it was swirling around her in a haze of speculation. 'No, Oliver.'

'At least think about it.'

'You deserve someone you adore, and who loves you back.'

'Maybe you would come to love me,' he said, his voice small and flat.

Maybe I already do, her skippy heart and flushed neck told her. 'But you're trying to get back in the air, to risk your life.'

'Even better. You would have a widow's pension.'

'How could you say that?' she snapped, jumping up with anger. She could have hit him. 'I would *never* marry someone with a death wish. I would never link myself to someone who cared so little for me, and my children, that he would break our hearts—'

'I just thought—'

'Well, don't. Don't throw your future away because you feel *sorry* for me.'

It was a relief when Emma brought in a casserole dish and placed it on the table, putting an end to their argument.

35

PRESENT DAY, 22 MAY

Monday had been spent finishing hems to the highest standard and packing up stuff to take out of the cottage. Uncle Ed had turned up with two men his own age, who demanded tea and biscuits every twenty minutes but moved an amazing amount of rubble from underneath the kitchen wall. She could see the bedrock they were going to build off – solid granite.

'By the time we've finished, it will last another few hundred years,' Ed had said, wiping sweat off his forehead. 'Although it could do with a bit of wall in front to fend off the tides. Your grandad used to get pebbles thrown through the windows. He got a bit of transom off a smashed yacht once, came right into the kitchen. It still had the name on it.'

She'd had a sudden flash of memory and darted out into the front garden. 'Is this it?' she'd asked, holding up a big piece of driftwood.

'That's it, the *Diamond Betty*,' he'd said, showing it to one of his colleagues. 'Let's hope you don't get the rest of it thrown up in a storm.' He'd lowered his voice to a loud rumble – she was still sure they could hear him outside. 'So, apparently you're going on a *date* with Jory tonight?'

'How do you even know that? I might be going out, but just
as friends,' she had said, but was sure the heat in her face told a
different story. 'And then I have to go back to the mainland for
work.'

Now she was standing on the quay, waiting for Jory and staring
at the groups of patterned turnstones hunkered down on
moored boats, rustling their feathers as they settled to sleep. A
black and silver speedboat zipped between the islands. She
turned her back on it when she heard it throttle back, swishing
along the quay. She twisted around to see Jory standing at the
wheel, wearing sunglasses and a baseball cap. She caught her
breath for a moment – he looked fantastic, like a real movie star.

'Wow. Is that yours?' she said, to cover her confusion.

'Hardly.' His teeth flashed white as he grinned. 'A repair
job. I'm calling this its sea trials, so don't make a mess of the
upholstery. Come on down.'

'I have heels on,' she grumbled, but it was easy enough to
step onto the ladder down to the pontoon and into the boat. She
had chosen skinny jeans and a leather jacket in peacock blue,
which a previous boyfriend had said matched her eyes. She had
taken special care, despite the change in her feelings towards
Callum. 'Where are we going?'

'Petroc,' he said, the engine purring into life.

'You didn't get a table at Elegy, did you?' The most prestigious restaurant on the off-islands, it was part of the famous
gardens on St Petroc's.

'Better.' He focused on navigating between all the moored
fishing boats, so she relaxed into the cream leather seats,
watching fish plopping in and out of the water and a group of
seabirds bobbing serenely on the surface.

Once he hit open water he could power the boat up more,
and she was pushed back in her seat. It was exhilarating, if too

loud to have a conversation. She laughed and he smiled back at her, turning the boat in a slow curve around the broken water where rocks were just below the surface. She felt safe in his hands; he knew this water even better than most islanders.

She was surprised when he slowed and took the boat along the sandy eastern side of the island where the tiny town was, clearing a small cliff edge to turn to the back of the island. Here the tide was stronger, the waves choppy enough for the boat to bounce a little on the tops, spray flying out the sides. She could taste the salt. She leaned forward to watch the water racing past the sleek, shiny hull. He slowed the engine to a soft hum and drew the boat into a tiny cove, with a stone landing stage and a couple of old fishing sheds.

'Where are we?' she asked, as he tied the boat up.

'Our unit,' he said, jumping ashore and reaching back for her. 'Our business, Trethewey Designs. Watch your step.'

She walked with care over the old cobbles on the slipway, the odd hole where one had been washed out. The first building was stone, but had a shiny corrugated roof; the second one was a modern boathouse, with access to the sea. He clicked a button on his keys and the large doors slid open like a giant garage. Inside was an empty hull up on blocks, and beside it was an old yacht.

'These are the boats you're repairing?'

'Modifying. We have a commission to build a hull from scratch, though. A fifty-nine foot racing yacht, for an American buyer.'

The hull was as sleek and shiny as a beached dolphin, and it looked strangely bare and vulnerable without portholes or a superstructure. 'What are you doing with this one?' she said, stroking its underside with one hand. It was so lustrous she left fingerprints on its silvery shell. 'It feels amazing.' She brushed it with her sleeve to shine it back up.

'It's the latest fibre, blended with carbon. It's good in an impact. Some of these boats are phenomenally fast, and they can be trashed just by hitting a bit of wood in the water.'

'Or a whale,' she said, walking back to the work benches all along the stone wall. Everything was in its place, wires neatly coiled, safety equipment hung up.

'Or a whale. To be fair, I think the whale came off better in that encounter.'

'Well, I'm glad the whale survived, anyway. This is great.'

'It is and it isn't. All this equipment was expensive, and we don't earn enough just doing repairs to make a profit yet. Maybe never. It's a competitive business.'

She walked over to the older yacht, complete except for its masts. She could see them laid down on the edge of the dock, where the sea would come up.

'Does the dock work? I mean, can you float a boat right in?'

He shook his head, reached into a box and pulled out a bottle and two glasses. 'The gates need repairing, one of them almost fell apart in the storm last year. We've found someone to do it, but it's the usual problem, getting materials here. We manage. We have a little crane between the sheds, to lift the boats out.' He pointed out back towards the bay, and she followed him.

'You did say dinner.'

He walked across the little inlet to a cleared area with a barbecue and a picnic table. 'Kris and I sometimes stay over, if the job is time sensitive.' He started to light the charcoal.

'What about Amber?' She was surprised that her voice came out so sharp. 'I mean, isn't she your business partner?'

'Not now. We pay her a wage as a financial adviser. Who told you about...' He laughed. 'What am I saying? We're back on the islands. How's your film star?'

'Not really a film star,' she said. 'He's going to be one, though, he's landed a great role for a young actor. Tell me about Amber.'

'You know what it's like. Bristol is a big city, I met her when we were both students, on a placement at a design studio. We had a bit of a fling, but I'm not her type.' She couldn't work out if he was upset about it.

'What's her type?'

'Multi-millionaire,' he answered, reaching into a cooler. He put a bottle opener on the table as she sat down. 'Want to open the wine?'

She fiddled with the foil as smoke started to drift off the barbecue. The sun was dropping now, and she felt cold. He seemed to know and threw her a sweater. 'Kris always keeps layers here, he's a bit of a tropical creature.'

It was soft, handknitted and smelled like Kris's aftershave. She pulled it on. 'How is Kris?'

'Good, very good. Working on a repair job on West Island when he isn't knocking plaster off your walls.' He looked sideways at her. 'He has been talking a lot about you. Maybe he has a bit of a crush.'

'He's so young,' she said lightly. She suddenly felt a weird shiver down her spine. *We're alone here, just us.* It was exciting, but tingly, scary excitement. She breathed deep, turned to him. 'I wanted to ask you something.'

'OK. You want to know why I never asked you out.'

'No! I mean, yes, maybe that too. Didn't you like me?'

'Of course I liked you. But you were, like, twelve. You were Dorrie's best friend, playing with your dolls in a tent in our garden.'

'I am two years, seven months younger than you.'

She'd never seen him look embarrassed or awkward before, she couldn't read what he was thinking. 'Kris is two years younger than you and you just said he's so young. I thought of you as part of the family.'

'But then, you kissed me.' There it was, blurted out, lying between them. 'The day before I went to university.'

'I like to think we kissed each other.' Then he turned those dark eyes on her and she had to look away. An indefinable emotion was bubbling up inside her.

'How did you work that out? I was hardly going to throw myself at you, I was far too shy.' Oh. The emotion she was trying to name was rage. 'And you still thought of me as twelve?'

'Obviously not. It was seventeen days after your eighteenth birthday. I wanted to talk to you, kiss you on your birthday, but it took me seventeen days to find the courage.'

She jumped to her feet, walked over to the edge of the stone quay, arms wrapped around herself. 'I find that hard to believe. Why didn't you say anything?'

'I knew how shy you were, how clever and self-contained.' His words reached her through the soft pat of the tide against the stone wall. 'I'd mostly been out with older girls or much more experienced ones. I didn't know how to talk to you.'

She hugged herself, tears stinging in her eyes. 'I agonised over that kiss for *years*.'

'Then you threw yourself into university life.' He was right behind her now, she almost jumped, her heart skipping. 'The first thing I heard from your mum and mine was who you were dating, what you were doing, all of your triumphs. I wasn't even sure you would come back. You seemed to prefer your new life.'

The water was almost still at the stand of the tide, the sea looked oily and reflected the pink sky. She took a breath to calm down.

'I wanted a fresh start, with boys who liked me,' she said, the words coming out sharp. 'Who didn't know I was shy.'

'Then you came back for Dorrie's wedding as maid of honour. I was determined to go back to being a friend.'

She turned back to him. 'I *never* thought of you as just a friend.'

'Well, I had to think of you like that. You know how close our families have been.' He walked back to the barbecue, which sizzled as he laid something on it, smoke surging into the clean air.

'Despite all your reservations, you kissed me anyway.' She turned around to see him smiling.

'That time was all you,' he said. 'You looked amazing in that strapless dress, you were flirting with me all through the reception, and you'd had how many glasses of bubbly?'

She couldn't stop herself smiling back, a little ruefully. 'My recollection is I went into the garden to get away from all the noise and heat. You followed me and grabbed me, caveman-style.'

He brushed something onto two steaks on the top of the grill. 'You were pretty drunk, weren't you? I remember you stumbling all over the patio in high heels, looking like you needed a lie down. As a gentleman, I put my arm around you to steady you and you looked at me. Like that, like you're doing now. You should wear sunglasses or issue warnings.'

'What do you mean?' she said back. 'Me? You and your... laser-beam eyes. Anyway, why did you kiss me, then?' She could hear the childish hurt and longing in her words. She shook it off, dropped her voice half an octave. 'I'm sorry. It's old history now. I just didn't understand what was going on.'

'And you do now?' There was a little edge to his voice. 'Libby, I'm always confused when I'm with you. Are you that twelve-year-old in the garden, that eighteen-year-old off to conquer the world, or that drunken siren on the patio who drove me wild with her sexy kisses?'

'I did?' That was some consolation anyway. 'Why didn't you follow up?'

'Libs, you were *drunk*. What was I supposed to do, drag you off to my bedroom?'

'I don't suppose a drunk girl stumbling about was very attractive either.' She smiled. 'Sexy kisses?'

He threw on some vegetables and liberally basted them, too,

the drips filling the air with sounds and smells. 'I have kissed a lot of women—'

'A *lot* of women,' she teased. '*Thousands.*'

'Not thousands, thank you. Now you're sounding much more like Dorrie.'

'I'll shut up, then.'

'Thank you. Where was I?' He put out two plates. 'So, I have kissed all sorts of women. Some of them were clever, some were funny, some were beautiful, all of them were sexy when you got to know them.' She could feel the change of gear as he looked at her again, the eye contact making her catch her breath. 'No one ever made me feel like you did at Dorrie's wedding.'

'Why?' was all she could say.

'I don't know.' He dished up two plates as the silence spread out between them, the only sounds the sizzling of the barbecue and the lapping of the sea.

'Jory...' she stammered.

Jory, Jory.

'Eat.' He pulled open a drawer at the side of the barbecue and placed some cutlery on the table. 'Drink.'

She'd managed to open the bottle. He took it, his fingers brushing hers, and poured it into picnic beakers.

She looked at the top of his head as he leaned over his food. 'Jory,' she managed to say, her heart skipping in her chest; she was acutely aware of her hands in her lap, his on the table.

'Eat first,' he said, his smile crooked when he looked up. 'Please, Libs.'

She tried. The food was delicious but her heart was jumping, her hands shaking and she felt too hot in the sweater. She tried to calm down, let her jumbled thoughts sort themselves out.

What does 'no one ever made me feel like you did' mean?

She concentrated on cutting the beautifully cooked steak into small bits.

'You can eat it,' he said after a few minutes as she pushed the food around her plate.

'You can't just drop a bomb like that and then change the subject.'

He pushed his plate away. She noticed he hadn't finished either. 'I've always loved you. You know, like a cute little kid next door. The three-year-old who tried to ride the dog, the seven-year-old who got stuck on the top of the shed. That flute recital you did at school when you were twelve, all those Sunday lunches at my parents' house or yours.'

She couldn't remember ever seeing Jory as anything other than wonderful. He was the glamorous older boy who would take them to the park and get them ice creams. Then, in the years when she was lanky and spotty, he was growing into a man.

'So... why did you kiss me when I went to university?'

'Obviously, something changed. But I didn't know that until the night before you went away, and we were sitting out in the garden. Suddenly I realised how beautiful and grown-up you were. So I kissed you.'

'And then went back indoors.'

He shrugged, turned away to look over the water. 'Libby. It was confusing. You were so young, so inexperienced. Suddenly I knew it was wrong, I would be taking advantage.'

'Virginal,' she added. 'Is that what you mean?'

'Well, in point of fact,' he said, looking back at her for a moment, 'so was I. Whatever my friends at school thought. But the feelings I got, they were dark. They were a bit terrifying.'

'A virgin? At twenty?' *He felt like that too.*

'You know what it's like on the islands. You can't do anything you don't want your grandmother to find out.' He leaned back. 'I mean, obviously, I'd done everything *but...*'

'You could have talked to me. You could have told me.'

Jory took a deep breath. 'Think back, Libs. It was a big kiss.'

'Not that big.' She thought back. Nothing like the drunken, ravenous kiss they'd had at the wedding.

'Well, it was big for me. I thought about you every day for months. I couldn't wait for you to come back at Christmas, and then you came back with a *boy*.' His lips curled as he said the word.

She could hardly recall the face of the student she dated for a few months. 'It was an experiment. That whole year was trying new things.'

'Well, you were different. Less like my little sister's friend and more like a woman. And you were doing so much. What were you doing with the ballet company?'

'Our first commercial placement was making costumes for male ballet dancers. It was a baptism of fire. That was the end of my shyness, anyway.' She smiled at the memory. 'That's when I was sure this was what I wanted to do.'

'And I was working for minimum wage, painting and servicing old boats. I must have looked like an ape next to that young man. We came to yours for Christmas dinner, do you remember?'

She thought back. It was all a bit of a whirlwind, but she had still expected Jory to say something. Anything. 'I know you avoided me.'

He shrugged, buzzed a little meat to a gull watching him from the sea. 'So, I moved on, too.'

'I remember,' she said, his sister having sent numerous pictures of Jory with various girls over the years. 'Didn't you get engaged at one point?'

'Nearly. I escaped that one by a whisker. I finally caved and went off to university.'

She smiled at him as a few more circling gulls came down. 'To study boat building?'

'Boat design. It was called maritime engineering science, it was for high-performance yachts. Lots of science.'

She nibbled on a bit of salad. 'I'm sorry about the food,' she said ruefully, looking at the plate she'd barely touched. 'It smelled delicious.'

'It was just a ruse to get you over here,' he said.

'Why did you want to?'

'Like I said. I didn't know what to think about those kisses. About you. You used to be the little girl next door, and then you became this clever, lovely siren who kisses me and then goes away.'

She turned back to the sea, feeling the familiar shiver of excitement that she used to get when he was around. 'So, what do you want to do about it?'

'I thought we'd try again, see if there's anything there. But now you've got that actor hanging around.'

Actor. Brakes screeched on in Libby's head. Callum's face came back to her, those eyes, the expression in them. Here was Jory acting like he wanted to try her on for size, and Callum, the film star, *wanted* her. He had only met the present Libby, he wasn't part of her dorky past.

'Don't you think if there was something there, we'd both know by now?' she said, her sensible words vying with the attraction building between them as the dusk fell.

'Something *is* there.' His eyes were drawing her in. 'There's always been something special.'

'No.' She jumped to her feet, as much to shake off the reaction her body was feeling. Part of her just wanted to throw herself into his arms, for no other reason than she had always wanted him. But that wouldn't accomplish anything other than bursting that bubble for ever. 'I'm not that eighteen-year-old who had a huge crush on you. I'm certainly not the twenty-four-year-old who could only kiss you when I was blind drunk. I'm a grown woman.'

'Who came out here with me, on a date, tonight.'

Yes, she had. 'I wanted to see if the chemistry was still there,' she admitted. 'I'm sorry if that's shallow.'

'No. I think I had the same idea. So – no chemistry?'

She had to shut her eyes before she answered. Because the chemistry was dark and swirling around her like a shadow. 'Not the type I need,' she said. She opened her eyes. 'I'm in the middle of my new future,' she said, watching him clear up, scraping the plates into the sea for the flock of waiting birds.

'It is that actor, isn't it?' He stacked the plates and utensils into a washing up bowl and put them in a sink in the workshop, flicking on a light. She could see his expression through the open double doors. Not what she expected. Not angry – maybe hurt.

'I don't know.' It just dropped out. 'He really likes me, I really like him. It's nice to meet someone who doesn't know all your childhood secrets. He has to make an effort to find out who I am. You think you already know.'

He barked a little laugh. 'I'm realising that,' he said, his voice hard. 'I thought you would jump at the tide coming in, the moon on the water, the romantic meal.'

She walked to the edge of the quay, watching the birds squabble and dive for the food. 'Sorry.' The reflection of a rising sliver of moon was breaking into fragments, the waves lifting and dropping the gulls.

'Don't be,' he said, right behind her, startling her.

Her heart started racing again, and now she wanted nothing more than to turn, pull him to her and kiss him. She stared ahead.

'You're right,' he said, his words soft. 'I took you for granted, I can see that now. I was just taking you out, giving you a treat in the swanky boat.'

'Which isn't even yours,' she added.

'Which isn't even mine. I thought you were just the way

COMING HOME TO THE COTTAGE BY THE SEA   223

you were when I kissed you last time. Staring up at me with those adoring eyes—'

'Drunk eyes,' she added moodily, kicking a pebble into the water, the birds lifting and flying off to their roosts.

He walked away and sat on the wall at the edge of the dock. 'When I saw you at the cottage, I just thought there was a connection. I'm sorry.'

There was, there was! She wanted to say something, to ease his bruised ego or whatever was making his voice sad, but a bigger part of her needed to sever that childish link for ever.

'It's fine.' She looked over at him. 'Let's agree that the long history of me yearning for my best friend's brother and him being kind is over. Truce?'

He smiled then, his eyes shining black, like a seal's, in the low light. 'Truce. Do you want to go back? I'll wash up in the morning.'

'Thank you. I am sorry again about the food.'

'Maybe another time. But as *friends*.'

36

JUNE 1942

Nancy waited for the nod from the marshal on duty, then walked across the tarmac runway. She waved to the girls finishing the beds of leeks, which were standing in regimented rows, like vivid green pencils. Baby cabbages had started to form rows around them.

'Hi, there.' Walter from Ohio smiled at her, in his flying gear over his uniform, his peaked cap a long way back on his head.

'Hello yourself,' she said, giving him a broad smile in return. 'I hope you're not going to land over all our crops.'

'Me too,' he said, looking down the rows. 'That would mean we'd missed the runway by quite a way.' He laughed at the thought; it was infectious, and she laughed too.

'What are you up to?' she asked.

He pointed behind him at the gleaming Liberator. 'Just taking some trainees out. Some of them haven't been up in one of the big birds. We'll find out who's got the personality to fly with us.'

'I thought you had your own people.'

'Oh, we do. But we need regular staff to help train them.

Pilots, co-pilots, bombardiers, navigators, radio operators, waist gunners, nose-turret gunners and top-turret gunners, even ball-turret and tail gunners. The B-24 has ten crew.'

'So you are the pilot?'

'I'm the captain,' he said. 'Top of the tree. But my job is to remind them that the most important thing they will learn is how to survive if we lose the plane. We have thirty new trainees every six weeks.' He tilted his head towards the workshops and hangars. 'Your friend, he's joining us to train bombardiers. He's seen action, he'll remind them that someone their age isn't immortal, that surviving a crash or a fire is making the right decision, in a split second.'

Nancy caught her breath; she felt cold. 'Oliver? I thought he was rescued.'

'I've read his report. He acted on instinct, he did everything right and saved himself. It was only poor luck that his mate didn't survive.'

The idea of Ollie going up on a flight terrified her, even if they had left things in a bad place with him. A bad place where she had told him she couldn't bear the thought of him flying again, and had let her anger get the better of her fear.

'I'm sure you'll be careful with all your trainees. What sort of job do such big bombers do, anyway?'

'We're multipurpose but this one hunts down U-boats. We can see them in these waters, even if they are submerged. And then bomb the hell out of them.'

She felt sick. 'Does that work?'

'We got one on our first flight out,' he said, looking back at someone waving beside the plane. 'I have to go. Briefing.'

She nodded, then looked over at the young men running around. None of them appeared to be Ollie. 'Is Pilot Officer Pederick flying today?'

'He's already on board, making checks. This will be his

third flight,' he called as he walked to the edge of the runway. 'Wish us luck!'

As he jogged across the tarmac, she saw two people in the cockpit. The sunlight lit up the red side of Ollie's face. He looked out towards Nancy, but didn't wave. She thought he may have nodded, but she felt so sick and wobbly she turned away, towards the fence, before she realised tears were running down her face.

She concentrated on planting out wooden trays of seedlings, wincing and ducking as the giant plane rolled down the runway, just lifting off at the end. She was working far beyond the wing tips, but still, she felt the air moving around her, a wind hitting her as it took off, the noise deafening. She didn't want to look up and see Ollie in one of the windows.

She only looked up when someone called her name. 'Baldwin! You have *another* visitor.'

Miss Westacott looked severe as she approached. She moved closer so she couldn't be heard. 'Please tell me you haven't got another husband stashed somewhere. The Women's Land Army is for unmarried, childless women in the prime of their youth.'

Nancy didn't know what to say. Technically, she no longer had her children, and she was definitely not married.

'I am sorry,' she said, looking over at the aerodrome building. 'Is he in the office?'

'I asked him to meet you by the guard house,' she said. Her face softened. 'I hope it is good news, whatever it is.'

Nancy walked briskly over to the guard posts, where the social worker was pacing up and down. She shook his hand and invited him to walk along to one of several wooden benches.

'I expected a letter,' she said, twisting her fingers together as she sat, watching his profile. He pulled out a manila file, and glanced through it, then pulled out a folded piece of paper.

'I was on the island, and thought I would deliver it by hand,' he said, and allowed himself a small smile. 'There is good news and bad news, I'm afraid.'

She took the note but was afraid to unfold the sheet. She was shaking so much it flapped in the breeze. 'Tell me the bad news.'

'Your husband – I beg your pardon, your *ex*-husband – has applied for custody of the minor children of your bigamous marriage.'

It felt like a blow to the stomach that almost took her breath away. 'Oh,' was all she could say.

'The case will be examined in family court in two months' time, by which time either party will have to show secure accommodation and reasonable income to support two children.'

She felt dizzy and stared at her feet, muck all up her boots and puttees almost to the knee. She struggled to find the words. 'And the good news?'

'As a mother of a child under school age, you are entitled to be evacuated with your children. You will be eligible to apply for temporary accommodation and a small income for the course of the war, or their minority.'

Nancy gaped at him. She had never had any state assistance of any sort. As her mother had dealt with the evacuation, she had no idea that she could be included. 'But the adoption?'

'Your husband's claim came at a good time. The foster parents, while very willing to take the children into their family, have no claim over adequate, natural parents. His claim has stopped the adoption, but yours will be even more compelling.' He cleared his throat. 'Uh, initial enquiries have indicated that your husband is known to the police in Hammersmith, where he currently resides.'

'I thought he was still in the West Country?'

'He is staying in a hotel in Penzance, with no obvious means of support,' he explained carefully. 'If you wish to also apply for custody, we could start the paperwork now. You will need a solicitor to put your claim to the family court.'

A bubble of joy spread from her chest, warming her face. Her hands were still shaking but the emotion was different. 'Then, I could see my children?'

'As you are their next of kin, we would suggest a slow introduction, so as not to confuse or frighten them,' he said. 'We could arrange for you to meet them at school, and perhaps visit the foster family.'

'I won't be eligible to be in the land army any more,' she said weakly, as she was hit by a pang of realisation.

'Indeed. Once your claim is approved, anyway. It would be wise to talk to your area representative and give her advance warning.'

'I've just got the tractor working and I'm the only person who can drive it.' It seemed like the daftest thing, once it was out of her mouth. She started to laugh, and he shrank back, as if she was going to get hysterical. 'It's all right,' she said. 'You're right. I will give notice, and spend as much time as I can training people up. Perhaps I can continue to do war work, somehow.'

He smiled then, a genuine smile. 'So often my job is telling children they are being moved, or that their parents are missing. This war has been toughest on children, too young to understand what's happening. At least Edmund and Louisa may yet have a happy ending.'

It wasn't until he walked away that a terrible thought struck her: her own children might not recognise her, or even want her in their lives.

37

PRESENT DAY, 2 JUNE

Back in Cornwall, the fantasy that working on the production was going to leave time for long lunches with Callum was soon dispelled.

The whole costume department was packed with people dropping off mending, and extras and actors getting fitted for everything from hats to shoes. Half a dozen runners went backwards and forwards with materials, coffees, garments. Libby concentrated on whatever she had been given, glad that her years of being a runner were mostly over. The costume designer seemed to be everywhere at once, advising and adding small changes. Her words of praise made the twelve- and fourteen-hour days easier.

'I've got one of your shirts,' Magda said, mid-afternoon on the fifth day. 'Callum came off his horse hard, so there's a big tear. And it needs dry cleaning. Watch the blood there, handle per the body fluids protocol.'

'Real blood?' Libby squeaked.

'Some of it. Probably a nosebleed. We'd have heard if there was a big incident.'

Libby couldn't quite breathe. She checked her phone, but there wasn't a message. 'Can I go and see if he's all right?'

Magda sat on the edge of the worktable. 'Libby?'

'I just – we spent a bit of time together, that's all.'

'We all get a bit attached to our actors. Just be careful, Libby. He'll be off to his next job in no time.'

'No, it's nothing like that. We're just friends.'

'Ten minutes. I'll deal with the blood so you can start work straight away when you get back. OK?'

Libby was still stammering her thanks as she grabbed her phone and jacket and sped through the narrow streets of the tiny village beyond the headland where they had been filming the action scenes.

She saw the ambulance before anything else, then she caught sight of a small group of people examining the horse.

She skidded on the stone road that led down to the beach. Callum was sitting on the steps of the ambulance, having his face attended to by a young paramedic. She was laughing at something he had said, so obviously he wasn't badly hurt.

Her fear melted into anger. 'What on earth did you do?' she said.

'This is my friend, Libby,' he said. He was topless – of course, they had given her his shirt – and the sight of his body still gave her wobbles, especially as it was splashed with spots of blood. 'This is Anya, she is just sorting my stupid nose out. Horatio tossed his head back just as I leaned forward, we clocked each other. *Then* I fell off.'

'Why are they all looking at him?'

'I don't know.' He frowned and tried to stand up, only to be pressed back by Anya. His face was swollen on one side, and his nose was filled with gauze. 'Can you find out?'

Libby left him with Anya, who was flirting with him again, persuading him to sit still to stop the bleeding. She was hesitant to interrupt the conversation between the director and some of the horse people. When the discussion broke, she stepped forward.

'I'm sorry to... Callum was just asking if the horse is OK.'

'Who are you?' the director snapped.

'I'm Libby Elliott, I'm doing his costumes. He was just asking.'

'The horse will be fine. He just can't ride him, that's all.' His voice softened. 'Tell him we're working on the situation.'

When she returned to Callum, the bloodied gauze had been removed and he was making faces, scrunching up his nose to assess the damage. 'I think it's stopped,' he said when he saw Libby. 'Is he OK?'

'He's *fine.*' She didn't feel she was the best person to tell him what else they said. 'You could do with Blue. You were great with him on the island.'

'I don't like to say I think he's the wrong horse. I'm just saying yes to everything they suggest.'

She smiled at that. 'Imposter syndrome, we all have it to some extent. You are still auditioning for the role, in your head. But they already want you. They've done all the publicity shots with you, interviews are lined up, your costumes and scenes are ready. Just be honest with them.'

'Then *he'll* be sacked.' He grinned. 'I'm reluctant to ruin his horsey acting career before it starts.'

'He's probably an old hand at this. He was probably one of those horses in that big advert, you know, where the black horses run over the hill? I'm pretty sure I recognise him.'

He took a deep breath, nodded. 'You're right. You're always right. You're so wise.'

'Comes with my advanced age,' she quipped, but the joke fell flat.

'Age is just a number,' he said. He stood up as a couple of men came over.

'We're thinking you haven't really gelled with Horatio,' the director said. 'Would you be up for changing at short notice?'

'Sure,' he said. 'I was just saying to Libby, I had no problem galloping on a strange horse at the weekend.'

Both men turned to Libby. 'We went riding on St Petroc's,' she said.

'Well, OK then. Come down when you're ready, we'll try you with a couple of others. We have a very good mare, she's just a bit shorter, not as impressive as Horatio. But much more relaxed.'

'What about the footage we already have?' Callum asked.

'We'll sort it out in editing. We have a lot of close-ups already.'

The director nodded and walked off, the other man following with a clipboard.

'Thanks for backing me up,' Callum said, wiping his face with a couple of make-up wipes. 'Sorry about the shirt. I think it got blood on it.'

'Nothing a good dry clean won't get out. Have you got another shirt here?'

'I have.' He glanced at her. 'You were going to get some ancient history out of your system. How did that go?'

Jory. Her heart dropped into her stomach.

'I suppose, all right. I don't know...' She struggled to find the words. 'I asked a few questions I thought I knew the answer to. But it turned out I didn't.'

'I'm going to need more than that.' An assistant brought a chair over so make-up could work on his smudged face.

'I'm more confused than ever,' she said, finally.

'Are you confused about *me*?'

She smiled broadly. 'No, you're much simpler. You make things easy.'

'So, we can go on an *official* date?'

Libby was immediately aware of the make-up artist – a

young man with several dozen piercings – looking at her. 'Go on,' he said. 'We're both waiting.'

She laughed at them both. 'Maybe,' she said. 'Now, I have to repair a shirt someone trashed falling off a horse...'

Before she could think about going on a date, she had to finish a day's work in the sail loft. Several actors had torn clothes in the fights, and as the light fell, she knew they were setting up for a big scene in the town. Even knowing the script, she couldn't understand the shooting script. They were doing as much of the outdoor shooting as the weather would permit. One clifftop scene was being filmed miles away, and Libby knew she might be called to help out on that one. Cleaning costumes or making sure they were consistently dirty or artfully torn was part of the job she hadn't worried about before.

Magda had left the spot-cleaned shirt for her to quickly repair, although she could see by the surge of people down the stairs when she came in that lunch was available. She could grab a sandwich later but the shirt was time sensitive. She sat by the open window to see the torn stiches and where the fine linen had stretched out of shape.

Her phone beeped. The first time she ignored it, lost in the rhythm of stitching. The second beep caught her attention.

It was her dad. For one moment, her heart bounding and her mouth suddenly dry, she wondered if it was bad news. She called.

'Dad? Is everything all right?'

'Yes, love, of course it is. I'm just letting you know Uncle Ed has done a great job on propping up the corners. They did find solid rock, and they also found the boulder they had built the kitchen wall off. It must have been washed out, or maybe the wind blew the sand away. They think that destabilised the walls and caused those big cracks.'

'So they will be able to make it safe?'

'They've done a temporary repair but it needs proper underpinning all the way along. The whole thing is going to be very expensive, and Ed and I aren't sure it's worth it.'

'Dad!'

'I know, your mum feels the same. It was a good house for your grandparents and your mum growing up. But it's old and with the sand moving, the water will eventually be right up to the doorstep. Each winter the foundations are more at risk.'

'What about a sea wall?'

'The council won't pay for it, and it would be expensive. And it will probably only last a few decades at most. It's a big problem, Libs, and we can't afford to solve it.' His voice softened. 'You know I've gone down to part-time. I don't want to take on a huge loan at my age.'

Libby's hand was so tight on the case of her phone, her fingers were white. She relaxed the death grip a little. 'How about if you sold it? Then someone else would fix the problems.'

'No one would want it. And they wouldn't get finance to buy it – it's unmortgageable. And it's unsafe to let out, too.'

'How long would the underpinning last?'

'Ed thinks until the sea comes right up the dune. He's finishing putting props in today, but I still don't think you should stay there.'

'It's fine, I'm staying in the cabin,' she said, looking out over the street outside, milling with production people, actors and extras. 'I'd buy the cottage if I could.'

'Libs, I'd *give* it to you, but I'm telling you now, it's a pup in a bag. You don't know what you're buying.' He sighed down the phone. 'I haven't got much in the way of pensions. I'm worried about leaving your mother penniless. We rely on that holiday cottage, we were going to sell it in the future, to give us some security.'

'But you'll still have the revenue from the flat.' The family had inherited a flat from an aunt, over a small shop that also brought in a little rental income.

'That's shared between your mum and her brother. Of course, he's quite a bit older, he's leaving it to her now Aunt Louisa is gone,' he said.

'But you're not going to leave her penniless, because you're not going anywhere,' Libby reassured him.

'Of course, that's the plan. But I hate the idea of the cottage being swept away. Your mum was still living there when we were courting. Your grandma used to keep a very close eye on me, I can tell you. We didn't even kiss in front of them.' There was a sad tone in his voice, even as he laughed.

'Dad. There's nothing going on, is there? With the cancer?'

'No, I'm fine. It just made me feel very mortal, do you know what I mean? I've always been fit and well, I just took it for granted.'

'Hold that thought. You still are fit and well.'

'I heard good things about that young man of yours,' he added, before she could say goodbye.

'What young man?' The words were out before she could stop them. 'Callum? Very nice actor, doing really well even if he keeps falling off his horse.'

'I was wondering about Jory. Your mum said you had a bit of a date with him.'

She was glad he couldn't see the warmth spreading across her face. 'We just had some food and a catch-up. Nothing like a date.'

'After he ordered steaks from the mainland, fifty quid wine from the vineyard on West Island and borrowed a speedboat? Sounds like a date to me.'

'It's not like that, Dad. We've been friends since we were children. We share a lot of history, you know that.'

There was a long pause at the end of the line. 'Well, he's walking around like his dog got run over. But if you feel like that, I can understand. I just always thought there was something going on between you.'

'No. Well, just a bit of boy–girl stuff, when we were really young. But we're adults now. We're just friends.'

Even as the words rolled out of her mouth she knew it wasn't true. She said goodbye and sat in the sun, squinting at the people below.

Every time she wanted to kiss Callum, she thought of Jory. When she wanted to talk frankly with Jory, he brought up Callum. Libby rubbed her face with her hands. She was as confused as ever.

38

JULY 1942

Nancy had managed to get one hour with a solicitor, to make a claim to retrieve the children that would counter Richard's claim. It cost every penny of her savings and Hen lent her ten shillings against her next week's wages.

She explained her whole situation to Miss Westacott, as the latter walked her Labrador over the hill. 'I didn't mean to lie on the application. There just wasn't a space to explain everything.'

'You came from a factory,' Miss Westacott said, staring over the grass to the hill beyond, to a grey band of clouds coming in. 'The admissions officer probably assumed that those questions had been asked.'

Nancy folded her arms over the hurt in her chest, hugging herself. 'No one ever asked anything,' she admitted. 'Except, "Miss, Mrs?". I showed them my birth certificate, that was it.'

'But you left your children?'

'It was either give them to my mother, or let an orphanage take them. I was left destitute. I was even in danger of being sued by Richard's true wife.' She swallowed hard. 'I had no idea my mother wouldn't let me see them. She was embarrassed.'

'Poor thing. Poor children.' The woman whistled for her dog. She was tall and broad-shouldered, and Nancy couldn't work out her age or much about her. 'Your story has affected me, Baldwin.' She flashed a brief smile at Nancy. 'It made me check on my fiancé's credibility before our wedding in September.'

Nancy was astonished. Miss Westacott looked younger when she smiled. 'I didn't know. Congratulations.'

'Well, I'm not counting my chickens until the wedding day,' she answered, making a little face. 'We can't be sure of anything, with this wretched war. He's in North Africa at the moment.' She called the dog back and clipped on his lead before they walked back through the ewes and lambs skipping about in the field beyond the stile.

'So I will have to leave the land army,' Nancy said.

'Technically, I think you should be terminated immediately.' Miss Westacott looked at her. 'But our need is great and your situation won't change for many weeks, perhaps months. I suggest we don't hand in the final paperwork until we know you will have custody of your children. In the meanwhile, we can get as many of the girls proficient on driving the tractor as possible.' She lifted the dog over the stile. 'I'll warn head office of the situation, of course. They have had a lot of issues like this. Pregnant girls, women who have run away from husbands, applications from sixteen- and seventeen-year-olds.'

'Perhaps I would still be able to volunteer to help the farmer? If I have time.'

Miss Westacott started down the hill path through the sheep, fast enough that Nancy had to trot to keep up.

'I think you will have your hands full. And we won't know where you will be sent, once you are in the evacuation programme. Do you have any relatives you could all stay with? Friends?'

Most of their friends had been Richard's. Older ones still lived in the dangerous areas. Her mind drifted to Capstan

Cottage, to the gruff but warm Emma, and the man who made her pulse race when she caught a glimpse of him.

'No. I'm quite alone.'

She was back at the planting, her back and legs aching with the constant bending and standing, when she noticed someone standing at the end of the barracks. She stood up, pushed the sweaty hair out of her eyes and squinted into the sun. He was just a slim, tall silhouette. She knew it was Oliver even if she couldn't make out his face. For a moment, while her body tensed, she thought about ignoring him and returning to work, but he was the closest thing she had to a friend, and she was bursting to talk freely with someone.

'I wasn't sure it was you,' she said, as he approached.

He smiled at her. 'I wasn't certain it was you either,' he said, looking up and down at her filthy overalls. 'You look like a bear in all that mud.'

She smiled, but she was distracted by how kind he looked, how much she liked him. 'I'm sorry we left things on such a bad note,' she said in a small voice.

'I'm sorry we left things at all,' he said. 'I don't think honesty is ever *bad*, exactly. I've missed you.'

'I hear you got through your medical exam.'

He leaned up against the corrugated iron of the hut. 'Not exactly. I suppose I was being unrealistic. I *have* been accepted to help train recruit air crews, but not for combat.'

A wave of relief surged through her. 'I'm so glad... Sorry, I don't know what I'm saying.'

'Emma's the same. She baked a celebration cake when I didn't get through it.' His grin was lopsided. 'I was disappointed for a moment, but there was a useful result, too. I have a problem lifting my left arm, and the medic suggested an operation that might help it.'

She gasped. 'Then, would you pass?'

'Not by a long way.' He stared at her. 'I'm not as disappointed as I expected, but I'd like to get better function on that side. No, I love flying with the Yanks, they're good lads. I'm an object lesson for them all. How about you?'

She told him what was happening with the children, her voice half strangled in her throat when she said the words: 'I'm hoping to meet them.'

'I'm so glad. But that must be terrifying.'

She closed her eyes, tried to slow her breathing. 'Suppose they don't like me?'

'Anyone would like you,' he said, and she could hear him walking closer. The warmth of his hand made her jump as he took hers. 'Chin up, Nancy. They will love you.'

She looked up into his eyes, bright blue, under reddish eyebrows, delicately drawn on his wide, freckled forehead. 'I just wished they could remember me, know who I was.'

'They will,' he said, his grip firm. He let go and looked across the fields. 'I hope we don't flatten your crops with constantly taking off.'

'Just try not to land on them,' she tried to joke, but she couldn't take her eyes off his face. She'd never felt like this, so certain, so right. 'Are we friends again?'

'We were always friends. Friends argue, fight, laugh, make up.' He grinned at her. 'You can't get rid of me that easily.'

As he waved and walked off, she watched him limp fast across the grass towards the hangars. The thought of being sent somewhere else with the children made her feel dizzy, pulled in two directions.

39

Libby had spent a hectic five days sewing before she flew back, fitting Callum with a collection of fancy clothes for an action scene on a clifftop somewhere. She'd enjoyed a couple of nights out with the costume crew, who were a lot more fun than she'd expected, with a glass of something and a karaoke microphone, anyway. She and Callum met every day, for a quick lunch or a long dinner, or just a walk along the beach. He'd mastered the riding quickly with the new horse, and the shooting schedule was back on track after a few days of good weather.

Callum had two days off, and had pressured Libby to invite him back to the island for the weekend, but she was resolute. She hadn't slept with Callum, but the temptation was there, and she knew it would happen if they spent a romantic couple of days together. But she still had no idea how she truly felt about Jory. And she was enjoying the challenge and wanted to make a good impression on Magda and the team.

But most of all, she wanted to go back and see the cottage. Being there unlocked more and more memories about the house, her grandparents kissing in the kitchen when they thought no one would notice. Her grandma showing her how to feed robins at the kitchen window, the tiny feet tickling her fingers as they buzzed on and off her hand to take a bit of suet or buttered toast. She'd taught her to crochet wonky squares to sew into the blanket that ended up on the back of her grandad's chair. He'd wrapped himself in it for weeks when her grandma died, quite suddenly, of a stroke.

She couldn't bear the idea of losing the place altogether, and had made an appointment with her bank to see what finance would be available. They were kind but discouraging: all avenues would lead to a survey, and that would mean being refused loans to renovate it.

She had splashed out on a helicopter ticket, to save time, and her dad had already said he would meet her to show her the work Uncle Ed and the builders had done to make the house safe. She waved to him when she disembarked. 'Dad!'

Paul dragged her into a giant hug that almost lifted her off the ground. 'Good week?' he asked, then picked up the heavier of the two bags. She greeted the puppy, who was growing fast, bouncing around her feet.

'Very good.' She rattled off some of the jobs she'd done, from remaking a pregnant actor's corset to mending Callum's shirts, again. The sword-fighting takes had been vigorous; the seams stood up to most of the action, but Sam's sword had caught in the stitching at the most dramatic moment and ripped it. She was thrilled to find out the dramatic moment had made the final cut.

'It sounds like you're getting on all right with that young man,' Paul said, walking through the town, waving to people they both knew, while she held the lead.

'I am. I like him.' She shrugged. 'But he'll get other jobs, and I will do the same, so it can't last. That's theatre.'

'And Jory was OK?'

'He was fine. We just talked over the past and agreed to leave it there.'

'It's hard if you have feelings for someone and they don't share them,' Paul said, looking over at her. 'I used to adore your mum, but she was always off with older boys, getting engaged, changing her mind, going out with visitors to the island. I nearly gave up.'

She smiled at him, tucked her free arm into his elbow. 'I'm glad you didn't. You wore her down with your devotion.'

'So that's what Jory's supposed to do?'

She laughed. 'Maybe. He should make a bit of an effort.' She thought about Jory's face when they left each other. 'He just snapped his fingers and expected me to come running. Just because I was infatuated as a teenager.'

'I suppose he did.' Paul stopped at the top of the rise, and they turned to look over the sea. She let go of his arm and sat on the wall, letting the pup run on the beach. The sky was so blue it was reflected in the sea, just a shade or two darker and greener. 'Postcard weather,' he said. 'You'll get hot, working in the summer house.'

'There's always a sea breeze up there,' she said. 'Tell me about the cottage.'

'We've made a temporary repair under both back corners,' he said. 'It will do until we make a decision on proper underpinning. It needs new wiring, plastered walls and ceilings, the chimney's leaning, the roof could do with a revamp and some of the timbers are rotten. I can't get the costs down below fifty grand, maybe seventy if we have to make major repairs – we don't know what will happen when we take the rest of the render off. But even then we'd have to build a proper retaining wall, plus apply for permission to move some sand as well. That's silly money.'

'I wondered if we could do it between us,' she said. 'I've got some savings.'

'Yes, for your future home, in London or Bristol.' He whistled for the dog and strode away.

She had to jog to catch up with him. 'I could make the cottage my home, one day. I'm happy renting in London but I'll move around for work anyway.'

'One day you'll want to settle down.' He stopped, turned to look back. 'If we could afford it, we would. But things have changed. This cancer – it's made me think about the future. Everything feels like it's on shifting sands.'

'But you're OK now.' She could feel a bubble of panic building inside. The dog looked from one to the other, whining softly. She bent to pet him.

He did the same. 'It made me stop and think. What was I working so hard for? Joanna and I, we hardly saw each other except in front of the telly at the end of a long day. We get a little rent from the shop, more from the flat. But all that money would have to go into the cottage now. We still have some years to go on our mortgage – you know what island houses cost.'

'There must be something we can do as a family. Maybe Beth and I can help.'

He shook his head and they started back towards the house. 'Beth has a high rent and Stevie to think about. She's got enough on her plate.'

'There must be a way if we all pull together.'

He smiled. 'Or we can just let it go and it will be someone else's problem.'

Anger bubbled up in her. 'Dad! I want to help. I'm nearly thirty, I have savings and I have a good income. I'm not a child, and I don't want to lose the cottage. It will be gone forever. It's our history.'

He stared at her then. She swiped a strand of hair out of her face; it always slid out of her ponytail. 'I'll talk to your mother. But no promises.'

He refused to speak more about it, but when they pushed open the door she could see the bones of the cottage. All the plaster had gone from downstairs, the beams were bare, even the stray wires had gone, just leaving a few pipes. 'You'll still have a bathroom,' he said, stretching up to touch one of the beams. 'And the old oak is OK even if the softwood needs replacing.'

'What about the floorboards upstairs?'

'They need treating, but they're elm. Solid.' He sat on the window seat, empty now the old cushion had gone, the dog sniffing around the bare floor, stopping to sneeze in the dust.

She walked outside to look at the corners of the back wall. They were propped up by steel supports on mortared stone pillars. There was a deep opening where the kitchen window had been – apparently, efforts to save it had been in vain. She went back in to have a look. Apart from a corroded copper pipe along the window wall, dripping into a bucket, it was empty and smelled like soil. 'But it's safe for me to come in here, to use the bathroom? I'll be back to work on set by Tuesday.'

'For the summer, yes. Then we'll have to decide what to do. But I'm not hopeful, maid.'

Libby stared out at the sea, the same view her mother had grown up with, and the view her grandparents had known from their wedding. She couldn't give up on it. Not yet.

JULY 1942

The land army had got used to the bigger planes taking off. The girls still moved off the land they were working, often taking a few minutes for a quick cup of tea or cigarette, but now there were only five women working the entire site. The work was arduous and the ploughing happened in the evenings, when there were fewer flights. Nancy had taken note of the last training flight out at four in the afternoon, now she and Henrietta were ploughing. Nancy drove the newly repaired tractor – she was still the best driver – and Henrietta walked behind gathering the bigger stones into piles to be removed in the morning. There were a lot of rocks, but Hen seemed happy to do it. She seemed relaxed and happier now George had gone.

Nancy carried on, trying to keep the furrows straight. The farmer always walked the field after she ploughed, shaking his head and pointing out wobbles and curves, but on the whole he seemed to appreciate what they were doing. Despite his advanced age, he worked as hard as anyone and had driven the sheep away from the aerodrome to fatten on the good grass on the hill above. He was using all three horses to transport everything from seeds and stones to harrows and hay.

She felt good. She was healthy from the work and the simple food and looking forward to seeing the children. She had an appointment to visit Louisa at school and then meet Edmund and Mrs Pascoe when they walked up to the school to take her home. Nancy was both thrilled and terrified.

The low drone of the Liberator returning made her look into the sky. She was driving parallel to the plane and was a hundred yards away from the runway, past the line the marshallers had placed for the tractor. Still, she climbed down and waited for it to land.

A man in uniform blew a whistle so loud it almost hurt, and she and Henrietta were waved back. They retreated to the fence as the plane came lower, looking exactly the same as usual.

Then Nancy noticed one of the wheels was only partly down. 'Oh no...' she breathed, but Henrietta didn't seem to hear her over the engine. She tried to remember if this was a flight Oliver was on, and shut her eyes to start praying. 'Please be safe...'

The plane flew past, low and fast, and made a sweeping turn to face the end of the field. She opened her eyes and, irrationally, thought about the baby leeks, now growing strongly, and the rows of cabbages beyond the tarmac.

Henrietta screamed as the plane dropped lower over the airport observation tower, right at the end of the runway, heading towards the grass at the end. It hit the ground and the good wheel buckled, the whole plane sliding along, the fuselage hitting the soft ground beside the runway, the plane dipping its wing onto, then into the soil. A huge spray of earth and grass flew up, splattering the girls as it passed, then the wing itself buckled and a piece of propeller, still spinning, smashed into the fence. Metal fragments screamed through the air in all directions. Then the plane slid and flopped to a halt at a crazy angle.

'Ollie!' Nancy was moving, running in heavy boots to the plane even as the fire engines followed it down the runway amid sirens, shouts and screams. Henrietta caught her around the waist.

'Stop!' she shouted. '*Stop!*'

Nancy froze as a door on the plane was forced open, close to the cockpit. Because the plane was leaning, the man, in flying suit and backpack, struggled to climb out, then dropped to the ground. Another clambered out, too, then another, dropping ten or twelve feet onto the soft ground.

One of the fire engines parked right next to the plane, extending a ladder, and the evacuation became less hazardous.

Nancy struggled to get free of Hen.

'No,' Hen said. 'There could be a fire. Look, everyone's being cleared.'

The men jogged or limped away from the plane and let the firemen do their job. Finally, Nancy freed herself and ran to where the group had mustered. She could see the flash of red that must be Ollie's hair. And he was bloodied, the front of his uniform spattered.

She raced up to him, and he stepped out to grab her, pulling her into a tight hug.

'Are you hurt? Oh, Ollie...' She pulled back to look at him. She couldn't stop looking, scratches on his face, a red mark over his eye. Her knees wobbled as she realised how close she had come to losing him.

He shook his head. 'I'm OK. Nance, sit down, you've gone white.'

He sat down next to her. One of the recruits walked away from the others and vomited on the grass; others sat, covering their faces with their hands or burying them in their folded arms.

'The blood,' she stammered. 'Are you hurt?'

'I was behind the cockpit,' he said. 'The skipper bought it.

He landed that bloody great plane perfectly and saved all of us, but he's dead.'

She could see people working through the shattered window of the cockpit. A man was brought out, on a stretcher, wrapped in bandages.

'Maybe he's all right—' she began.

'That's the co-pilot,' he said, his face white, his scars stretched as he looked down at the blood on his flight suit. 'I think *he'll* be all right.'

Pilot.

'Is it Walter Baker?' she asked carefully, trying not to give in to the hysteria that was building inside her.

He nodded, his eyes brimming with tears. He sniffed and looked away.

'Sorry about your crops,' he said.

She almost laughed, a cough of black humour and relief. 'Who cares about that?' she said. 'You're alive. Walter said we were giving you a soft landing.'

'It almost worked,' Oliver said, reaching his arm around her shoulders and hugging, tight. 'I think the propeller shattered, some part of it came in the window. It's a miracle more of us weren't killed. He took the whole force of the impact.'

'There's no chance?' Her mind was filled with images of Walter's smile, his eyes crinkling up when he smiled, his laugh.

'No.' He gagged for a moment. 'It was instant.'

She leaned into him and felt his lips on her hair as she cried.

41

PRESENT DAY, 13 JUNE

Back at work on the mainland, filming was taking place on a cliff top along the north Cornwall coast. As Libby technically had finished for the day, she was invited to watch Callum film a pivotal scene, where he would meet a possible love interest.

He gave her a little wave as he got his hair done, then she watched as he was introduced to his nineteen-year-old co-star. Hardly more experienced than him, she was willowy and pale-haired. She shook hands and within minutes they were looking at her script and laughing. Libby walked around to where the crew were setting up the tracks for the camera that would run alongside the action. The team explained how the final shot would be a drone close-up of the actors' faces and then it would pull back to show the cliff. Safety nets would be obscured along the edge in case either fell, but they could be smoothed out afterwards if they showed. Both actors would wear harnesses under their clothes for the most dangerous shot.

'He's pretty anxious,' one of the crew said, looking back at him. 'I think he's more worried about the kissing than the action, though.'

She laughed. 'He probably is. He's quite shy.'

'At least his mother isn't here,' he said, rolling his eyes. 'Last year one of the actors had his wife, his mum, his agent and his assistant on set for each intimate scene.'

She thought back to the previous series. 'Wasn't that a rape scene, though? I think I'd want some support.'

'*Attempted* rape. And it's all acting, you know. It's just pretending. Although those two do seem to have hit it off. That always makes it easier.'

Startled, she looked back. The actress, Josephine, was lightly swatting him with the script while he pretended to fend her off. 'That's good.' She walked back over and was nabbed by Magda, who was carrying some fine lawn fabric.

'Libby, do you have a minute? We're having a problem.' Libby could see the problem: the lights were shining through Josephine's chemise in places.

'It looks a bit thin,' she said, holding it up to see her splayed fingers through it. 'Do we have time to line it?'

'I think we need to. Can you help me? I'll cut if you tack.'

A truck had been set up at the back of the car park and Libby and Magda cleared out a space to start making a bodice to go inside the chemise.

'Why is she walking around the cliffs in her petticoat anyway?' Libby asked, biting off some cotton.

Magda glanced at her. 'Why do you think?'

'The script!' they both said, and laughed. The storytelling was sometimes in conflict with the historical costumes, or common sense.

Magda slid some shears around a curve, effortlessly guessing where the line should be.

'Wow. I'd be marking up and checking several times,' Libby said.

'Practice. You'll be like this in a few years. Your work is excellent.'

Libby's cheeks grew warm. 'Thank you,' she mumbled, pinning the front bodice pieces together.

'Except...' Magda said, slicing another piece of cotton for the back. 'Oh, we need to keep the neckline very low so it doesn't show if they want any heaving-bosom shots.'

'Except?' Libby looked at her.

'We all do it,' Magda said. 'But it doesn't give the best impression.'

'Do what?'

'Get a crush on the actors.' Magda stopped, glanced over at Libby. 'People are talking about you and Callum.'

'Nothing's happened.' Which wasn't even true, she realised as she thought back to the kisses.

Magda smiled, a bit sadly. 'It doesn't matter, it just *looks* like it has. Just because there isn't an explicit rule about fraternising, it's still a black mark against you if you do.'

Libby started bringing the seam together with tacking stitches, small runs of gathering stitches to help with the fit. 'Have I got a black mark already? We're not sleeping together.'

'But it looks like you are. Here you are on your day off and you're watching him film a love scene.'

Libby focused on the stitches for several moments, getting the seam straight and matching each side perfectly. 'I need to press this,' she mumbled, hoping the heat in her face had subsided as she moved.

'I'm not telling you off,' Magda said. 'You're a grown-up. But it's a gossipy industry—'

'Like an island,' Libby said. 'I grew up on an island where everyone knew everything.'

'It's a lot like that. The people you work with today are the people you are going to bump into over and over again. If you get a reputation now, you'll only be asked to work with women. And I don't need to tell you there are more male actors than female.'

Libby hadn't thought beyond how sweet and kind and good-looking Callum was. 'Am I hurting his reputation, too?'

'Not really. As long as he remains professional and – more importantly – acts his socks off, no one minds what he does. It's tough to inhabit someone else's head for the camera. I just think...'

'What?' Libby picked up the two back pieces as Magda started to hand-sew, very fast, perfectly accurately. The stitches sank into the weave of the cotton, the tension perfect, even though they would never be seen.

'He had just got his dream job, and the first few scripts. He's playing a romantic character; he will have to act falling in love with a beautiful girl. It kind of puts him in that mindset. Then you turn up, looking fabulous. Looking like the kind of girl he couldn't get at school. Of course he's attracted to you.'

Libby pinned and tacked. She didn't really think of herself as looking *fabulous*. 'I feel a bit like that about him.' She smiled weakly. 'I'm trying not to get overwhelmed and starstruck.'

'Acting is hard, it's complicated. No matter how hard they try, real emotions are tied up in there.' She smoothed a seam. 'Most actors are a little neurotic when they are filming.' She shook out the bodice front before Libby handed her the tacked back. 'Go and get Josephine, we'll try it on her, see where the neckline needs to be.'

Libby's head was full of questions as she walked across the car park and onto the grassland along the top of the cliff. The sun was dropping, casting long shadows; she knew they wanted to start filming in less than an hour.

Both actors were now studying their scripts and someone was talking through a line with Callum.

'Hi, Josephine?' Libby said. 'We're ready for that bodice to be fitted if you're free.'

'I can be,' she said, smiling at Callum. 'See you on the front line.'

'So, how's it going so far?' Libby asked the young actress.

'Brilliant so far,' Josephine said. 'And Callum's so nice, isn't he?'

'He's a teddy bear,' Libby said.

'I was just a bit worried about kissing him,' she confided as they crossed the car park, walking between the vans and trailers. 'I mean, I've only done that sort of thing on the stage. Not in close-up.'

'I didn't know they wanted an actual kiss,' Libby said, waiting for a reversing car.

'They want us to *almost* kiss, for the script. Then *actually* kiss, in case they change their mind. They want both in the can.' She rolled her eyes. 'I'm carrying breath mints and mouthwash everywhere at the moment, just in case.'

It made Libby feel strange, with unexpected unease. Maybe it was jealousy. She glanced down at Josephine as she waved her up the stairs to the mobile workroom.

'I'm sure it will be fine,' was the least clichéd thing she could manage.

42

JULY 1942

'I'm coming with you,' Ollie declared, adjusting his tie in the mirror at the cottage. 'Don't argue.'

'I wasn't going to,' she said, checking in her compact mirror that she looked tidy, although her hair desperately needed a cut and had escaped from her bun. 'That's why I walked up to meet you.'

'I mean, I want to get to know these children too. I've heard so much about them, and I know how much they mean to you.'

'They are my world.' She looked over at Ollie. He still had a bruise on his forehead. Despite his assurances, debris from the propeller blade had spun all over the inside of the plane. 'They are the most important people in *my* world.'

More even than you. Who I've grown to care about.

He lurched easily in time with her; she wondered what it would be like to hold his hand. 'How's your leg?'

'As good as it's going to get. I'll probably get a bit of rheumatism when I get older, but I don't mind.' He was quiet for another few steps. 'I would like to help, if I can.'

'You can't lend me rent and food money every week until I get a job,' she countered, feeling empty inside. 'How can I make a home for the children if I can't support myself? I don't want to be evacuated off the island.' *Away from you.*

He carried on past the aerodrome, where girls were still replanting the beds the plane had hit. Thank goodness it hadn't burst into flames, she thought for the thousandth time, for all of their sakes. Amazingly, newly transplanted cabbages and leeks just needed putting back in the right way up to start growing again. Hen was watering them from a tank pulled by Minty and Star. She waved as they passed. A little patch of flowers rested beside the tarmac, where Walter had died.

'Please don't think I'm proposing anything inappropriate,' he began. She looked to him, hoping he wouldn't repeat his suggestion of marriage. 'I know I did the wrong thing speaking up that day – I was acting out of very muddled feelings.' He put a hand through her arm. 'I did have a death wish, you were right.'

'Oh.' That was all it was then, the last hurrah of a man determined to die in the skies like his crewmates.

'But I realised something in those few seconds when we knew the plane had to land. My crew wouldn't want me to die to be with them. They'd want me to live.'

She pulled him to a halt. 'So...?'

'I'm going to go back to ground crew. I was slow to get out of the plane, because of my injuries. In a worse emergency, like a fire, the men behind me would be delayed by my stupid arm and damaged leg.'

'I'm so glad.' She really was, it made him as safe as anyone could be in this cruel war.

'So, if I ever ask you to marry me again, it won't just be to give you my widow's pension.'

She smiled, but it pulled at her heart. 'Which wasn't much, anyway. And if I had said yes, wouldn't it just be to help me get my children back?'

'Exactly.' He smiled at her. 'Although it's a good reason.'

She smiled and her eyes filled up with tears at the same time. 'I am glad you've changed the way you think about it. Let's do this meeting and see what happens.'

'But I still do have a proposal for you,' he said, starting back along the road, a little faster now they could see the blue dot that was the boat coming around the neighbouring island.

'If you can think of anything that would help...'

'My cousin Emma rents a room to me, so that my mother and aunt aren't overcrowded in the flat. And so that they don't both fuss over me all the time.'

'That's good. And you get to live at the cottage.'

'But I have accommodation on the base. I can ask for a bunk any time I like. You could take up the rooms in Emma's cottage instead.'

'Rooms?' Her mind was turning over possibilities, problems, difficulties. 'I don't have money for rent, I couldn't just move in, I hardly know her.'

'She likes you. I can't tell you how rare that is,' he said, smiling at her as they walked through the town. 'The rent is hardly anything. She enjoys the company.'

'But the children?'

He shook his head ruefully. 'Emma is great with children. They seem to understand her better than adults do.' He dropped behind her as a group of people walked off the big ferry. 'I have talked this over with her. I couldn't just spring it on her.'

The idea was an explosion in her head, making her stammer. 'But... this is too kind...'

'She would enjoy the company, when she's home. And with you there, she could spend whole weeks with Lily and the baby when James is away. I know she would love that, but she hates leaving the house empty. And the cat.' He walked over to a queue for the Morwen boat. 'Here you go. My treat. Forty-five minutes of sea spray and nausea.'

. . .

The teacher of the tiny school, Miss Cartwright, was kind but very firm. Nancy and Ollie could sit in the school 'library', an alcove with a few shelves of books, many from the previous century. There was a wooden bench to sit on, and a few pictures on the wall. The teacher returned with a tiny girl in tow, in a faded dress that was too long for her and an apron over the top.

Nancy froze.

'This is Miss Baldwin, and Mr Pederick, her friend,' the headteacher said, before Nancy could speak. 'This, as you know, is Louisa Shore.'

Ollie crouched down to her height. 'Hello, Louisa,' he said, his face in as broad a smile as his scars would allow.

Louisa stared at him without flinching. 'What happened to your face?'

'I was hurt in the war,' he said. 'But I'm getting better.'

'My mummy and daddy were killed in the war,' she whispered. Nancy's heart was beating so hard she was convinced they could hear it. She put her hand on a shelf to steady herself.

'That's very sad,' she managed to say, trying to contain her emotions so she didn't scare the child. Her arms cramped with the effort to not snatch her baby up. Louisa hadn't changed much, except that the blonde silk on her head had grown into a mass of fair curls that looked too big for her small face and thin neck. Louisa looked up at Nancy. Her eyes narrowed.

She turned to her teacher. 'Can I go now?'

'Of course, dear,' Miss Cartwright said, then mouthed, *Sorry* to Nancy.

'I hope... I hope I can see you again,' Nancy said, as soft as she could.

'Did you come from London?' Louisa said, her focus suddenly sharp.

'I did. My mother lived there.'

Whatever memories came to the child seemed to confuse her; she was looking back and forth between the women, looking more and more anxious. 'I remember you.' Her little knees were trembling, she caught at the teacher's skirt to hold herself up. 'You visited my mother.'

'I did,' Nancy said, choking back tears. 'But she was really your grandmother.'

She could almost see the cogs turning in the child's head. 'Are you Eddy's mummy?' she finally asked.

She looked at Ollie, who was still at eye height, as if he could explain it all.

'She is,' he said, smiling again. 'She's your mummy too.'

Louisa flinched, tears running down her face.

The teacher dabbed at her face with a clean hankie. 'Goodness, all these tears when it's such good news! Your real mother has come to see you. Louisa, run to Miss Ellison, she'll let you sit in the office. If you're good she might give you a barley sugar.'

As the child slid past Ollie and out of the door, Miss Cartwright nodded to Nancy. 'All in all, that went well. Give her time to adjust; she hasn't got over being evacuated yet. Time will be the big healer. We will ring the bell in half an hour, and Mrs Pascoe will be bringing young Edmund up to pick up Louisa. Now, you must excuse me, I have a class.'

Ollie stood and opened his arms. In the privacy of the library, Nancy hugged him and cried.

'Well, that went better than I expected,' Ollie said, into her ear, and she managed a watery chuckle.

'That was good? She didn't remember me.'

'She didn't scream because she thought you were the ghost of her dead mother,' he said. She turned away, dried her face and blew her nose on her handkerchief.

'My mother must have told her I was dead. I was – to her. I'd managed to have two children out of wedlock.'

'What was she like?'

Nancy leaned back against him. 'Puritanical.' She started to cry again. 'Strict. Still, I didn't want the Germans to drop a bomb on her.'

'I'm sorry.'

Held in his arms, she felt different. People saw his scars, the young face, the broken leg, not the man he was now. She knew he wouldn't be much different at forty, or eighty, for that matter. She knew then she loved him, like she did the children. How could she not have realised it before?

They sat next to each other on the bench. 'Are you ready for the next round?' he asked, taking her hand. His better hand was freckled, long-fingered, a line of black grease under the quicks, just a ridge of scar down one side.

She took a deep breath, squeezing his fingers back for a moment. 'I have to be,' she said. 'I can't run away now. Not again. I only left the children with Mum to get a job.'

'Your mother could have helped, babysat them while you went out to work.'

'She didn't want to give up her own job,' she explained. 'So when evacuation was offered, she took it.' She sniffed, straightened her back, let go of Ollie's hand. 'But you're right. I shouldn't have let it overwhelm me, and I shouldn't have trusted her.'

'There's a way now,' he said, fiercely. 'We'll find it and that – blighter – won't have anything to say about it.'

'I need to do it for myself,' she said. 'This can't be about someone else saving my bacon so I can have Louie and Edmund back.' She smiled at him. 'Even you.'

'But you'll think about Emma's offer, won't you?'

'I'll think about it...'

A bell clanged and children's voices erupted. A dozen children of various ages streamed past the open door and they followed them out into the small playground beside a field. A woman maybe ten years older than Nancy was standing at the gate. Miss Cartwright brought Louisa by the hand to them. 'Perhaps you'd like to escort Louisa to Mrs Pascoe, have a chat with her?'

Nancy held out her hand slowly, and equally nervously, Louisa put her fingers in it. She glanced up for a moment, and Nancy smiled.

'I'd like to meet Mrs Pascoe. She's been so nice to you, everyone tells me.'

'She has rabbits,' Louisa confided.

'I love rabbits,' Nancy said.

Louisa led the way across the path to the gate, the last child in the playground. She let go of Nancy's hand and reached for Mrs Pascoe's. The woman was alone. Nancy's breathing quickened at the thought that she wouldn't see Edmund today.

'Mrs Pascoe?' she said.

'Mrs Shore.' They shook hands and Ollie stepped forward and was introduced.

'It's Miss Baldwin now,' Nancy said, with less assurance, unable to explain.

'Of course. Eddy isn't here, he's at home, he's got a bit of a cough.'

It was like a thump to her chest. 'It's good to see Louisa looking so well,' she managed to choke out.

'I thought you might come back for tea, to see him,' Mrs Pascoe said, looking away. 'If you'd like.'

'That would be lovely,' Nancy said. 'Is it all right if Mr Pederick comes too?'

She seemed more comfortable with Ollie, asking him a few questions as they walked into the town.

After a few moments, Louisa reached a hand for Ollie's, and Nancy walked behind them, in an agony of jealousy.

43

PRESENT DAY, 14 JUNE

Libby, in her shared room at the guesthouse, ignored the third text from Callum. She'd already told him she was too busy to go out that evening after work, and he didn't seem able to take her rejection. 'You've got to eat...'

She had a plan to research Capstan Cottage. The house had been called Cardy House at the 1921 census, so she paid for a few credits with a genealogy site and looked it up.

The whole island had barely a couple of hundred houses then, but so many more people than now. She wondered where they all lived. The whole area of the old aerodrome was owned by Chyandour Farm, with no less than three labourers and two household servants, presumably all squeezing into the farmhouse. She had babysat for the present farmer when she was a teenager and knew the house wasn't *that* big.

There had once been three cottages on the road; one was now just a bit of wall by the bus stop, and one had sat just off the road, which must have been knocked down to build the heliport. Cardy House's head of household had been Adam Verran, born in Cornwall, thirty-four years old. His wife Meg, thirty-three and... she counted the children. Seven children from fourteen down to four months. She sat back, wondering where on earth they all slept. Adam was listed as a mariner, on a pension – perhaps he'd been injured. Meg Verran was listed as a washer-woman. Well, she'd certainly be able to dry laundry – it was the windiest part of the island. There were Verrans all over the islands, presumably all coming from this one Cornishman. She thought Beth might even have gone to school with one.

Her phone beeped and she checked it on reflex.

A text from Callum. 'What's wrong?'

She had to write something back or he'd never stop. She didn't want to give in to temptation, after what Magda had said. She typed in a few words. 'Speak tomorrow. I'm busy. Night.'

When her phone rang a few moments later she nearly ignored it, but the number was unfamiliar. She picked up.

'Hello?'

'Libby! Hi, it's Jory.'

Her heart jolted. 'Oh. Hi. Is everything all right?'

'Of course. I'm just up the road. I wondered if we could meet up for a drink, now we're just *friends*.'

She pressed her hand over her thumping heart. She wasn't even sure what fear she'd been hit with. 'It's just, I didn't expect you to call me.'

'Well, I didn't need to before,' he said, reasonably, with laughter in his voice. 'But I'm just up the road and on my own. I'd love to see your face right now: "Is everything all right?". The drama's going to your head, Libs. Stop sewing and come and cheer me up. I'm over here picking up a specialist part for a yacht and it's coming in by train tomorrow morning.'

We're just friends, old friends. Childhood friends. Even though she reminded herself of it, it didn't stop her heart bumping. 'There's a pub down the road, the Pickled Pilchard. Can you get there?' she said.

'Sure. See you in half an hour?'

'OK, but not for long. Some of us are working.'

She jotted down the information of the family on the screen, then hesitated. Jory would be a few minutes yet, so she scrolled down to look at the previous census. Mr and Mrs Gaunt and their three children lived there in 1911, he worked as a butcher and slaughterman. A decade before, they were newlyweds with one baby. She sat back. It seemed such a shame that this cottage with so much history might be lost to the sea.

Jory was waiting at the pub when she got there. It was more of a walk than she'd expected, but the night was still warm, if threatening to drizzle, a few spots landing on her face.

'What's your poison?' he said, sitting back down after getting her attention.

'A soft drink, no alcohol. I have a seven o'clock start.' She was tense after the awkwardness of their last meeting.

He came back with two drinks, which she raised an eyebrow at.

'I'm looking after my health,' he said, unnecessarily. 'Zero sugars, zero alcohol.' He sipped the drink and made a face. 'Zero flavour.'

'Why are you watching your health?' she asked, looking over the rim of her glass at his perfect, powerful frame.

'I'm in training.' He sipped, grimaced again. 'Amber's got me a place on the crew of a racing yacht between jobs. I'll be sailing by day, polishing the boat by night. Every little bump and scuff damages performance, and we need to keep the speed up.'

'Good grief.' She nudged his shoulder. 'Well done, you. I always thought you were the lazy one, working with Grant, anyway.'

'I do conserve energy for when it's needed. I was going to order some food, do you want some? It looks like they do a chicken salad.'

She laughed. 'Lightly grilled, no dressing?'

'Deep fried and smothered in dressing,' he said. 'What about you?'

Callum was right, she had to eat. 'Same. Thanks, Jory.'

'I'll put it on the company expenses, let Amber sort it out.' He disappeared around the corner and she looked at her phone while he was gone, vaguely registering new voices as a group entered the pub.

She looked up to see Callum and Josephine and two of the other younger actors chatting and laughing as they found a table. When he saw her he stopped smiling, his mouth went hard. He came straight over. 'I thought you were busy.'

'You were right,' she said a little awkwardly. 'I need to eat, at least.'

Jory walked over, straightened when he saw Callum. 'Do you want to introduce us, Libby?'

'This is Callum Michaels. He's the actor I'm working for. Callum, this is an old friend, Jory Trethewey.'

'Ah.' Jory put out a hand and shook Callum's. 'The horse rider. I heard about that.'

'How?' Callum said, looking at Libby.

'It's the island gossip telegraph system,' she explained.

'My mum does yoga with Frankie's mum,' Jory explained. 'So everyone knows about your weekend at the hotel, the double en suite room overlooking the sea.' He waggled his eyebrows suggestively and Callum tensed, leaned forward.

Libby tutted. 'You know perfectly well I stayed at the cottage with my great-aunt Catherine.' She smiled up at Callum. 'Don't take any notice of him. We were brought up almost like brother and sister. Very annoying big brother and very patient little sister.'

Callum turned his attention to Libby. 'I just wondered if… You seemed a bit off with me earlier.'

Josephine waved to Libby then walked over to introduce herself to Jory.

'I had to do some work for Magda, the costume designer. She gave me some very useful career advice.' She stepped away from Jory.

'You don't care about all that, do you?'

'But I have to. I'm at the beginning of my career and you are at the beginning of yours. We need to act completely professionally at all times. Which is what you are doing, socialising with people who do the same job as you.'

'Who bore me.' He glanced at Jory, who was chatting with the whole group now. 'At least can we talk tomorrow?'

'Of course.'

He stalked back to his group. Jory came back and sat down. 'Who's the girl hanging on his every word?'

'That's Josephine. She plays a maid who falls for Callum's character.'

'She's pretty,' he said. 'Which I could say if you were really my *sister*.'

'I'm sorry. I just wanted to calm him down. He's acting a bit odd.'

He leaned closer and looked at her intently. 'Who can blame him? He's jealous.'

She dropped her gaze. 'He has no right to be.' She sipped her drink. 'I'm sorry you and I left it so awkwardly,' she said, looking down at the table. The waiter made her jump when he came over with the food.

'It's not awkward,' he said, frowning at a pile of crisp salad leaves and one, golden chicken breast. 'It's just unfinished. You don't know me any more, Libby. It turns out, I underestimated you, too.'

'You thought I would fall into your arms now you were ready for me.' She felt like walking away, she even put her hands on the table. Something stopped her. 'I don't want to argue,' she said.

'How about we accept that I was an arrogant arse for expecting to schmooze you with steaks and wine, and should have talked to you first, instead?'

That made her smile, despite the tightness in her throat. 'If you have the words *arrogant arse* tattooed where everyone can see them, I think we'd be even.'

'You are different, now,' he said, half smiling, picking up his cutlery. 'I like it. Eat up.'

She took a bit of the rather tough chicken, struggled to get it down. 'When are you going back to the island?'

'I pick up the part from the train tomorrow. It comes from Germany, they wouldn't ship to the highlands or islands. I'll get a helicopter back, if there's space.'

'Then what?'

'Hard graft at Capstan Cottage. We have to get all the rubbish into dumpy bags and drag them up to the van. If your mum and dad are going to sell, we need to clear all the debris. Which reminds me. I think it would be better and safer if you stay out of the house altogether, until it's fixed. The outhouse still has a flushing loo and sink.'

'I know.' She looked down at her plate, suddenly not hungry. 'I was wondering who lived at the cottage before, how long it's been standing there, right at the edge of the sea.'

'I only know the ghost story.'

She stared at him. 'How can you know a ghost story about the island that I don't?'

'It's not a very nice story, maybe your parents didn't want you to know. It's more of a gruesome murder than a ghost story, anyway.'

'*Murder?*' She was intrigued, but he looked more than a bit awkward.

'I didn't want to freak you out. Your grandparents never said anything had disturbed them, but before that people heard voices and odd tapping there. There was a man who lived there, donkey's years ago.'

She picked up her phone and brought up the genealogy site. 'Gaunt? Or Mr and Mrs Verran?'

'No, nothing like that.'

She looked back through the results. It was hard sorting by house – she had to search by the common surname Ellis then work her way around the houses on the census. 'How about Angwin? There's a Gwen here.'

'That's it! Angwin,' he said. 'I think she was the last woman hanged in Bodmin jail.'

'Wow. She's here in the 1840 census. It just says she is married to a Thomas Angwin, labourer, born in Plymouth.' The tiny record was sparse, two whole lives between the lines. 'Why was she hanged?'

'For murdering her husband. I think he was cruel, beat her regularly. Is there anything about the story?'

She pushed her plate away; Jory speared her chicken and put it onto his. 'There's an article here, on the jail's website,' she said, reading rapidly. 'She was found guilty of killing her husband and throwing the body into the sea. But her son disappeared too – they couldn't find him. But bloodstains were found in the washhouse.' She looked up, stricken. 'Oh, Jory, is that my outhouse?'

He shook his head at the thought. 'I suppose so. How old was the son?'

'Four years old. She claimed her husband killed the boy and she lashed out in self-defence. But what happened to him? They didn't find a body.'

'Did they think she *killed* him too?'

Libby felt a pang of grief and sadness for the woman. 'She never confessed. But if someone killed Stevie, I'd probably kill him. It must have been a tough life, she was only thirty-three.'

His warm fingers curved over her clenched hand. 'Well, I'm certain she's at peace now. I've never heard a ghost there. Have you?'

She remembered the bird calls, all night.

Have I?

44

JULY 1942

Nancy walked through the open door of Mrs Pascoe's cottage on Morwen, just off the quay. A young girl sat on a rocking chair with a toddler on her lap. His cheeks were red and he was sleeping. The front room was the only downstairs room, she realised. An archway led from the small front room, with a table and chairs and a couple of fireside chairs squeezed in next to an unlit fire, to a tiny kitchen. Between them was a set of stairs, bare and narrow.

Louisa scampered up the stairs, and Ollie slipped in beside the table to allow Nancy in.

'It's not big, but it's a loving home,' Mrs Pascoe said defensively.

'It's *lovely*,' Nancy said, eyes watering. 'Your own front door, a chair for everyone. Perfect.'

'We have a yard, too, for the little ones to play in,' she said, more neutrally. 'I'll put the kettle on. Have a seat.'

Nancy walked to the rocking chair to look down at Eddy. 'I don't know your name,' she said to the girl.

'I'm Beattie,' she said, shifting the weight of the little boy.

He was fairer than Louisa, but like her, had wildly curly hair. 'Do you want to hold him?'

'I would love to,' Nancy said, as Beattie slid out of the rocker.

'Sit there, he likes it,' she said. 'He's teething, he's been a bit sick.'

He grizzled for a moment in his sleep as Nancy sat in the rocking chair and took him. He burrowed his head against her and started to relax again as she rocked.

'He looks so bonny,' she said, marvelling at the downy curve of his cheeks, his tiny ear, the plump little legs.

'We heard you was his mam,' the girl said, sitting close. 'He's such a good baby. Except when he pulls all the washing down.'

'I haven't seen him since he was a few months old,' Nancy said, hardly daring to speak above a whisper in case she woke him. When he would no doubt want the woman he thought of as 'Mam'. 'I missed him so much. They didn't tell us where they had evacuated him to.'

'So they sort of... stole him?' The girl was dark and small, with chocolate-coloured eyes.

'My mother did.' She looked over at Ollie, who was listening intently. 'She thought she was doing the right thing, but it wasn't fair. Not for the children, or me. Babies need their mothers.'

Mrs Pascoe walked past her, glancing down, then walked to the bottom of the stairs and quietly called 'Louie'. A creaking and the patter of feet was followed by the bump, bump of bare feet on the stairs. 'Do you want to show Miss Baldwin – your mam – one of the rabbits? You can give him some carrot tops.' She wiped her sleeve unapologetically across her eyes.

'What did they tell you?' Nancy asked. 'About their parents?'

'Just that they had none and their grandma was killed. Then they said we could apply to adopt if we liked.' She put a steaming teapot wrapped in a tea towel on the table as Louisa walked through the kitchen and out into the yard.

'It wasn't true. Except that my mother *was* killed.'

'I'm sorry for your loss,' she said, staring at Nancy. 'You don't seem like a bad 'un, but you ain't married.'

'I believed I was,' Nancy said, wiping one of her tears off Edmund's curls. 'He was a bigamist. He lied to everyone.'

Mrs Pascoe seemed to be working something out in her head. 'Well, the children have suffered.'

'They have,' Nancy whispered. 'We all have.'

Louisa stood in the archway between the two rooms holding an enormous rabbit, its back legs dangling almost to the floor. 'His name's Hector,' she announced to the room, sneaking a look at Nancy. 'He's my friend.' She bent over to slide him to the floor, then went into the kitchen for a handful of greenery, which she fed to him.

'I've never seen such a big rabbit,' Ollie said, breaking the silence.

'We raise the kits for meat,' Mrs Pascoe said, 'but we keep the adults for breeding. The does are skittish but he's daft, very gentle.'

She smiled at Louisa, now stroking his head as he worked his way up sprigs of leaves.

'I'm not sure what will happen,' Nancy said, revelling in the sight of her daughter and the heavy warmth of Eddy, held in her arms. 'I know... that there's another party who has applied for custody, but he's unlikely to get it.'

'So, it's between us and you,' the woman said, kneeling down to stroke the animal, smoothing his ears through her fingers. 'So, you better call me Margery, then. My husband is Kenal, we call him Ken. If I thought they wanted to go with you... I'd want the same if it was one of mine. But they've had enough being pulled away from people, screaming. It's what

Louie remembers in her dreams, night after night, being taken away.'

Nancy couldn't bear the thought of losing them now, not now she had finally found them again. 'Please, can I get to know them? We can hear what they want. I mean, it will have to go through the courts, but surely we can settle it between ourselves?'

The little boy in her arms started to wriggle. He had opened his eyes, and when she set him on his feet, he sat down next to the rabbit.

Margery poured out dark, steaming tea into mismatched cups without saucers. 'I do think it would be best if they could choose,' she said, finally. 'I'm sorry, we're out of milk, I gives it to the babies.' The tears slid down her face again.

Nancy couldn't stop the tears either. 'No matter. Thank you.'

'Only I can't bear the thought that I will never see them again,' Margery said.

Ollie caught Nancy's eye. 'We hope they will stay here, on the islands,' he said, which made Nancy jump. If they were evacuated together, there was no guarantee of that. 'So you would be able to visit, if you liked. Because Nancy is going to be living on St Brannock's in Capstan Cottage, with Miss Emma Chancel.'

45

PRESENT DAY, 17 JUNE

Back at the summer house, Libby was just putting the last pieces of the sleeves and their linings together when something blocked the sunlight for a moment.

'I didn't expect to see you,' she said, her heart jolting.

Standing in the doorway was Callum, looking broodingly handsome in a flowing white shirt loose over jeans and what looked like motorcycle boots. 'You didn't answer my messages,' he said, staring at her with that intense stare. 'I need to talk to you.'

'So you came all the way to the island?'

'We need to talk,' he repeated.

'I don't have any more to say to you,' she answered, but she was still surprised at how warm she felt. 'Magda is right,' she said, folding the pieces on the table in order, holding them down with the scissors.

'The damage is already done,' he said. 'People already think we're sleeping together.'

'But we're *not*,' she said, staring at him, drinking in his perfect face, those amber-hazel eyes glowing in the afternoon sun.

'I've learned a lot over the last few weeks,' he said, leaning against the door frame. 'I thought I'd been employed as just a pretty face, to be honest. I'm not too modest to know that people like the way I look, at least while I'm young.'

She could envisage the man he would mature into. Even more beautiful. 'But you're an actor.'

'Actually, they love my acting, too. Everyone seems to.'

'Except Horatio the horse,' she joked before she could stop herself. *I'm nervous, why am I nervous?*

'Maybe he was intimidated by my talent,' he said, smiling back. 'Anyway, you made it much easier for me to relax into the job, feel like I looked the part. That made it possible to act the part. Thank you.'

'My pleasure,' she said, standing up. 'But you didn't have to come all that way to say that.'

He stepped inside, close enough for her to smell him. *Why does he always smell so good?* 'No. I wanted more than that.'

She met him halfway at the kiss, her head spinning as he put his arms around her. 'I can't—' she began, as she pulled back to look at his face. 'I'm essentially living in an old shed.'

'Is anyone at the cottage?' His thumb brushed her lips, and he kissed her again.

She pulled away to look out of the window, the evening sun streaming in, making everything look more colourful. 'No. They've gone for the day. Jory is coming back to fix the steps tomorrow.'

'So, who is going to know?' he said, kissing her shoulder where her stretched T-shirt had slipped off. 'If I stay.'

'Everyone,' she whispered. *Jory.* 'The whole island. Everyone who saw you walk up here, everyone who will watch you walk back.'

'So no woman can ever have a relationship on the island?'

She put both hands on his chest. 'I really like you, and you are very handsome and funny and kind. But I don't want to have a relationship with you, not really.'

'I thought the unfinished business was finally over.'

'It is, it was. I don't know,' she said, helplessly. 'I'm not ready to move on yet.'

Callum looked down as she pulled back. He managed a lopsided little smile. 'But you don't see me like that. Not any more.'

She looked at him. 'No. I'm sorry,' she said, feeling the words out as she spoke. 'I suppose I don't. Maybe I'm just meant to be on my own, at least for now.'

'I can't believe that,' he said. 'Which leaves me wondering, what do we do now?'

'I was going to suggest we walk down to the town, have the best seafood platter I can afford, then I could get you a room in a hotel.'

'I had to come.' His eyes gleamed through his long lashes. 'I just thought it was worth a try.'

'It was the most romantic thing that has ever happened to me,' she admitted. 'I'll be boasting about this when I'm an old lady, and you are a world-famous film star...'

'I'll get the next helicopter back,' he said, with a huge sigh. 'I was so sure you'd fall into my arms.'

'I did,' she reminded him. 'But it's not going to work out, and I'm too grown-up to risk my whole career. You do understand?'

'I wish I didn't,' he said. 'But I do. Can I kiss you? Goodbye?'

It was a good kiss, she thought later, one of those long kisses she'd seen in films. But even in his arms, one thought intruded.

If this was Jory...

· · ·

The next morning, Libby was full of doubts. She was drawn to Callum, and while she couldn't see a future, she was very tempted to take what was on offer. But he had caught the next helicopter off the island and she had slept alone in her nest in the summer house. She was woken by some tuneless whistling outside the door. When she looked towards the cottage, she met Jory's gaze for a moment, then remembered she was in shorts and an old T-shirt.

'What are you doing up here?' she called through the open window. She wrapped the blanket around her shoulders.

'I came to have a look at those steps. We've got a dozen dumpy bags of rubbish to move but we're borrowing a van for that. We'll recycle the hardcore.'

'Where's it all going to go?' she asked, suddenly aware she hadn't brushed her hair. She reached for a brush. 'What time is it?'

'Eight thirty. Your boy has gone.'

'He's not my boy.'

'I can't imagine why not. If you're over your childish crush on me, anyway.' He started scooping out sand and grass roots with a shovel. 'I mean, he's very attractive, isn't he? Or so all the girls tell me, including my sister and my mother.'

'He's a colleague, I think we're friends. He just wants more.' She pinned up her hair to get it out of her eyes. 'I'm making tea and toast if you want some.'

'I wouldn't mind some of that coffee,' he said, frowning as the spade hit something metallic with a loud thud. 'What's under here—'

'What is it?'

'Libby, don't move,' he said, frozen in place, the spade still in the ground. 'Don't laugh at me, but I think I've found a mine. Or maybe even a bomb.'

'What? A *bomb*? No, don't be silly.' But his face was white, his eyes wide with fear. 'Don't move,' she said. 'I'll call for help.'

She reached for her phone and called the emergency services; she was immediately instructed not to move, not to stand on the floor of the summer house or move her weight. She was warned that any vibrations could set it off. All she could do was stare at Jory, frozen in place, beads of sweat on his forehead, while she listened to the phone operator.

'Libby. Can you climb out of the side window and get away?' Jory hissed.

'No. I've been told not to. I could set it off.' She pulled her feet back onto the bed, as if getting away from the danger.

'I need you to. I can only worry about one of us at a time,' he said.

'I don't want to blow you up. Blow us both up. We don't have a choice,' she said, listening to the voice at the other end of the call. 'No, it's Jory Trethewey, he was digging in the dunes above the cottage and he hit some piece of metal.'

'Tell them it's cylindrical, at least a foot in diameter,' Jory said. She relayed the information.

'They say to stay absolutely still. Both of us.'

He grimaced up at her. 'Please run for it,' he said. 'Then when you're clear, I can run for my life. At least I'd be going downhill, I can dive over the dune.'

'Just wait, please, Jory.' A siren squealed, far off. 'Someone is coming.'

'What do you think it is? Could it be a mine, washed ashore?'

'All the way up here?' she said. 'No, I don't think so. I think it could be a bomb left over from the war. Do you remember at the museum, as a kid, seeing the debris from the nurses' home that was hit? Maybe a bomber dropped some over here.'

'Your grandad would have known, surely?'

'Not if it buried itself in the sand,' she said desperately, staring at him.

His hands were trembling. 'This is a really awkward position, leaning forward like this.'

'Just a bit longer,' she said, pleading with him. 'Jory...'

'I know. I'm staying as still as I can. I'm just scared.'

'Me too,' she said, as a car screeched to a halt up on the road, and boots clattered down the path to the cottage.

'Don't move a muscle,' someone shouted. 'Is it just you two?'

'Just us,' Libby said. 'But it's hard for Jory to stay still, he was digging.'

'We'll get you out of here as soon as we can,' the voice called back. She recognised it after a long moment, the same coastguard who had come over to warn them off the beach when the mine drifted in. 'The fire brigade will be here in a minute.'

The minutes ticked by. She could hear a helicopter coming in, landing at the nearest end of the aerodrome. She locked eyes with Jory. 'Just hold on,' she begged him.

'Get out of the summer house,' he pleaded. 'Libby, I can do anything if I know you're safe.'

'I'll be safe if you don't move,' she said, watching as he fought to keep the spade in the same position. 'We both will. But if I move, it could go off.'

'The summer house has been here for eighty years,' he said. 'It's not going to move now.'

A grotesque figure in a padded fire suit stepped out from the shadow of the cottage. 'Libby? Jory? Are you all right so far?'

'I can't hold this position much longer,' Jory said, panting. 'Get Libby out. She can climb onto the table and out of the side window, get out of the way.'

The man skirted right around the summer house until he was almost behind it. Libby climbed from the bed onto the table and crept towards the window. Her heart was thudding so hard she thought everyone must be able to hear it.

'We can't wait for a bomb disposal expert,' he said, pulling open the side window. 'Can you step out the window?'

'Just about,' she said, before she realised tears were streaming down her face. Her breath was coming short and fast, the terror locking her fingers into fists. 'But what about Jory?'

'He'll be safer with you gone,' the man said. 'Then there's just one person who might accidentally set it off.'

'It's making a noise,' Jory said, his voice squeaking out higher than usual. 'It's vibrating. I can feel it.'

Libby stretched onto the windowsill, moving her weight as gently as she could. 'Jory,' she started sobbing. 'Stay still.'

'I'm trying.'

She reached her arms around the suited rescuer's padded neck, and he lifted her down, past Jory, pulling her through the long grass and onto the side path.

'Now!' he said urgently. '*Run!*'

46

AUGUST 1942

Nancy walked up to the cottage, her kit bag over her shoulder and a suitcase under her arm. Henrietta had offered to come with her, but she wanted to make the first introduction by herself. She also had the idea that Emma didn't like surprises, or extra people.

The door was open, and a scruffy ginger and white cat sat outside. Nancy tapped on the door as the cat hopped into the long grass.

'Oh. It's you,' Emma said, putting her head out the door. 'Ollie will show you your room.'

'This is so very kind of you,' Nancy said, her voice thickened with emotion, but Emma swatted the compliment away as if it were a wasp.

'Well, it's for the kiddies,' Emma said roughly, before vanishing into the kitchen.

Oliver appeared from around the side of the cottage. 'I'm glad you came,' he said. 'I moved out today but couldn't miss Em's rabbit stew.' He lifted her suitcase. 'We've been shooting them on the aerodrome. They were nibbling on your cabbages. Shall we?' He led her up the narrow stairs, pointing to the three doors. 'Right, Emma's room is the big one at the top of the stairs. She wanted to give you that one but I persuaded her to stay put.'

'I should think so too.'

'Then the space at the far end would be free for the children. It's very narrow, we'll have to make some bunks, but it's a sunny room.' He pushed the two doors open, and walked into what would be Nancy's room. The low window gave an uninterrupted view of the sea in one of its turquoise moods, dappled with cloud shadows that were blue. The smaller room was long and thin, had a window at each end, and was the full width of the house. The sills were low, she touched one. 'Would it be all right to...?

'Lily had already suggested you put a couple of window bars there,' he said. 'Since Edmund is only little. Well, they both are.'

'I wanted to talk to you about something,' she said, catching her breath and looking into his light blue eyes. It had been a long time since she had noticed his scars. 'You know this doesn't put you under any obligation. Or me.'

'Which is why I moved into a crowded barracks,' he answered softly. 'So neither of us is compromised in any way. You will be free as a bird.' He put the case on the bed.

'It's not that I don't want—' she began, but clammed up. 'I mean, I don't know what will happen with the war. Or with the children. But I don't want you to feel that anything has changed between us.'

'We're still friends, aren't we?' he said, looking at her with a smile. 'I'm the sort of friend who will go to appointments with you, you're the sort of friend who cares whether I have a death wish or not.'

'And do you?'

He sat on the corner of the brass bed, which was covered with rich blankets. There was also a pot cupboard, a large chest of drawers that only just cleared the door and a chair by the window. 'Not any more.' He winced and looked out of the window. 'In those moments in the Liberator when we knew we were going to crash – I knew I wanted to survive, I wanted to be the one that got out again, no matter what the cost. Of course, I hoped everyone else survived too, but...' He looked at his spread fingers. 'I would have given an awful lot for the skipper to have survived too. But not my life.'

'How is the co-pilot?'

'Surprisingly well. He'll make it back into service, but maybe not fly again.'

She sat beside him on the high bed, the springs creaking. It seemed like a good mattress, worthy of the big house Emma had come from.

'You've both been very kind,' she said, bumping his shoulder with hers. 'More than I deserve.'

'I could pretend I'm doing it all – we both are – for two little children who didn't ask to have the whole war dropped on them.'

'Pretend?' Her breath caught in her chest. She was afraid to look at him. Emotions and possibilities swirled around them like a breeze.

'One day, I am going to ask you to marry me. I don't want you to be influenced in any way by my giving up my bedroom, that's for Louisa and Eddy, really. Poor little scraps, and poor you, to have them dragged away like that.' He shuffled his feet. 'I know you had a love before, and that went horribly wrong. Maybe you don't think about me like that—'

'I think I do,' she said, surprising herself. 'But I don't know my own mind right now. My first and main priority is the children.'

'Exactly right. And phase one being complete, now you need to find a job and claim them back.'

She smiled at the words, 'phase one'. *What is phase two, three and four going to be?*

'Dinner,' Emma called up the stairs.

'We'd better go down. She only calls once, then the cat gets it.'

Nancy stood up and stretched. 'I'm not sure I've ever had rabbit.'

'This is the time of rationing. It would be very surprising if you *haven't* had rabbit,' he said with a smile.

47

PRESENT DAY, 18 JUNE

As Libby sprinted down the slope, barely keeping her feet, she heard a high-pitched screaming. She realised it was coming from her. '*Jory!*'

Urgent shouts sounded all around her. A firefighter reached for her as she got to the corner of the house.

'Run!' he shouted, dragging her by her arm along the main wall of the cottage.

She had just reached the doorway, the door standing open, when the world turned upside down. The sky made lazy circles and she was deafened instantly as the bomb went off. Debris whirled around them: sand, dirt, bits of stone from the cottage. The door slammed shut, shattering the timbers, and the windows blew out in slow motion, splintering into stars, glitter, falling on everything. She shut her eyes.

'Jory!' She knew she was screaming his name but couldn't hear anything. More debris rained onto her as she put her hands up to guard her face. Her hearing slowly returned, first a humming that turned into a buzzing, then distinguishable sounds creeping in. When she dared look, she was covered in inches of sand, broken shells from the beach, bits of painted timber from the summer house. She even recognised a tatter of the coat she had been finishing.

'Stay still, lie down!' She heard the command, as if from far away. She shook her head, looked around to see a uniformed man advancing towards her, arms out. She realised she was covered in glass shards, glinting in the sun. The man who had saved her was lying beyond her, attended by a paramedic; another man knelt beside her. 'Don't move, yet,' he said, his voice louder as her hearing returned. He took her hand, the glass digging into her skin. 'Stay still.' Then he shouted, 'More help over here!'

Her voice was gone in the dust and sand she'd breathed in. 'Jory,' she mouthed. 'My friend.'

'I know Jory.' He wouldn't meet her gaze. 'I don't know,' he said. He let go of her hand and the paramedic started asking her questions. He put her neck in a collar, washed glass shards off her exposed skin, felt her pulse and listened to her chest. Eventually, he helped her sit up against the cottage wall. Great chunks of old plaster had been shocked off, and lay all around; her back was against the bare stone.

All she could think about was Jory standing right on the bomb, sweat on his face, his eyes staring into hers as if recording the moment for ever. She was caught by an attack of coughing hard enough to make her sick, her body trying to eject the dust and sand in her throat and lungs. Someone put a mask on her face. She shut her eyes and leaned back, dizziness descending upon her, amplifying the buzz in her ears.

In the distance, through the droning, she could hear more shouting, more commotion, but for the life of her she couldn't make her arms and legs do what she wanted. She felt like she was falling into sleep, right when something was happening. Maybe they were saving Jory. Or maybe he was dead.

'Wake up, Libby,' someone said, maybe later, she wasn't

sure. A stinging pain in her arm made her cry out with a hoarse yell.

People were all around, lifting her onto a stretcher, moving things, listening to her chest, then she was lifted through the sliding door of a helicopter. It was only then that she could look back at the corner of the devastated cottage, roof half gone, bare stone walls, shattered door.

But no Jory. She couldn't see him. She made one more effort to shout at them, the word escaping as a squeak into the mask, and then she fell into darkness.

48

SEPTEMBER 1942

'And this will be your room,' Nancy said to Louisa, lifting the small case onto the bigger of the two small beds. Since they were so young, Ollie had helped her build two child-sized beds, which laid end to end, neatly fitting the space, once it was confirmed by the family court that she would have full custody of the children. He'd also fixed bars to the low window at the back, and between them they had managed to bring in a small chest of drawers from downstairs. Emma had spontaneously produced a wicker basket from under her own bed, with a few old toys in it.

'Mine and Charlotte's,' Emma had explained, and left the room before any thanks could be offered.

Louisa walked to one of the beds and sat on it, shoulders hunched, looking miserable. 'Where will I go to school?'

'You'll start your new school on Monday. You'll have a new teacher.'

'I need to go to the outhouse,' Louisa mumbled.

'I will take you down and show you. Come on, Edmund, we can show you too. You can see the sea!'

She helped Louisa, lifting her when she realised she would

need a step, then took the children around the back of the garden, to see the beach.

'Now, you promise me you won't go past the fence unless you have a grown-up with you,' she said, crouching down to their level.

'Don't you have any rabbits?' Louisa asked, turning her back on the sea.

'We have wild rabbits, you'll see them come out when it gets dark. Maybe we could hatch some chicks, we could bring up some chickens and have eggs,' she suggested, not sure if she could kill a rabbit when the time came.

'Where's that funny lady?' Louisa said, looking over her shoulder.

'She's our landlady. You can call her Auntie Emma, if you like. She's very kind, but...' She struggled to explain Emma's abrupt manner. 'Sometimes she seems quiet.'

'I want Mam,' said Eddy, sitting down hard in the sand and spiky grass.

'She's gone,' Louisa said to him, stony-faced. 'This lady is our mam now.'

Nancy felt like her heart was being crushed. She had dreamed of this moment for so long. 'We will visit Mrs Pascoe next Saturday. We'll go on the boat, you'll like that, won't you?'

'I want my mam!' he shouted, tears and mucus erupting as he threw himself into Louisa's arms.

She could hear Emma bustling in the kitchen, the window pushed open. 'Cake,' she called, just once.

'Come on, Louisa,' Nancy said, sniffing back her own tears. 'Ollie said she only says it once then she gives it to the cat.'

As Louisa dragged Edmund to a standing position, she lifted her eyebrows. 'There's a cat?'

'Yes. He mostly lives outside, but...'

'Come on, Eddy,' his sister crooned to him. 'Let's go see the cake lady and the cat.'

Nancy longed for Ollie, his certainty that it would all work out. She was left in the garden, feeling like the wind was blowing straight through her.

The children were up at the table; Eddy was sitting on several large books and tied to the chair with a scarf. 'They like the cake,' Emma said, sitting with them at the table.

'I'm going to help feed the cat,' Louisa said.

'That's good,' Nancy said, glad that at least Eddy had stopped crying for 'Mam'. 'I thought we could go upstairs and unpack your things, maybe we could look at the toys. What do you think, Edmund?'

She put her hand out to touch his head but he leaned away from her fingers. 'Cat,' he said, shoving more cake in his face.

Nancy sat with them, the tiny round table feeling crowded. 'Shall I pour some tea?'

'We've got milk for the children,' Emma said. She pushed the last piece over towards Nancy. 'You need to eat too. You've been off your food. Ollie said.'

Emma's kindness was ponderous but heartwarming. Nancy cut the slice into three, gave the children a sliver each and ate the last one herself. 'I don't know where you get all the ingredients from,' she said, and sipped the tea.

'It's just tinned milk,' Emma said, standing up. 'And we've got some canned fish for the cat. They have leftover tins at the cannery, Lily sends me them. And we've got a nice bit of haddock from one of the boats for our tea. One of the fisherman's wives dropped it by with some potted crab. Everyone knows Ollie,' she explained as she walked back into the kitchen.

Louisa jumped down from the table, which set Edmund off wailing until Nancy untied him. She wasn't hopeful that the children would even see the cat, and was surprised to see him purring and rubbing his head against Louisa's hand. 'Here you go,' Emma said, passing down a cracked old saucer.

The cat, somewhat daintily, started eating as the two children crouched down and stroked and crooned to him

'He likes children,' Nancy said.

'They don't judge,' said Emma. 'Like me, I like children too.'

'You're good with them.'

'But the boy smells,' Emma said, without polite preamble.

'I'll bath him. It was a long trip for him in a nappy.'

There was a tin bath in the outhouse. Nancy thought about bringing it in then looked at the back garden, lit by the hot sun. A couple of buckets of warm water later – the water apparently came from a spring up the hill and the stove was already lit – the bath looked so inviting Nancy was tempted herself. She got her last bar of castile soap and fetched the reluctant children, who had just discovered the toys in the basket. Edmund was leaving unpleasant damp patches on the floor, mercifully not on the rug.

'Come downstairs, see the bath in the garden,' she said, cajoling the children downstairs and outside. 'You can have a bath and pretend you're swimming in the sea,' she said, undressing Edmund. He shrieked with delight, glad to get the wet and dirty clothes off and to splash in the tin bath, stamping up and down until even Louisa wanted to go in. Nancy soaped both children, from their hair to their toes, and washed away the Pascoes, their old life, her own grief.

Rinsing them with a metal tooth mug from the outhouse, and drying any residue of soap away from their eyes, she felt like her breath would stop. She could die here, with the sun in her eyes, perfectly content. An especially violent splash from one of the children brought her back to herself, and they both giggled.

'Little monkeys!' She slipped off her stockings and dress, leaving her undergarments. Ollie would be at work for hours, and who else would see her? She was as well covered as in her swimming costume. She lifted Edmund into her arms, and stepped into the bath, sitting him on her lap. 'Now we're all wet,' she laughed. Louisa sat up the other end, observing without comment. Nancy soaped and rinsed herself, the six inches of greying water rising higher around them.

'It's nice to be clean,' she said, smiling at Louisa. 'Perhaps one day, we can go for a paddle in the sea together.'

'I like the beach,' she answered very shyly.

'Beach! *Beach!*' Edmund shouted, splashing even more of the water out of the bath.

'Me too. I took you to Margate on the train once,' she said to Louisa, 'when Eddy was in my tummy.' The memories stalled, and she stopped, unsure of the little girl's reaction. She looked like she wanted to say something, but was afraid. 'Right, then,' Nancy said, to ease the burden on Louisa. 'Now we all have to get dry – and I only brought one towel!'

She managed to rub the children down and let them run naked up to the bedroom. She wrapped as much of the small towel around herself as she could, then walked in the front door in wet underwear with as much dignity as she could muster. Emma stared up from her book, then looked down, but Nancy had the impression she was amused.

Mrs Pascoe had cut down old dresses from her children for Louisa; every seam was sewn by hand and with care. Little extras like flower-shaped buttons and a bit of smocking enlivened her clothes. The heat from the sun had warmed the bedroom so much Louisa only needed fresh knickers and a clean, if threadbare, summer dress. Edmund needed sitting on the porcelain pot, and to be put into a clean shirt. She would just have to follow him around until he got the hang of potty training.

Once free, he immediately ran to the toys, finding an elaborate wooden train made up of layers of brightly painted wood that fitted together. There was an old, one-eyed doll, which he took to as well, and a dozen blocks that formed puzzles. Right at the bottom, he unearthed something soft.

'Hector,' he shouted, in amazement and some triumph. 'Found him.'

Louisa took the cloth rabbit, holding it at arm's length. 'He's just rags,' she scoffed, but she put it on her own bed. She peeked through her hair at Nancy. 'I do remember going on the train,' she said. 'To the beach.'

49

PRESENT DAY, 18 JUNE

Libby woke up in hospital after a lot of medical attention. No one could answer her questions about Jory, so she stopped asking. It felt like her brain was stuttering, unable to proceed with the rest of her life until she knew whether he was all right, or... She couldn't think about what else might have happened.

In this strange world, nothing seemed real, nothing mattered. She drifted away again on a pillow of pain relief. Now she was in the hospital she couldn't identify each individual pain, but she was aware that her head and neck hurt more sharply than anywhere else.

When she awoke again, her mother was beside her. 'Hi, lovey,' she said softly, as if the sound might hurt her. 'You're all right, you're going to be fine.'

Libby opened her mouth, but the words wouldn't come. She wanted to stay in this almost-place, where she didn't have to face what had happened.

'It's all right. Everyone is alive, everything will be all right,' her mum said, holding her hand tightly, but the words didn't seem to land.

'J-Jory?'

'Especially Jory. He managed to throw himself off the sand dune, straight down onto the beach. He'll be fine. He's being patched up in our local hospital, back on the island.'

Waves of emotion washed through Libby, but she couldn't identify them. *Jory, Jory. He's alive...* That look in his eyes, just before she jumped into her rescuer's arms and left him with a ticking bomb, seemed to have drilled into her. She knew she would never forget the expression on his face, his desperation to make sure she was safe.

She tried to look around the room, but her neck was still rigidly encased in a collar. 'Where am I?' she said, her voice small and rasping.

'Plymouth. You've chipped a vertebra in your neck and had a bump on your head, but you will be fine. We'll take you home tomorrow.'

'Can they take this stupid thing off?' Tears were tickling her face. Joanna patted them dry.

'In a minute, when they've looked at all your scans. Did you hear me, lovey? Jory is OK, the fire officers are all safe. One of the coastguards was knocked onto the beach with Jory, but he's going to be fine once his broken arm mends.'

'Jory's OK,' Libby repeated, but the words still wouldn't sink in. All she could see in her mind was the panic in his eyes as he shook, trying to hold the spade – and the bomb – still.

'He's desperate to see you, Libs.'

'I *need* to see him,' Libby whispered, tears rolling down her face. 'I've been stupid, getting starstruck by Callum, by my job.' She swallowed hard, her throat still feeling like sandpaper.

Joanna held up a cup with a straw in it, and Libby sipped the lukewarm water. A nurse started undoing the collar, releasing her from the rigid pressure.

Overwhelmed and exhausted, Libby lay back and slipped into the darkness once more, tears still rolling down her cheeks.

· · ·

When she surfaced late in the evening, she could barely believe that Jory was standing in her curtained hospital bay, covered in plasters, and with a bandage on his hand. He still had sand in his hair, and his face was dirty. She stared at him for a moment, unsure if he was real.

'I had to come,' was the first thing he said, his voice rough. 'I needed to see you were all right with my own eyes.'

'You're... *alive*,' she managed to croak.

And in that moment, she knew.

It has never been anyone else. It is just Jory.

'We jumped off the edge of the dune,' he said, just as hoarse. He sat gently on the edge of her bed and took her hand in his. 'Well, I did. Nick landed harder, but he's OK.'

As Libby stared at him, she realised he must have been blown or fallen twenty or so feet onto the soft beach. She couldn't stop looking at him, the tiny cut beside his ear, the bruise over his eyebrow. He was *here*. He was *alive*. She gripped his hand in hers, his fingers reassuringly warm. They interlaced their fingers.

'You're going to be all right,' she said in wonder. 'We're *both* going to be all right. So it really was a bomb?' She almost laughed at the idiocy of it. 'Of course it was a bomb.'

'The army are coming over to check the area out for more,' he said, curving his fingers around hers, staring at them. 'It was dropped during the Second World War, a whole line of them went off back in the 1940s, but that one must have buried itself straight in the loose sand. The storms have been slowly uncovering it ever since.' Even his fingers were still a little gritty in her hands, and she noticed the sand under her nails, too. 'I thought you were dead, Libs. By the time I saw you, you were being packed into a helicopter.'

'We're not dead, Jory. We're OK.' She looked at his profile as if she'd never seen it before. 'Look at me.'

He had been staring at their intertwined hands, but now he

looked up and their eyes locked. It was all she needed to know, the golden flecks in his dark eyes were still there, the intensity of his gaze on her like she was his whole world.

'You're the one, Libby,' he said, his mouth lifted slightly at the corners. 'I've realised that now.'

Her smile grew so wide it almost hurt. She couldn't stop looking at him, every tiny detail, his eyelashes, the golden hairs on his forearms and the brown tan line on his neck. 'Me too,' she whispered, as he leaned towards her.

It was a little kiss, lopsided and quick, but it was the best kiss Libby had ever had. Sparks of light went off inside her head, all her thoughts stalled, and she was lost in the moment.

He sat back, smiling properly at her. 'I'm sorry about the summer house. And all your work.'

She waved it away with her free hand. 'It's all insured.'

He shook his head. 'Maybe not.'

'What?'

'Your dad was told the cottage and contents might not be insured at all. It doesn't matter,' he added quickly. 'We'll replace your machines and stuff.'

'Why isn't it insured?' The cottage, too, all her clothes and laptop, her materials...

'The dropping of the bomb is technically an act of war. It might not be covered.'

Libby stared into his eyes, and started to laugh. 'You are *kidding*?'

He looked confused. 'Not the reaction I was expecting, but OK.'

She leaned forward again, and this time he put his arms around her and managed a bigger kiss. She pulled back, looked into those eyes, felt the pull between them. 'I've got *you*,' she said. 'I don't have a crush on you any more, and you're not as good-looking as Callum. I just know I love you.'

Libby reached out to touch his face and noticed the dozens

of tiny glass cuts on her hands; after a moment, Jory took her hand again. His fingers curved around hers perfectly, and despite the cuts, he lifted her hand to his lips and kissed it.

'Thank God you're all right,' he said, with conviction. 'I thought you must be dead.' His eyes were red, sandblasted perhaps. They had rinsed them out, there were remnants of rivulets streaking through the dirt on his face. 'Can we draw a line under all our history?' he asked, abruptly. 'Could we just start again, from this moment?'

'When we were reborn,' she said.

'Sort of. I love you, Libby. I knew that the second I realised what that chunk of metal was. All I could think about was that you were trapped in the cabin, sitting on a bomb. I realised how much time I have wasted when I could have been with you.'

'Me too,' she said, suddenly exhausted, shivery, shocked. 'I was never with Callum, by the way.'

'I don't care,' he said.

For a few moments she just rested with her hand in his, feeling warm and safe. Then the thought hit her.

'What about the cottage?'

'Missing some of its roof slates, it's pretty well a skeleton but the walls are still standing. But the summer house is completely gone, smithereens.'

'Which would have been me,' she said slowly. 'And you.'

In that moment, it did feel like she'd been reborn into a world where Jory loved her and everything else could be managed.

50

SEPTEMBER 1942

Something woke Nancy deep in the night. It sounded like someone banging on the door before she realised it was the anti-aircraft guns on the other end of the island. She could hear an engine noise and jumped out of bed, pulling the door open to the children's room.

'Is it the Germans coming?' Louisa sobbed, sitting up in bed, illuminated by a half-moon beyond the window.

'They aren't trying to hurt *us*,' she reassured, as Louisa crept into her arms. 'We'll just hide in the dark and they'll soon fly away home.'

But the heavy droning was coming nearer, covering the three miles quickly. Then she heard more thuds – and an explosion. Something had blown up on the airport or the farm.

The engine sound, deep and malevolent, seemed to be coming straight for them, as if it would crash into the cottage. A dull thump sounded, followed by an explosion over the beach and a scattering of splashes.

'What is it?' Emma said, standing in the doorway, looking scared in the moonlight.

'It's a plane dropping its spare bombs as it flies over. It

missed us,' she said, but her heart was jumping almost out of her chest. 'There, darling, it's all gone.'

Louisa pressed so close she was curled up like a hedgehog against her, her face completely hidden. Edmund started grizzling, not sure what was going on but unhappy. Nancy could hear the air-raid siren sounding now.

'Mummy!' Louisa whimpered, and even through the panic, Nancy was thrilled to hear the word again. She pressed a kiss on her curls, smelling of the soap. It was imported, she remembered her mother buying a box before the war. Now it was one of the last things she had of her mother.

Edmund was efficiently put back to bed by Emma, who then pressed a finger lightly against his forehead and said, 'Sleep.' To Nancy's amazement, he lay down; he was so impressed with Emma he did anything she said.

Emma leaned to look out of the window. 'There's some smoke and flames on the beach,' she said. 'But I can't see anything else.'

'I think something hit the sand,' Nancy said, surprised at how wobbly her voice was. 'Maybe an incendiary.'

'Well, least said, soonest mended,' said Emma. 'No point upsetting the kiddies. Get some sleep and we'll see what Ollie thinks in the morning.'

They didn't have to wait that long. Within half an hour Ollie had cycled along the aerodrome road, his bike clattering as he threw it down by the front door. 'Nancy?' he called. 'Emma!'

'For goodness' sake, you'll wake the children again,' Nancy said, who, unable to sleep, had heated up powdered milk and cocoa in an attempt to reset her bedtime routine.

'Are you all right? The boys launched a couple of Hurricanes, and they reported something burning at the top of the beach, close to the cottage.'

'A hundred yards away,' she said. 'We're safe. There was an explosion back towards the town.'

'It hit your leeks,' he said, pushing back his cap with one hand.

'Not my leeks any more. They'll just put them back in,' she said, barely able to see him by the one candle. 'Can I interest you in a small cocoa?'

He stared at her, and as her eyes adjusted, she could see the fear on his face. She took a step forward and walked into his arms. He was shaking.

'I was bombed before,' he said. 'All I could think was that my whole life is here, in this cottage. I couldn't bear it if I lost you.'

'It's all right,' she said, much as she had to Louisa. But then she looked up, and when he reached for her, it was different. The first kiss was light, gentle, as if he didn't know if it was allowed, but couldn't resist. No one had made her feel like this. Certainly not Richard, who took his kisses when he chose and withheld them if she questioned him. The thought that this should have been her first kiss crossed her mind.

'Is this all right?' he murmured, and she kissed him back.

'Yes.' She pulled away a little at the smell of burning milk. The coal stove had long gone out; she was using the enamel paraffin ring that sat beside it.

He put his arms around her waist and leaned his face into her hair. 'You smell nice,' he said, as she stirred the milk.

This could be my whole life.

'We all had a bath,' she said, and unexpectedly giggled. She explained having a bath outside, overlooking the deserted beach.

'That's very risqué of you,' he said, but she could feel him laughing too.

'I only stripped down to my underwear,' she said. 'But it's a corselette and bra... in cream.' She couldn't help laughing again.

'It must have looked like I was running through the house naked, except for a towel. Emma did raise an eyebrow.'

'I wish I'd been there. I would have loved to see her expression.'

She could feel the heat in her cheeks and she turned the flame off and poured the cocoa into two mugs. 'Well, I was very glad you weren't.'

'Maybe when we're married, you can do it again. We'll all take our baths in the summer sunshine.'

She pulled away a little, took a breath and handed him his drink. 'Are we going to be married?'

'Since the entire island – and Morwen too – expect our engagement imminently, I should think so.'

'Don't I get a say?' she teased.

'I could have proposed, and then agonised while you made up your mind. But the entire land army, including that rather terrifying Miss Westacott, have it all organised. Henrietta's making a dress with some fabric her mother sent, and my aunt Bernie is already planning the reception.'

'I'd like that here,' she said. 'For close friends and family – if Emma allows.'

'And Lily is making a bridesmaid's dress and sailor suit for the children, and you'll get to meet James. Many of my friends will be there from the town and the base.'

She sipped the hot chocolate. 'What about Joy?'

The darkness was a blanket of quiet as he paused. 'If I'm going to break someone's heart, it's not going to be mine,' he said, finally. 'I'll let her friends talk to her. It's not as if we were ever really officially courting.'

'You were in her eyes. And she's told everyone in her circle.'

'Yet they all know it's been you, right from the moment I saw you trying to farm by the fence.' He put his cup down in the enamel bowl with a tiny clink. 'The bigger problem is – I'd really like us to live here at the cottage, with Emma, after we're married. At least at first. I know the space is tight...'

'It's perfect.'

'We won't have much privacy.'

'You do understand I have two children, don't you? There won't be much privacy anyway.'

He reached for her hand, kissed her wrist. '*We* have two children. I intend to be a very good father. And husband.'

Cold gripped her stomach, and she leaned against the cooker, holding her cup in front of her to keep him at bay. 'You deserve someone unblemished and innocent. I've been married,' she said, wishing the last years away for a moment. But she didn't regret the children.

'Don't you deserve some whole and unblemished man, too?'

'No! That's not what I meant.'

He pulled his shirt out of his waistband. The soft candle-light flickered over his scars. 'You should know what you're getting.'

Every tightness, every ridge had been formed in fire and months of suffering. She let herself look, properly look, for the first time. 'Poor you,' she breathed. 'Does it still hurt?'

'Sometimes. It's more uncomfortable than anything. The door frame burned me right down to my leg. Apparently, you can still see the rivet marks.' He tried to smile but it looked tragic. 'I don't know why I think you would want to marry me—'

She walked up to him and kissed him, both hands on his warm skin, the texture under her hands, his arms tightening around her. 'I really don't care,' she said, shaking her head. 'I'll marry you, Oliver Pederick, and be proud to be your wife.'

EPILOGUE

PRESENT DAY, 21 OCTOBER

Libby sat astride the new summer house roof, lifted a nail from the pouch on her tool belt, and hammered it in. The wooden shingles were a bright orangey red, but would soon soften and bleach down to silver. The council had given permission for a replacement cabin, with a little more floor space, which would be better as Libby would be living there for the next year or two while the cottage was completely renovated.

When she wasn't off working. She had just come back from filming the inside scenes on set in Bristol, Callum's new superfine coat having been finished just in time, although she hadn't managed a spare one under the circumstances. The sewing crew had been amazingly supportive, she was so grateful that they had all helped her get back to work after the bomb.

'I'm back!' shouted Jory, matching his words to the steps on the ladder against the wall.

'Did you speak to my dad?'

'I did,' he said, finding a spot to sit beside her. 'He heard from the insurance people. They'll appeal but—'

'They are refusing the claim, as we thought, saying that the bomb was there because of an act of war.'

'Well, we knew, didn't we?' He looked out over the sea. 'This is the best view on the island. We should put seats up here.'

From the roof, she could see back over half the island, right to the town and her parents' house. The other way, she could see the misty shape of the neighbouring island and, beyond, the open sea.

'The view from inside the summer house will be great, too,' she said, wistfully remembering the old cabin.

'And double-glazed windows and doors,' he reminded her, having only just finished fitting the latter. 'And a decent bed.'

The cabin would have enough space for a bed with storage underneath, high enough to look out at the sea in the morning. They had also squeezed a tiny wet room under a mezzanine floor, which was big enough for storage or for nephew Stevie to stay.

Libby felt history repeating itself, and imagined Oliver and Nancy building the summer house out of driftwood and scraps. Libby thought it was probably the only place they could get a bit of privacy, as Nancy had two children when Ollie married her.

She smiled at him. Not only had their entire romance taken place under the eye of the community that advised them, talked about them, but loved them, but they'd also had to travel to the mainland to find some privacy. Now they would have a little space of their own. 'When's your catamaran coming in?'

'High tide tomorrow, so about eleven. Do you want to come and watch?'

'I'd love to.' She leaned in for a kiss, then pulled back and stared at him.

The real Jory was so different from the boy she'd had a crush on, and they were still finding out about each other. One thing she'd discovered was that he was less confident about his new business than he appeared, while also being more talented than he let on. He'd been approached by several boat builders about doing designs for them, and Libby had found she could be useful in business meetings. It was easier to boast about someone else's work than her own.

'What about the roof?' he asked, looking around.

'Once you get off, I'll be finished in a couple of hours. Dad's coming over to help me sort out the ridge while I take Stevie and Rocket onto the beach.' The dog had finally found his explosive name.

'I'll stay, then,' he said, reaching for the top of the ladder. 'How's Callum?'

'He's fine. He's bringing Josephine over to the islands for Halloween, before they head off to do publicity. I said we'd do dinner.'

'We'll be properly in the cabin by then,' he said, standing at the top of the ladder. 'Then we can start on the cottage.'

Libby smiled. 'I do have some news,' she said, waiting to see his expression change.

'OK, surprise me.'

The cottage roof had been temporarily repaired by friends and family from the town; even people she hardly knew, or residents fresh from the mainland who wanted to get to know their neighbours, had helped. The islanders had reached into their pockets as well as labouring for free, and Grant was going to rewire the house at cost.

'I talked to the heritage people.'

'Brilliant. Is it going to be listed?' He looked down at the cottage, shrouded in scaffolding below the summer house.

'I think Grandad Oliver and Grandma Nancy would have been proud of us, you know? Rebuilding this place. I know it isn't quite the same cottage where they were in love, but it's our version of it. Don't you think?'

'I do,' he said, smiling, leaning in for a kiss.

'So, Dad has offered to sell *us* Capstan Cottage. If that's what you want. For us both.'

His mouth was open for a moment, unable to speak. 'How? That would be wonderful but...'

'We can find the money over the years, to pay them back. And we can apply for grants to help rebuild. Did you know it's over three hundred years old?'

He laughed then, reached for her and hugged her until she had to protest that they would both fall off. 'Let's give it another hundred years, at least,' he said, grinning, then climbed down the ladder.

She reached into her jeans pocket, for a heavy twist of metal that had come from the garden of the cottage. She looked down at it, knowing it was there when Ollie and Nancy had lived here, and feeling that she needed it to watch over her relationship, too. A part of the past, preserved for her new future.

She tucked it under the next shingle and hammered the nail into place.

A LETTER FROM REBECCA

Dear Reader,

I'm so glad you found *Coming Home to the Cottage by the Sea*. I hope you enjoyed meeting Libby and Nancy, and revisiting the islands. You can keep in touch with future island stories by following the link below. Your email will never be shared and you can unsubscribe at any time.

www.bookouture.com/rebecca-alexander

For this book, I researched many personal stories of the effect that the Second World War had on rural and village life, from the Women's Land Army women growing food to the experiences of evacuated children. Living under the shadow of war made heroes of everyone who staunchly got on with life. Now, we can find peace in visiting beautiful places, and so many of those are islands. In liminal places surrounded by the sea, life seems concentrated and intense, and our senses seem stronger. To go there even in my imagination makes me happy.

If you want to support me and the Island Cottage books, it's always helpful to write a review. This also helps me develop and polish future stories! You can contact me directly via my website or Twitter.

Thank you and happy reading,

Rebecca

KEEP IN TOUCH WITH REBECCA

www.rebecca-alexander.co.uk

 twitter.com/RebAlexander1

ACKNOWLEDGEMENTS

This book wouldn't be in your hands without the patience and skill of my editor, Jess Whitlum-Cooper. Writing each book is a pleasure, but editing them into shape is a lot of work, and Jess does most of it.

Thank you also to the wonderful team at Bookouture, for continuing the process of shaping the novels and making the stories and my characters consistent across the series. They also design the lovely covers and organise the publishing, which is a mystery to me.

Many thanks to my son Carey Bave, my first reader and editor, who knows all my books. He keeps me writing and challenges me, asking all the right questions

As always, much love goes to my patient family, especially my six-year-old granddaughter Lily. And to my husband Russell, who will take me to a remote island or moor or beach just because I need inspiration.

Made in the USA
Middletown, DE
03 September 2023

37891877R00189